M000296802

SALTY DOG

PHANTOM QUEEN DIARIES BOOK 7

SHAYNE SILVERS
CAMERON O'CONNELL

ARGENTO
PUBLISHING

CONTENTS

This is a work of fiction. Names, characters, businesses, places, events, and incidents are either the products of the author's imagination or used in a fictitious manner. Any resemblance to actual persons, living or dead, or actual events is purely coincidental.

Shayne Silvers & Cameron O'Connell

Salty Dog

The Phantom Queen Diaries Book 7

A TempleVerse Series

ISBN 13: 978-1-947709-22-5

© 2019, Shayne Silvers / Argento Publishing, LLC

info@shaynesilvers.com

ALL RIGHTS RESERVED. This book contains material protected under International and Federal Copyright Laws and Treaties. Any unauthorized reprint or use of this material is prohibited. No part of this book may be reproduced or transmitted in any form or by any means, electronic or mechanical, including photocopying, recording, or by any information storage and retrieval system without express written permission from the author / publisher.

SHAYNE AND CAMERON

Shayne Silvers, here.

Cameron O'Connell is one helluva writer, and he's worked tirelessly to merge a story into the Temple Verse that would provide a different and unique *voice*, but a complementary *tone* to my other novels. *SOME* people might say I'm hard to work with. But certainly, Cameron would never...

Hey! Pipe down over there, author monkey! Get back to your writing cave and finish the next Phantom Queen Novel!

Ahem. Now, where was I?

This is book 7 in the Phantom Queen Diaries, which is a series that ties into the existing Temple Verse with Nate Temple and Callie Penrose. This series could also be read independently if one so chose. Then again, you, the reader, will get SO much more out of my existing books (and this series) by reading them all in tandem.

But that's not up to us. It's up to you, the reader.

You tell us...

DON'T FORGET!

VIP's get early access to all sorts of book goodies, including signed copies, private giveaways, and advance notice of future projects. AND A FREE NOVELLA! Click the image or join here:
www.shaynesilvers.com/l/219800

FOLLOW and LIKE:

Shayne's FACEBOOK PAGE:
www.shaynesilvers.com/l/38602

Cameron's FACEBOOK PAGE:
www.shaynesilvers.com/l/209065

We respond to all messages, so don't hesitate to drop either of us a line. Not interacting with readers is the biggest travesty that most authors can make. Let us fix that.

When I was a little girl, my aunt used to have to drag me out of bed. I don't mean that metaphorically, either. She'd holler at me a couple times from the kitchen most mornings before clomping up the stairs, flipping on the lights, snatching me by the ankles, and yanking me out of bed. I'd spit and hiss like a cat, try and kick free, but no matter how hard I fought I'd end up standing in front of the bathroom mirror, glaring at my reflection, bleary-eyed, my red hair a tousled, tangled mess. I wasn't a morning person, back then.

And I sure as hell wasn't one, now.

"Where on God's green earth are we goin'?" I asked, rubbing my arms to generate heat. My breath fogged up the air, barely visible in the faint light of dawn. On either side loomed Boston's pitch-black skyline, buildings rising up like dark monoliths against a twilight sky. The streets themselves were largely deserted at this hour, aside from a few clinically insane morning joggers. One bustled past us as I spoke, pumping her arms so fast her neon-colored attire could have given seizures to an epileptic.

Scathach, legendary warrior and my sadistic Faerie godmother, admired the industrious woman as she passed, nodding to herself as if it were the most natural thing in the world to wake up at the asscrack of dawn, in the heart of winter, and run. "Come on," she said, ignoring my question.

I followed after the smaller woman, grumbling under my breath. Once, I might have refused to tag along until I knew exactly what Scathach had planned, but lately I'd resolved to have more faith in people and embrace a more positive outlook. Which is perhaps the only reason why, when Scathach woke me an hour before sunrise by banging relentlessly on my door, I'd elected not to shoot her. Although, now that we were wandering the streets of Boston in below-freezing temperatures, I was beginning to regret that decision.

Scathach angled us towards the Massachusetts Bay, seemingly unfazed by the frigid weather. Winter had arrived in force this year, leaving the vast majority of Boston's inhabitants to huddle around their fireplaces and loved ones. Meanwhile here I was, trailing after an immortal, shoving my hands deeper into my pockets and cursing the Fae half of my biology. Sure, I could outrun a car and arm wrestle a gorilla, but apparently my genetics didn't make me immune to things like hypothermia. Lame. "No, but seriously," I said, "where are we goin'?"

"Cold?"

I fought to keep my teeth from chattering as I replied, "Of course."

"Good."

"What?"

Scathach paused to look at me, having to crane her neck to fix me with her full glare. Despite the fact that I stood significantly taller than her at six feet even, the woman was remarkably imposing, her features crisp and angular, pale skin a sharp contrast to her hair, which was a shade more orange than my own. She huffed, breath pluming, then continued on. "Remember, this is entirely your fault."

"What's me fault?" I spluttered, taken aback.

She growled under her breath, but never slowed. Guess neither of us were morning people. I sighed but trailed behind as we marched down first one block, then another. At last, Scathach slowed, angling towards Norman B. Leventhal Park, one of those aesthetically pleasing divergences from the hustle and bustle of Boston's financial district, an area laden with stately banks, sleek condos, and high-rise office buildings. Of course, by this point all the greenery had long since died away, leaving little behind but bare, skeletal branches, wide brick thoroughfares, and a deactivated fountain. Or it would have, if it weren't for the brief, bright flashes of color peeking between the trees. I frowned and squinted, wondering what could possibly be happening in the middle of the park at this hour.

"Jesus, you're not havin' us run another half-marathon, are ye?" I asked, glancing down at my attire; I'd dressed in a hurry, throwing on a pair of jeans, fur-lined boots, a long-sleeved thermal, a heavy sweater, and a pea coat.

"No." Scathach resumed her march without further elaboration, casually ignoring the glowing orange hand and any oncoming traffic. I hurried after, cursing as I dodged what few morning commuters there were on the road. By the time I caught up to her, we were in the heart of the park, the trees blocking out what little sky could be seen above. It was somehow even colder here, the breeze more forceful without the windbreaks to shield us. I ducked my head and picked up the pace, letting my long legs cover the short distance between us.

"I'm sorry!" I called out. I was forced to jerk to a stop to avoid running into Scathach, who'd halted mid-stride. She stared at me, mouth hanging open. "Whatever it was I did," I said, panting. "I'm sorry."

Scathach's eyes narrowed. "You're just saying that because you're cold."

"So?"

"Bah." The legendary warrior waved that away and resumed walking, though she seemed a little less aggravated than she had before, the tension in her shoulders gone. As we neared the spot where I'd seen the flashes of color, she slowed. "Don't worry. You'll be warm in a second," she said.

I scoffed, taking in our surroundings, none of which included a fire or, better yet, an Irish coffee. "And how d'ye figure that?"

Scathach frowned, turned, and shoved me as hard as she could towards a cluster of trees.

Except I didn't hit them.

Instead, I fell, and fell, and kept falling.

I landed on my ass in the middle of nowhere. Well, not nowhere. I was definitely *somewhere*. And, wherever it was, there was sun. A lot of it. I grunted, squinting against the glare overhead, and took stock of my body, making sure I hadn't broken anything in the fall. Once I was fairly sure I could manage it, I tried to sit up, only to be assaulted by a wave of crippling nausea. I fell back immediately, taking deep breaths to keep from losing my breakfast. What the hell was going on? Where was I? And why was it so unseasonably warm, here? Before I could begin to answer any of those questions, however, a face appeared in my vision, materializing to reveal a pair of impossibly bright blue eyes hovering below a crimson base-ball cap, pale mug otherwise largely obscured by a luscious beard that brushed the top of his windbreaker.

"You've looked better," Robin Redcap, fabled storybook creature and notable friend, said. He grinned and fidgeted with his bloodstained cap, the repository of his power. Once, I'd mistaken it for a Red Sox ball cap, the embroidered "B" a dead giveaway. Recently I'd learned the "B" stood, not for Boston, but for Blood. Personally, I thought it lacked imagination, sort of like naming a Dalmatian "Spot".

"Well, that settles it," I croaked. "I'm definitely not dreamin', if you're here."

Robin frowned. "And why's that?"

"You're not sexy enough. Not by a long shot."

"Cute."

"See, that wasn't so hard, was it? Complimentin' me, I mean."

Robin grunted a laugh, then reached down to help me up, drawing me gingerly to my feet. "Move slow and you'll be fine. The queasiness will ease up soon."

I did as he suggested, letting the Redcap support my weight while I waited for the nausea to fade. By the time it finally did, sweat prickled my brow, and I realized I was being roasted alive with all the layers I had on. I struggled out of my pea coat, draping it over one arm, the sun beating down on us both. "Where am I?"

"Home," Scathach said, from behind us. I whirled, then immediately regretted it; without Robin holding me upright, I'd have collapsed and started retching. I pinched my eyes shut, taking deep, soothing breaths.

"Easy," he cautioned.

"Home?" I asked, once I got my bearings back. I looked up to find Scathach staring out at a gorgeous coastline: cerulean waves licked the edges of a sun-dappled beach, a sandbar connecting our grassy knoll with another across the water. Several dozen figures milled about on that distant spit of land, so far away they registered as little more than dots on the horizon, though some seemed far larger than others, somehow. Faint, haunting tunes played on the wind. Bagpipes.

"Scotland," Robin said, nudging me. "St. Ninians, if we're splitting hairs."

"My home," Scathach added, hugging herself.

I opened my mouth, my first instinct to yell at Scathach for launching me several thousand miles from Boston without my permission, but then I caught sight of Robin's chiding expression. I clamped my mouth shut and took in the view once more. "Ye have a beautiful home," I said, at last.

Scathach swiveled round and smiled. And I mean really *smiled*, her eyes brimming with pleasure, cheeks flushed. In that moment, I could see her as she must have once been, thousands of years ago: a proud, beautiful woman. A mother. A lover. Mortal and fragile and bold. "Isn't it, though?" she said.

"Well played," Robin whispered. He gave my arm a squeeze and disengaged slowly, making sure I could stand on my own before stepping away. He'd probably have babied anyone else, making sure they were acclimated before letting go, but then Robin knew how I felt about having my personal space invaded—even by my friends. "So, I assume Scathach filled you in on what's going on?" he asked.

I gave him the look that question deserved. "Ye know what they say about assumin'..."

"I wanted it to be a surprise," Scathach called back to us, having returned her attention to the coast.

Robin's eyebrows went up. "Well, surprise." He waved a hand at the sandbar and its mass of occupants. "Welcome to Scotland. And the High-land Games."

"The Faeland Games," Scathach amended.

"Right. That."

rom the sandbar below, I could make out a vicious rain line in the distance, a curtain of swirling grey looming a hundred feet further inland from where Robin, Scathach, and I had stood not so long ago. Beyond it lay nothing but sunshine and clear blue skies. "What's that?" I asked, trailing behind my two companions.

"The fence," Robin replied, drifting back to keep pace with me. "A little glamour to keep the Regulars from finding us. Turns them around if they press on towards the beach." Regulars, those human beings who lacked supernatural power of any sort, as opposed to the Freaks who made up the majority of my acquaintances—vampires, werewolves, psychics, witches, you name it—were largely unaware of our existence. And it looked like the Fae meant to keep it that way.

"Clever," I admitted, noting the way Robin puffed up as a result. Guess it'd been his idea. "So, what—"

But I never got to finish the question. Instead, Robin grabbed me by the waist and yanked me sideways, forcing both of us to the ground. I cursed as we landed, spitting out sand as it hit my face. But—before I could lash out at Robin for tackling me—a log the size of a Californian redwood came spinning end over end through the air, burying itself only a few feet away, one side planted firmly in the ground. It quivered there for a moment, then toppled, a cloud of sand exploding into the air.

A cheer went up, drowning out the moaning bagpipes, guttural roars and ear-splitting howls that raised the hairs on the back of my neck. One voice, in particular, I recognized. Not long after, the chorus faded, the bagpipes resumed their wailing, and a shadow fell across Robin and me. The Redcap sat up, brushing sand off his jeans, and glared up at the oddly proportioned, green-skinned monstrosity who stood menacingly over us.

"The caber toss is over there," Robin insisted, jerking his thumb towards a wider, more isolated stretch of beach and its slew of brawny, bulky Faelings, many of whom were busy flexing. It reminded me of Venice Beach, if Venice Beach were full of disproportionate, comically large meatheads with unnatural skin tones...oh, wait. Nevermind.

The bridge troll, a piss-poor poker player named Paul, straightened and scratched at his chin where one long, white whisker poked free from a massive mole, bobbing up and down. He grunted, then grinned, his yellowed teeth thick as bricks. "Oh," he replied. He left us there, staring after him as he ambled towards the log. He bent over, the broad muscles of his back straining as he hefted the caber. In moments, he had the log hoisted over one shoulder, seemingly unfazed by its prodigious weight. He spun to wave at us, forcing Robin—who'd begun to stand—to dive back to the ground a second time to avoid being hit by the log. "Bye, boss!"

Robin cursed under his breath and made a show of wiping himself down. "Damn trolls," he muttered.

"Boss?" I asked, raising an eyebrow.

Robin flicked his gaze at me, then Scathach, who stood watching the gentle waves lap against the beach, seemingly unfazed by the whole incident. "You didn't tell her?" Robin asked.

Scathach turned and shrugged.

"We took the job," Robin explained as he rose to his feet. I followed suit, brushing away errant sand, praying none of it had slipped beneath my jeans; it'd be bad enough trying to brush it out of my hair at the end of the day. "Which," he added, "is why we're here."

"What job?"

"Adjudicators," Scathach replied, glowering at me. "On *your* recommendation, it would seem."

"Oh, right," I said, wincing as I recalled the day I'd gone into the law offices of *Hansel, Hansel, and Gretel*—the legal representatives of the Faerie Chancery, an organization responsible for governing the Faelings who inhabited the mortal realm—and made my pitch. It *had* been my idea to see Scathach and Robin take on the roles. Part judge, part executioner, Adjudicators typically weighed in on policy decisions, looked after the Chancery's interests, and provided both protection and unassailable authority in times of crisis. Or that was the idea, anyway. Unfortunately, the previous Adjudicators had gone off on a crusade months ago and hadn't been heard from since, which had left the remaining Chancery members both unprotected and uninhibited.

Until now, it seemed.

"I do not appreciate having to do this." Scathach's stare had an almost physical weight, her earlier smile a very distant memory. But at least now I knew why she'd been giving me the cold shoulder all morning; she was grumpy because I'd promised the infamous Hansel and Gretel I could get her to cooperate. I grimaced, prepared to offer an apology I wouldn't mean, but Robin held up a hand before I could.

"She says that," he began, "but trust me, it's for the best. Thanks to that, we've started doing things a little differently. There's no pitting one side against the other, no infighting, no vying for influence. We've gotten away from the politics and focused on the members, instead. Which means Scathach has her role, and I have mine."

Scathach pursed her lips but nodded. I realized in that moment that she wasn't actually mad at me so much as she was annoyed to have a role in which others depended on her. For as long as I'd known her, she'd been a bit of a loner, always willing to lend a hand, but twice as eager to ride off into the sunset. For someone like her, getting stuck looking after people had to be agonizing in its own way. I guessed I could relate. "And those roles would be?" I asked, cocking an eyebrow at the Redcap.

Robin jabbed his chest with a thumb. "Carrot." He pointed at Scathach. "Stick."

"What did you just call me?" Scathach's hand edged towards the knife on her hip.

"It's an expression," I explained before Scathach decided to saw off Robin's beard and feed it to him. "He means you're the one who punishes the Fae who get out of line, and he's the one who rewards 'em for good behavior."

"I see. Fine." Scathach planted her hands on her hips. "But don't ever call me a stick again."

Robin cleared his throat. "Of course."

"So, I take it this was your idea?" I asked the Redcap, breaking the tension. I waved a hand idly at the gathered Fae, then realized I recognized a surprising number of them from past dealings. As I watched, a small contingent of Faelings began a game of tug-o-war, lifting a rope of braided silver, trying to force each other over a line drawn in the sand. A half-dozen pixies, so small that at this distance they seemed little more than dust motes hovering in mid-air, bobbed and weaved through the competitors, wings buzzing, seemingly cheering them on. The whole spectacle was blatantly ridiculous, and yet I had to laugh; it was good to see so many of my people happy. And they *were* my people, I was beginning to realize, despite our biological and cultural differences. In fact, the more I got to know them, these outcasts and exiles who reveled in their petty feuds and two-faced bargains, the more I saw of the woman I'd become. I mean, a black magic arms dealer with a reputation for drinking the night away, starting fights on a whim, and who just so happens to be the daughter of a Fae goddess? Somehow, I doubted that was pure coincidence.

But did that mean my whole life had been predetermined? That I was just an inflexible, one-dimensional demi-goddess, destined to live this way forever, to repeat the same mistakes over and over again?

Or could I change?

"It was," Robin replied, chuckling alongside me even as my laughter faded, smothered by the weight of my own thoughts. "I thought it might be good for them," he explained. "Team-building, if you will."

"He's been reading human books," Scathach said, eyeing Robin out of the corner of my eye.

"Oh?" I cocked my head, noting Robin's reddened cheeks. "Did Camila get 'em for ye?"

The blush crept further up his face. Camila Velez, Robin's human paramour, was a bruja—a particular sect of witch who helped run a paranormal paraphernalia shop in Boston. I still wasn't sure how I felt about her or their budding romance but had to admit most of that uncertainty was tied to my complicated relationship with her brother, Max—a hunky brujo who seemed adamant that he and I were meant to spend the rest of our lives together. Well, maybe not in so many words, but the offer had been there, all the same.

"Camila thought it might help to take a few classes, actually..." Robin admitted.

"You're goin' to school?" I asked, gaping.

Robin frowned at me. "And what if I am?"

"Nothin'," I replied hastily, raising my hands in surrender. "Can I ask what your major is?"

"Business administration."

I grunted, stifling a laugh.

"What?" he asked.

I waved that away. "Nope, that's great. I'm sure you'll look great in a cap and gown. Get it? Because ye like caps?" I gestured at his namesake.

Robin groaned.

"Wait! Have ye thought about startin' a Fae-ternity?"

"You're a child, you know that?"

"Ye don't even need to get a house. Just find yourselves a hill on campus, throw some parties, lure unsuspectin' passersby. Ye could call yourselves Fee Phi Fae Fum!"

"Are you done?"

I held up a hand, considering Robin's question. "Hold on. What's a fairy's favorite subject?" I waited, but all I got was Robin's disdainful stare. "Fae-losiphy," I said, giving him the come and get it gesture with both hands.

Robin turned on his heel and walked off.

"Oy! Come back, I came up with a better one!" I called.

"I'm glad you're enjoying yourself," Scathach said. "But it's time you did something useful."

"Somethin' useful?" I echoed. "What d'ye mean?"

"The race." Scathach nodded towards the sprawling Fae, many of whom were milling towards what looked like a starting line at one end of the beach. "We went ahead and entered you."

"Ye did what, now?" I glanced down at myself, then back up. "Why didn't ye warn me?"

"What fun would that be?" Scathach asked as she waved, trailing after her fellow Adjudicator.

Well, shit. Guess the joke was on me, after all.

3

The starting line was really more of a loosely configured boundary, beginning where the grass met the sand on the far side of the sandbar. Which meant, by the time I arrived, I found several of the brighter Faelings crowded along those few spots that extended further onto the beach, eager to take whatever advantage they could. As I worked my way through the crowd, I spotted a familiar pooka loan shark sporting a track suit instead of his three-piece, hopping in place, bunny ears flopping. It might have been cute if it weren't for the menacing, fiendish expression on Alby's face, not to mention the creepy way he slid his impossibly long-fingered, monkey-like hands over his chest. I watched as Alby leaned over to speak to his one-armed enforcer, an ogre named Ennis, pointing out a few other competitors. Probably trying to rig the race, if I had to guess; some Faelings simply couldn't help themselves. I sighed and turned my attention to the race itself.

A straight shot from one end to the other, the race was a winner-take-all event. Whoever made it to the finish line first won a no-questions-asked boon from the Chancery's two Adjudicators. It was a brilliant bit of market-ing, not to mention the reason why so many of the Chancery's members had opted to participate. Frankly, I had no idea what the rest of the Faelings were gunning for—better healthcare? Dental? Was the tooth fairy not pulling her weight? Regardless, I knew exactly what I'd ask for if I won: a roundtrip ticket to Fae.

Ordinarily I'd have liked to arrange that on my own, but I'd been wracking my brain for months now trying to come up with a way into Fae so I could fulfill a promise I'd made to a friend, with nothing to show for it. At first, I thought it'd be easy; I'd recently learned how to make Gateways that opened portals from one place to another, and assumed I could use one of those. But it turned out the Gateways I created were linked to this world, exclusively. But I knew for a fact Scathach had the means to travel to and from Fae, although she'd been cagey about the details. Of course, that meant —if I won—I could finally fulfill my end of the bargain and see Eve, my resident houseplant and budding Tree of Knowledge, planted in Fae.

"You don't stand a chance, I hope you know that."

The voice was feminine, high-pitched. I turned and found it belonged to a Faeling I didn't recognize, though something about her seemed familiar. Maybe it was her classification; she was an elf, practically human aside from the pointed ears, the obscenely long lifespan, and the fact that she looked like she'd come fresh out of the pages of a fitness magazine. Blonde, beautiful, and ridiculously well-proportioned without even trying, I was inclined to loathe her instinctively. But then I wasn't about to let a total stranger get under my skin that easily, no matter how blemish free hers was.

"What was that?" I asked.

"I'm just saying. Half-breeds like you are notoriously bad at things like this. They lack…experience."

I raised an eyebrow. A half-breed. Hadn't heard that before. A few of the smaller Faelings around us drifted away, sensing a fight brewing. Of course, many more took their place, eyeing the two of us eagerly. "Do I know ye?" I asked.

"I doubt it. You hardly *know* any of us." She cocked her hip and planted a perfectly manicured hand on it. Her jogging suit was bright pink and so form-fitting it might as well have been bubblegum. And yet, the instant she stood like that, head tilted just so, derision written all over her face, I realized I did know her, after a fashion.

"Ye were one of Ryan's girls," I said, too surprised to keep the thought to myself. Ryan, a former friend turned murderous Faerie henchman, had been quite the lady-killer before leaving Boston over a year ago. Interestingly enough, whether that lady was Fae or human hadn't seemed to matter much to him, so long as they were both available and attractive; I'd seen him with dozens of such since I first met him, though none for very long.

"Excuse me?" the elven girl spat.

I waved that away and turned back towards the race. "Nevermind. Look, whatever issue ye have with me, I suggest ye keep it to yourself. I'm not in the mood to hear it."

"It wasn't true. What you said about Ryan," she insisted, ignoring my advice altogether. She grabbed my shoulder and spun me around, the strength of her grip enough to leave bruises. "Quinn MacKenna is a liar!" she declared, loudly and angrily enough that even the Fae who'd been eager to see a fight opted to take a step back.

I shrugged off her hand. Once, I'd have knocked her flat on her ass for touching me, let alone accusing me in front of dozens of my peers. Hell, I might have dropped her for something as trivial as her calling me a "half-breed." But the unfortunate truth was I could sympathize with the poor girl. Hell, even *I* had initially refused to believe Ryan capable of kidnapping and torturing his own kind, and I'd seen it with my own eyes. "Sometimes, aye, that's exactly what I am," I said, at last, sighing. I met the elven girl's eyes, letting her see how much it pained me to admit my friend had traded in his morality for vengeance. "But not this time. Not about what he did."

Her eyes hardened, jaw-bunched, fists balled up at her sides. "You still won't win," she hissed. Then she spun away, pushing through the crowd so violently I could hear cries rise up in her wake long after she'd disappeared from sight.

"She really loved him, you know." This voice belonged to a much smaller creature, a pixie the size of my fist, fluttering only a few feet away. Petal— one of the Faelings I'd helped rescue a couple months back, including Ennis and a host of others—flashed me a sad smile.

"Aye, well, I suspect she wasn't the only one," I replied, trying my best not to sound too bitter; Ryan and I had never had anything like a romantic relationship, but his betrayal had stung all the same.

"Maybe, but he always paid a little more attention to Mabel than the others."

"Oh?"

Petal nodded but didn't seem inclined to comment further. "Anyway," Petal continued, "forget what Mabel said. I'm sure you'll do great, my lady."

I winced at the moniker but didn't correct her; she simply ignored me whenever I tried. "Wait, ye aren't competin', then?" I asked.

"No, flying isn't permitted, and I'd rather not get stepped on," Petal replied, chuckling, her laughter ringing in the air like the chiming of tiny bells.

I glanced over at some of the other participants, including Paul and his contingent of Monsters, most of whom outweighed me by several hundred pounds. "Me either," I acknowledged.

"Gentle Fae!" Robin called out, getting everyone's attention, his voice so clear and carrying so far, I knew it had to be aided by some sort of glamour.

"Good luck!" Petal whispered before buzzing off. I waved and dug my foot into the sand. I'd decided to run barefoot, rather than risk blisters from my boots. Of course, running in jeans wasn't exactly ideal, but for a chance to get back to Fae, find some answers, and honor a promise, I'd do whatever I had to, even if that meant a little chafing. I took a deep, calming breath and turned my attention back to the Redcap.

"...on the count of thrice," Robin was saying. "Once, twice, thrice!"

And, with that, the race was officially on.

4

*I*n my opinion, the first ten yards in any given race are always the hardest to run. Sure, some might argue the last big push is what really defines champions, but anyone who says that hasn't had to separate themselves from a truly aggressive pack of fellow competitors, jostling their way past the plodding masses, trying to set a good pace while avoiding those overeager racers whose only goal is to blast past everyone. Frankly, when you aren't running on a track, with convenient lanes to follow, the initial moments of a race are often a chaotic mess. Now imagine running with creatures half your size, or even twice your size. Creatures who can leap ten feet in the air over another racer on a whim. Creatures who can and will slip between your legs as you run. Do that, and you might have the *slightest* idea of what I had to go through the moment the race began.

Basically, it was pure, unadulterated mayhem.

I launched myself forward, diving beneath the outstretched arms of two trolls who'd decided to wrestle rather than race, coming up smoothly from a well-executed shoulder roll to resume jogging towards the finish line. I wasn't running, exactly. The sandbar was long, even for those of us with increased endurance, which meant I had to conserve energy if I wanted to have anything left in the tank. Fortunately, now that I was clear of the pack, I could make out the few figures who were ahead of me, led by two runners well in front. One was Alby. The other had bound her long, blonde hair into a ponytail, though I'd never have mistaken her thanks to all that pink.

Mabel.

I gritted my teeth and pumped my arms a little faster, picking up the pace. Up ahead, the pooka raised his fist to the sky, pumping it once. Almost immediately, one of the frontrunners went down with a howl, spilling into the sand as the one-armed ogre he'd been running alongside trudged on, oblivious to the Faeling's curses. So, the pooka wasn't simply rigging the race, he was trying to win it by having Ennis take out the competition. Great. Just great.

Over the next few minutes, I passed three more downed runners. One, a kelpie, seemed merely to have cramped up; she looked like a caught fish flopping about on the sand, desperate for a glass of water. The other two had been knocked unconscious. Which left the large pack of runners behind me, none of whom were close enough to cover the distance in time, and those in front. The ogre, the pooka, and Bubblegum Barbie.

I put on a burst of speed, dipping into the reserves I'd built up while training with Scathach. Say what you wanted about the lady's sadistic training methods, but I was pretty sure I could run the Boston marathon on a whim, at this point. Or kick it into a gear so high it'd make Usain Bolt look like Chris Farley.

The instant the distant shoreline came fully into view, I did exactly that. Every fiber of muscle in my body sung with tension as I kicked off, lengthening my stride even as I increased my turnover, sending waves of sand soaring behind me as though I'd been revving my engine this whole time. But I hardly noticed; I focused instead on the ogre's back, pulling up alongside in moments. Ennis turned towards me, raised his arm as if to strike, saw my face, and lowered it. He flashed me a hideous grin and purposefully tripped himself as I hurried by, collapsing dramatically onto his good side rather than risk his boss' anger. Smart ogre.

Now that all I had left to do in order to win was to race past the pooka and his running mate, I decided to take stock of both runners. I watched the elven girl's ponytail bob as she moved, her gait even and smooth, making up for a lack of pure speed with her flawless form. Mabel ran the way all true professionals do, without a hint of wasted energy. In fact, I found myself admiring that toned, tan body—appreciating it perhaps a little too much.

Maybe in another life…I shook that off, turning my attention to Alby, who kicked awkwardly from one foot to the other, his strides absurdly long, the way a triple-jumper might, clearing huge swathes of land in the process. Still, I knew I could beat them both if I could only pick up the pace, even just a little.

No flying, Petal had said. And yet Alby was using his powerful, rabbit-like legs to his advantage. Plus, no one had called foul when Ennis knocked out those other competitors. Did that mean we were allowed to use our own abilities to our advantage? I grinned, an idea forming even as the finish line became clearer and clearer.

I needed an edge if I was going to win…so I gave myself one.

I concentrated and tore open the Gateway with the flick of my wrist, extending it in front of me like a road, relishing the sensation of a smooth grassy slope beneath my feet, so much less abrasive—not to mention less draining—than the sand I had been running on. I pressed on, letting the slight decline aid me, gaining ground thanks to the improved terrain. I felt my energy diminish a little with every step, the Gateway exhausting my accumulated power supply. Thankfully, I had a fair amount to expend; since learning I was essentially a magical siphon, I'd gone out of my way to soak up a little residual magic here and there, which meant I could afford to keep going a little longer. I checked the sundial on my wrist out of the corner of my eye, watching it tick down as my magic depleted. Just enough. Maybe.

I continued running, so close now I could practically reach out and flick Mabel's ponytail, even yank on one of Alby's ears. Then, in the space of a breath, I was running between them. Alby turned to stare at me in utter shock, the black fur around his face matted with sweat and coated in sand. Mabel barely glanced at me, but when she did, I thought I caught the faintest glimmer of satisfaction. But I didn't have time to question it. The shoreline was just ahead. So close I could practically taste victory.

Something silver shimmered in the distance, and I thought I heard voices whispering behind me, but figured that was merely the blood pumping in my ears, the light nothing more than sweat running into my eyes. At this point, I was so close I could taste it. I kicked that much harder, puffing out my chest, willing the others to fall back. And that's when Alby made his move, leaping in front of me, hoping to use my Gateway to his advantage. Except he never made it; Mabel crashed into him from the other side, veering left so quickly she almost took us all out. The two tumbled into the sand, rolling away. I grunted, utterly confused, but kept running, letting my Gateway wink out of existence as I took those last few steps, whooping for joy.

I crossed the finish line.

And fell into a sea of blood.

5

I came up flailing, coughing and spitting, completely disoriented for the second time in as many hours. By the time I recovered enough to tread water, my every muscle screaming, I knew I wasn't in Scotland anymore—not unless Scotland had a blood-drenched loch out there I'd never heard of. In truth, it wasn't so much the water was red as it was illuminated from far down below, the waves stained crimson by whatever was down there. I kicked in slow circles, taking in the moonless night sky, panic making my beating heart race that much faster even as faint, distant memories tugged at my subconscious. I'd been here before, somehow.

The Scarlet Sea.

The voice inside my head, my constant companion, my wild side, spoke with more authority than I'd heard in months. It was like someone had cranked up the volume, turning the knob until her voice was somehow louder than my own. Of course, that voice wasn't really a her. If anything, she was me, if only a part of myself I couldn't trust. The part of me that acted without thinking, the part that always got me into so much trouble. *The part of you that you won't forgive.*

I shook that off, my body leaden, weighted down by the clothes I wore, including a heavy and currently impractical sweater. I slipped out of it, peeling its limp mass off my upper body to leave me in nothing but a black tank top to go with my jeans. Oh, and no shoes. For some reason that felt familiar, too.

No shoes. The Scarlet Sea. A memory tugged at me...an old, blind man covered in bloody bandages. An impossible island city. A golden boat and a horse with a seafoam mane—perhaps the loveliest creature I'd ever seen.

And all beneath the ruins of a blood red sea.

Had I traveled back to Fae after all this time? But how? Before I could begin to dwell on either of those questions, however, I spotted something from the corner of my eye. I twisted as fast as I could and saw the prow of a dinghy not far from where I swam, the craft carving its way smoothly through the water. Something trailed after it, spilling behind the stern like motor oil, except whatever it was painted the passing waves in monochrome shades of grey as if sucking the very color from the water.

It took me exactly ten seconds to make up my mind and paddle towards the boat. The voice inside my head hissed a warning, sensing the potential for danger, but I ignored it. It wasn't that I disagreed, but at this point a boat was a boat; if I stayed out here much longer, I'd be too exhausted to swim, and end up at the mercy of whatever lived in these waters.

Soon, it became clear that no one was steering. That, in fact, there was no one aboard at all, which only intensified the warnings blasting inside my head. I gritted my teeth and swam until I was alongside the hull, then reached out, wrapping a hand around the gunwale. A sensation so slight I hardly noticed it rode up my arm, sort of like the low thrum of electricity, but too faint to do more than raise the hairs on my arm. I almost jerked away all the same, but the sensation was gone in an instant, leaving me with nothing but the feeling of wood beneath my hand. I took a deep breath, drew my body up against the boat, and then, very gingerly, dragged myself out of the water, doing my best not to capsize the damn thing in the process.

And that's when I noticed the body.

"Jesus Christ!"

I released the boat and kicked away, heart pounding, but nothing chased after me. Instead, the row boat righted itself and continued inexorably forward as if I'd never touched it. *Told you so*, the voice whispered. I grunted, then hurried to keep pace with the craft, kicking up water in my wake. Once I caught back up, I repeated the process I'd begun a minute ago, careful not to disturb the body this time as I clambered into the boat, accounting for the extra weight as best I could. The instant I was sure we wouldn't capsize, I scrambled as far from the body as possible, still prepared for something, anything, to go wrong.

When it didn't, I began squeezing water out of my tangled hair, letting the crimson liquid splash over the side as I studied my fellow passenger. The body belonged to a young man. At first, I'd have said he was simply sleeping—his face flush with color, long, copper-colored hair cascading over one muscular arm. The rest of him was like that, too. Muscular, full of life. Hell, that's why I'd fled the first time I saw him; I'd half expected the bastard to leap up and attack me for trying to hitch a ride on his boat. But he hadn't. In fact, now that I was close enough to notice, I could see he wasn't even breathing. And yet he looked pretty good for a dead man; he wore clothes woven from gold cloth, sturdier than silk, and yet somehow more vibrant. Around his arms were thick gold bands with silver inlay, pressed against the flesh of his biceps so snug it was as if they'd been made for him. Oh, and he was beautiful.

Like, really, stupendously beautiful.

"If I kiss him, and he wakes up, do I get to be Queen, ye t'ink?" I asked aloud. The voice in my head purred, daring me to give it a try. I sighed, visions of the last man I'd kissed dancing in my brain. Well, not dancing. What Max did inside my head was rarely so choreographed. Of course, those were just fantasies; we'd only ever shared the one kiss. I still vividly recalled the instant our lips had touched—how he'd lit up like the Fourth of July, veins throbbing with iridescence, with unbridled, inexplicable power. Unlike Sleeping Beauty here, Max was handsome. Like so masculine it hurt *handsome*. The kind of guy who you let crawl naked under the covers of the bed he'd built with his bare hands after he kindled a fire from scratch.

"Bad luck, boyo," I said, admiring the quiescent creature for the beauty he was, but feeling not even an ounce of the attraction I'd felt in the circle of Max's arms that night, "no kisses for ye." I sighed for a second time and turned my attention to the horizon and its unfamiliar sky, wondering how the hell I'd ended up here of all places. The boat continued on, seemingly unhindered by my added weight, though towards what destination I could only guess. "Unless, ye know, we run out of options," I added, under my breath.

*a*t some point, I fell asleep. I'd have loved to blame the exhaustion of running a breakneck race only to find myself in another realm, stranded in an impossible boat on an inexplicable sea, but the truth was probably simpler than that: I was jet-lagged. After being thrown forward a few hours into Scotland's time zone, I'd been shoved into a plane of existence that probably didn't even *have* time zones. My circadian rhythms had been hijacked, swerving from the easy bounce of jazz to the raucous clash of punk music so fast it'd given me the mental equivalent of whiplash.

I had no idea how long I slept—mere minutes, maybe, though it felt like hours. Either way, by the time I woke, the sun hung high in the sky. Well, *a* sun, at least. This celestial body was both smaller and brighter, casting harsher shadows than those I was used to. I groaned as I shaded my eyes from it, my body stiff and aching, the muscles I'd used so casually during the race protesting my every movement. I sat up, though I made sure to check on Sleeping Beauty first—had to make sure the bastard hadn't been playing possum this whole time. Once I'd confirmed he hadn't so much as twitched, I sighed and stretched, squinting as I scanned the horizon before us; I was pleased to note the waves had returned to a familiar shade of blue.

Had we left the Scarlet Sea behind? How long had I slept? Taking stock, I realized I wasn't hungry, yet. Or thirsty, for that matter, though I wasn't sure how that was possible since it'd likely been hours since I'd last had anything to drink. Did hunger not exist here? If so, at least I wouldn't die of starvation or thirst. Not that it mattered; my body might survive here, but my sanity wouldn't hold up under the pressure of being lost at sea forever.

"I will *not* start talkin' to meself and callin' ye Wilson," I muttered to my fellow passenger. Before I could note the irony of that assertion under the circumstances, however, a shadow fell over our boat from behind. I spun, mouth ajar, to find the skyline of an ancient city looming over us—I recognized it as the old man's island, the one I'd visited in what had felt like a dream.

And it was getting closer.

The boat was going backwards, I realized, which put me at the stern. I moved gingerly, twisting around to study the decrepit island metropolis, still awed by the sheer gargantuan size of the place; statues so large their proportions were difficult to make out rose among the skyscrapers, some so tall they rivaled those found in major cities. In fact, at times I felt I could almost recognize their shapes. In a way, the whole island reminded me of a necropolis, each building or edifice honoring something, or someone, by standing vigil. But wait...if we were here, then that meant I hadn't been transported to Fae at all.

It meant I'd crossed into the Otherworld.

Except that was inconceivable; home to the forsaken Tuatha de Danann —the Fae gods—the Otherworld was supposed to be nearly impossible to reach, like Mount Olympus or Valhalla, a locked realm, inaccessible to all but those few mythological champions featured in songs written by long-dead bards. How had I ended up here? And, more importantly, *why*?

Someone waited for us on one of the docks—several of which seemed to spread out from the island like spokes on a wheel—a cool sea breeze tugging on the ragged ends of the bloody bandages which obscured most of the man's face and throat, leaving only his stubbled chin and chapped lips bare. He wore a tattered shirt and breeches, exposing his sun-kissed skin and a body that had long since been whittled to nothing but bone and sinew. Still, I knew better than to get within his reach; the old bastard had whipped me around like a ragdoll the last time I was here, and I wasn't interested in a repeat performance.

After what seemed like an eternity, during which I could do nothing but watch, the boat finally bumped into the dock, mooring itself as though that were the most natural thing in the world. The old man, meanwhile, stared out at the waves as though we weren't even there, seemingly lost in thought. That, or maybe he was blind, after all. I bit my lip, trying to decide if I should make a run for it, or wait things out. Before I could make up my mind one way or the other, however, the body at my feet stirred.

Sleeping Beauty's eyes fluttered open as he drew first one breath, then another. The rise and fall of the man's chest tugged at the fabric of his shirt, almost as if he'd outgrown it. He raised himself onto one elbow, face slack, bleary-eyed and groggy, and met my eyes. I shied away, disturbed by what I saw reflected there—a fierce and deliberate intelligence to match that almost indescribable beauty. In some ways, I had to admit, I was attracted to the man, if not drawn to him. But there was something there, something brutish and *alien* about the man, that set off alarm bells in my head. I waited for him to speak, holding my breath, all of the sudden dreading what he'd say, what he'd ask me to do, because I knew I'd have to listen and obey. But then, just as he opened his mouth to speak, a wrinkled, knobby hand pressed against the man's forehead.

"Sleep, me son," the old man whispered, his voice deep and resonant, yet somehow soothing. In a way, it reminded me of the wave settings on those white noise machines, and I felt my own body responding to his command, my eyelids suddenly inexplicably heavy. "Not yet, Lugh. Not yet," he said.

I flinched at the name, surprise alone keeping me from curling up for a nap of my own. Lugh? *The* Lugh? As in Lugh of the Long Arm, the spear-wielding hero of the Tuatha de Danann? I'd been sharing this tiny rowboat with a freaking *god* this whole time? And wait, had this old buzzard called him *son*? Feeling entirely too exposed and completely out of my depth, I shook off what little lethargy remained, saw my opening, and scrambled out of the boat onto the dock just as Lugh's head fell back into the crook of one arm, face peaceful, chest unmoving.

I made it halfway down the dock before I felt someone grab my arm.

I froze, memories of the old man's strength as he tossed me around making me hesitate. Should I try to fight him off? But then it occurred to me that—while he'd tossed me around like a child the last time we'd met—he'd also sent me back to Fae. Could he, would he, do it again? I turned, slowly, and faced the senior citizen, noting the wisps of grey hair that he'd missed while shaving, and opened my mouth to ask—politely—for a one-way ticket home.

"Could ye—" I began.

"I've been waitin' for ye," the old man interrupted. "Come on." He released my wrist and started hobbling down the dock, his movements stiff. I simply stared after him, a growing sense of dread building in the wake of what he'd said.

Waiting…for me?

That didn't sound good.

"Well, are ye just goin' to stand there for all eternity?" he called over one shoulder, then chuckled as if he'd made some sort of joke.

"And why's that so funny?" I yelled back, still unsure whether to follow after the old bastard or cut my losses and make for the boat. Sure, I'd be risking my sanity in the process, but—staring at the sprawling, dilapidated skyline ahead of us—I wasn't sure it'd make much of a difference.

The old man halted, cocking his head to look back at me, staring at me through those bloody bandages, his stick-thin arms folded behind his back. "Because, if ye don't come with me now, that's exactly how long you'll be standin' there for."

6

*E*ventually, I followed the damn geezer. Together, we moved slowly among the ruins, the old man brushing his hands over the worn stone and rusted steel as he went, murmuring under his breath. At first, I'd considered confronting him, demanding that he tell me what I was doing here, but something about the patient way he strolled among the dilapidated remains of a once sprawling metropolis gave me pause, as if I were being ruled by the same instincts that led me to whisper in a library or stay silent at a funeral. Soon, the questions roiling about inside my head faded, momentarily forgotten against the intimidating backdrop of the island city.

"Where are we?" I asked, at last.

"This is the Gate," he replied, matter-of-factly, though he didn't elaborate further.

At least he was answering my questions.

"The Gate to where?" I asked.

The old man chuckled. "To everywhere. A few different whens, as well, in fact."

"I don't understand."

"Few do." He waved a hand as if none of that mattered. "If it helps, t'ink of this place as a waystation. A realm between realms. A port of call for wayward travelers."

"And what would that make ye, exactly?"

"Me?" The old man shrugged, angling towards a smaller, less decrepit building in the distance. "Depends. Sometimes I'm the doorman. Sometimes I'm the bouncer."

I grunted. "Aye, that bit I remember," I admitted, rubbing at my aching wrist where he'd grabbed me, the memory of his inexorable strength last time we'd met still fresh.

The old man glanced back at me over one shoulder, frowning. "Pardon?"

"When ye kicked me out, last time I was here. Although, truth be told, I was t'inkin' it might be right nice of ye to do it again," I said, hopeful. "I promise I'll go quietly, this time," I added.

The old man was already facing me, shaking his head. "Afraid I've never seen ye before in me life."

"What d'ye mean you've never seen me before in your life?" I asked, exasperated. "Ye dragged me off the island, threw me in a boat, and told your horse to throw me out!" I raised my hands skyward, my voice getting louder and louder until I was practically screaming at the doddery git. I took a deep breath, trying to calm myself down, even as the voice inside my head egged me on, demanding we make sure the old man never forget us, ever again.

My would-be guide paused, hands planted on his hips, studying me carefully despite the bandages wrapped over his eyes. He pursed his lips. "Oh, right. You're the one I sent off with Enbarr. Have ye done somethin' different with your hair?" The old man tapped one of his fingers against his lips, then held it up. "Wait, nevermind. Ye went and changed your soul, that's it. Clever." He abruptly spun round on his heel and continued weaving between structures. "Like mother like daughter," he added, sounding amused. "Should've known."

"I did *what?*" I yelled before hurrying after him.

"Changed your soul. Don't ye worry, it's common enough, even among our kind. Though we tend to reflect the change a bit more, generally."

"Wait, who the hell are ye, really?" I asked, a small migraine building just behind one eye, making it twitch sporadically. But again the geezer avoided answering. Instead, he jerked his chin towards the doorway of a squat, blockish building even as he shuffled through it himself. I hesitated, then followed him into the dim recess beyond, determined to find some answers now that I'd gone this far. Changed my *soul?* What the hell had he meant by that?

A single flame arose almost immediately, and I realized we were in a living room of sorts, a room dominated by a single table surrounded by a few wooden chairs, none of which looked alike. The old fogey set the candle he'd been holding down and took one of the chairs for himself, moving ever more slowly, as if in a great deal of pain. "Low tide," he explained, catching my baffled expression.

"What?"

He smiled, flashing surprisingly white, healthy teeth. "Nevermind that. Let's get on to business, shall we?" With that, the bastard dismissed me entirely, staring into a dark corner of the room as if it were the most interesting thing in the world.

I felt the migraine growing. "What the hell are ye on about?" I asked, exasperated. "What business could we possibly have?"

"Oh, this isn't between us," he replied.

"Then what—"

"Name your price, Manannan mac Lir," a voice interrupted, emerging from the corner of the room as a murky figure rose from the shadows. She spoke entirely without accent, utterly uninflected, and yet chills rose up my spine as I recognized my mother's face materializing from that dark recess, flames dancing behind her eyelids. And yet, there was something different about her since we'd last interacted; she appeared translucent, ephemeral, if not insubstantial.

The old man grunted and leaned forward onto the table. "Ye know what I want, Morrigan," he replied, voice thick with emotion. The man's—no, the god's—body suddenly sung with tension, despite looking frailer than I'd ever seen it. And yet, I suspected he wasn't frail at all, because—according to my mother's ghost—this was Manannan mac Lir, perhaps the strongest among all of the Tuatha de Danann, if you believed the hype. A necromancer and magician, prophet and gatekeeper, Manannan had once been worshipped as god of the seas among a people for whom the sea held the key to all life.

"It is not yet his time," my mother's ghost replied. "Nor ours."

Manannan's fist banged against the table and a blast of distant thunder shook the heavens outside. "And yet ye brought this one here?" he hissed, waving a hand at me dismissively.

My mother shook her head. "It was not my power which called her here."

"Then whose?"

My mother was silent.

"That's not possible," Manannan spat scornfully, leaning back into his chair.

"We will all have our parts to play in what comes," my mother replied. "It has been many years since I knew my former husband's mind."

"And what will your part be this time around? Warmonger? Scavenger? Murderer?" Manannan glared across the table, but my mother's ghost seemed unfazed by the sea god's accusatory tone. Instead, she held out her hand, palm up, and floated forward until she stood a mere foot away.

"Read my future, Manannan mac Lir."

The god's mouth fell open, too surprised to remain entirely angry. He hesitated, then reached out, sliding his hand along her own, his knobby fingers sliding through her flesh as if he were running them through fog. The two gods fell still, neither speaking, the only sound the beat of the waves against the island, so distant it registered as little more than a hum. I considered interrupting, if only to demand someone tell me what was happening, but before I could, Manannan jerked to life, snatching his hand back as if he'd been burned. He cradled it, and I realized his blood-soaked bandages were stained further with tears. "You'd do this for her? But why?"

My mother's ghost smiled as she made her way back towards the shadows, gaining solidity the further she went from the light. "I do it for us all, Manannan."

The sea god grunted, then cleared his throat. "Passage granted."

"She will need a guide," my mother's ghost added.

"Excuse me?" I said, raising a hand. "Would either of ye be so kind and tell me what the fuck is goin' on?"

"D'ye want me to explain?" Manannan asked.

"No, I'll tell her," my mother's ghost replied, turning those haunting, fiery eyes towards me. "Not long ago, you were abducted against your will. I do not know by whom, or for what purpose. All I know is that another force interceded on your behalf and brought you here."

"What force?"

My mother's ghost shook her head. "If he wishes you to know of him, he will show himself to you. Until then, know that while you are a guest here among us, you are also a stranger. In this realm, some will be kind to you, others will not. Some may try to obstruct you, though their motives are often as mysterious as their means. In essence, you must use your best judgment if you are to succeed."

"Alright, hold on," I said, rubbing at the bridge of my nose. "What d'ye mean 'succeed'? Succeed at what?"

"You are here to find me, Quinn."

I shook my head. "Listen, I do want to see ye, ye know I do. And I appreciate whoever or whatever stepped in to help. But seriously, can't ye just send me home like ye did last time?" I glanced over at Manannan, who was already shaking his head.

"Last time ye were a trespasser," he explained. "This time ye were invited, and by a power beyond mine, no less. Besides," he studied my mother's ghost for a moment, "I'm with her on this one."

"With her on what?" I asked, exasperated.

"It's time," my mother's ghost replied.

"For what?"

"For me to fade away."

I felt the blood drain from my face. "Wait, you're dyin'? And ye tell me this *now? Here?*"

"We can talk more once you arrive," she said, ignoring my question entirely.

"Let me get this straight. You're about to die, and ye want me to what, pay me last respects? But to do that, I have to cross the *Otherworld?*" I started laughing, suddenly struck by the sheer absurdity of the situation. I laughed until my stomach hurt and I felt vaguely nauseous, tears pricking the corner of my eyes. "But...I just wanted to go home," I whispered.

"I can return you home from where I am," my mother's ghost replied, pitilessly. She turned her attention back to the sea god. "You will have to send her with someone you trust."

Manannan leaned back in his chair, staring first at her, then at me. He studied me for a long moment, then grunted. "Ordinarily, I'd send her with Enbarr. He's the fastest option, not to mention the tamest."

In that moment, a brief vision of Manannan's horse flashed before my eyes—a cerulean thoroughbred with a mane formed from frothing waves, the creature as large and majestic as the ocean itself. I sat up a little, still reeling from the idea that my mother's ghost might be fading, but also thinking it might not be so bad having to go on an extended field trip to find my mother's realm if it meant I got to ride Manannan's legendary steed in the process.

"But...she strikes me as a pain in the ass who'll need a lot of hand-holdin'," Manannan added. "So I'll send her with Cathal."

"Ca-what?" I spluttered.

"Ah, the hound. Excellent choice," my mother's ghost interjected, ignoring my outburst.

"You're sendin' me into the Otherworld with a freakin' *dog*?" I demanded, rising to my feet.

Manannan grunted, sounding amused, a light grin playing at his lips. "You'll get along great, I'm sure. You're perfect for each other." Before I could say anything to that one way or the other, however, my mother's ghost dissolved, disappearing among the shadows from whence it came.

"Hurry, Quinn," she whispered, eyes dimming as the darkness swallowed her face whole. "We're running out of time."

7

I had about a million questions, but Manannan didn't give me time to ask even one before we abandoned the blocky domicile for the sunlit outdoors. If anything, he seemed exceptionally eager to kick me off his island. Unfortunately, I was still reeling from the notion that my mother's ghost—the last tangible connection I had left to family of any sort—was fading, which meant I wasn't exactly thinking straight enough to ask the important questions.

"Ye never did explain this place," I said, waving at the ruins as we passed in an attempt to fill the silence. "Not the Gate bit, but why it looks like this."

The sea god nodded absentmindedly as he shuffled towards the docks, his steps more certain the further we went, his feebleness dissipating even as I watched. "This is where civilization comes to die," he explained, as if that cleared everything up. "As time wears down the structures created by both mankind and Fae," he went on, perhaps noting my irritation, "they come here, little by little. Ye might even recognize some." He gestured towards a distant structure poking out from between two statues, its apex practically unmistakable even from far away.

"Wait, is that the Great Pyramid?" I asked, gaping.

"The bones of it, that's all," Manannan replied. "Eventually, the whole pyramid may reside here, swept beneath the sand in your realm, a testament to civilization."

"But why here?" I asked, baffled, marveling at the many statues and towers that stood fully formed, awed by the pathos of this vast, cluttered landscape.

Manannan grunted. "I collect 'em."

"Ye what?"

"I'm sure you're familiar with the concept," Manannan replied, chagrined. "In your world, humans collect stamps and rocks and what have ye. I simply t'ink bigger than they do." Manannan shrugged, glancing at me with a placid expression. "Even gods need a hobby. Somethin' ye should remember, little one."

I bristled a little at the title but held my tongue. For all I knew, the term of endearment was literal, not patronizing; I'd seen more than a few gods now, and I was beginning to think being larger than life was part of the gig. "Back there," I said, changing subjects, "what is it ye wanted?"

"From your ma? It's not important."

"Ye keep sayin' that, but I didn't ask if it was important," I replied, barely holding my anger in check. "I didn't ask if it mattered. I just asked." I stopped walking, forcing the sea god to either talk to me or continue on without me in tow.

Manannan slowed, turned, and finally leaned against what looked to be the skeletal remains of the Chrysler Building, all that steel and stone eroding slowly into this realm. "Ye have her stubbornness, ye know."

"Quit tryin' to sweet talk me and answer me question."

Manannan grunted a laugh. "Fair enough. Do ye remember the man in the boat that brought ye here?"

"Ye mean Lugh," I said. "I heard ye say his name when ye came to…" I paused, wondering how I should describe what Manannan had done. "When ye tucked him in."

"Aye, that's one way to put it. Although I t'ink you'd be better off sayin' I bespelled him. Somethin' I've been doin' for centuries, now." Regret played around Manannan's mouth, visible somehow in the lines of his deep frown.

"Ye wanted to wake him up?" I offered.

"Aye."

I thought back to those brief moments in which Lugh and I had exchanged glances, remembering the heat behind his eyes, the waves of power that had practically roiled off the storm god, and shuddered. "But why?"

"Because he's needed."

"Needed for what?"

"That is none of your business," Manannan replied. I opened my mouth to protest, but the sea god held up his hand. "I don't owe ye answers, little one. What I tell ye, what any of us tell ye, is a gift to be respected. Best remember that." A distant crack of thunder made me flinch.

"Well," I said, drawing out the word. "Could ye at least tell me what ye meant about me soul?"

"Souls change. They grow. That shouldn't surprise ye." The sea god gestured for me to follow once more.

"Of course," I replied, falling in step. "But *how* has mine changed?"

"Your boat's down that dock," Manannan said, pointing. I huffed at the change of subject but shifted directions all the same; no sense getting smited over a little Q&A, no matter what the topic.

In less than a few minutes, we stood over the little row boat that was supposedly going to carry me to the Otherworld's mainland. The sun, meanwhile, had begun to set, though it struck me that I'd seen no moon to take its place. "How d'ye have waves without a moon?" I asked, absent-mindedly.

"The waves will never still as long as I'm here," Manannan replied, as if that made all the sense in the world. But then, maybe it did. The sea god nudged me towards the boat, and I noticed a bit more of his face peeking through the bandages, as if they'd fallen loose, somehow. The face beneath seemed smoother, too, the grizzled lines around his mouth faded, the stubble darker, less grey.

I stepped into the boat gingerly, wishing I had more time, or that Manannan would have answered more of my questions. But then, before I could settle in, I felt the sea god's hand on my shoulder, drawing me around. The arm attached to that hand, I noticed, was significantly more muscular, so much fuller, than it had been only a few minutes before.

The sea god pointed at my chest. "Loss." Then my stomach. "Fear, which breeds caution, but also self-doubt." Then, finally, my head. "Purpose. None of which ye had when ye were here last. Those are the changes I see."

"I—" I began.

"Remember this, Morrigan's daughter," Manannan interrupted, his grip tightening, "the Land of Youth is a temporary place, a realm unto itself. Do not dwell there long, no matter what. Listen to your guide, do exactly as he says, and ye may yet survive this journey intact."

"Intact?" I settled my hand over his. "What d'ye mean 'intact'?"

"This is the Otherworld," the sea god replied. "Many have dreamt of this place, perhaps even longed to find it. But ye should know by now that not all dreams are good dreams, and not everythin' ye look for should be found."

"What the—"

"Listen to your guide, and don't forget your purpose!" Manannan called as the boat beneath me sped off into the water, the force of it causing me to tumble backwards. I watched from the flat of my back as the sea god, no longer old at all, really, became a mere speck in the distance.

Don't forget my purpose, he'd said.

But what *was* my purpose?

8

The mainland's shoreline, when the sun rose and it finally came into view, was quite literally breathtaking. Which, considering the stunning view of Scotland's coast I'd had so recently, meant it hardly seemed real. From leagues away, I could make out white cliffs rising up into the early morning sky, so tall I suspected they'd be snowcapped, like mountains. But, as I drew closer, I spotted flashes of vibrant green instead—lush forests shrouded in mist. By mid-morning, I noticed a ravine bisecting the nearest cliff, from which a beach of pure black sand spilled out, its edges rimmed by jagged, obsidian rocks which seemed more and more imposing the closer I got. Fortunately, Manannan's boat seemed to have a mind of its own; it weaved through the eddies until the dinghy ran ashore, jerking to a halt amidst the surf.

I rose, body aching slightly less than it had the last time I'd taken stock, but—between the cramped confines of the boat and the uncomfortable sleeping position I'd been forced to adopt—far from one hundred percent. That, and I still hadn't eaten—a fact I became exceedingly aware of the moment I stepped onto the beach. The pitch black sand was fine and powdery beneath my feet, although surprisingly cold, as if untouched by the sun above. I clutched at my grumbling stomach, licked my impossibly dry lips, fought to breathe through my parched throat, and searched the beach for signs of my guide.

"Where the hell is that mangy dog, anyway?" I grumbled, turning, only to jerk back in shock as something rose from the sand only a few feet away.

A black beast I'd mistaken for one of the rocks, its flanks and chest scoured with faint druidic markings the color of smoldering coals over fur a shade of black so deep it was almost purple, climbed to all fours and shook, flinging sand in all directions.

Which included mine.

I sputtered and backed away, coughing and cursing as I tried to cover my face from the barrage of sand. By the time I looked back up, the creature stood a foot away from me, its brooding face—somewhere between dog and panther—even with mine, piercing amber eyes peering directly into my own. This close, I could see its massive canines flash, its powerful jaws bunching as it spoke. Yes, spoke.

"You the Morrigan's brat?"

I took an involuntary step back, opened my mouth, then closed it. I was too surprised, and perhaps—though I hated to admit it—too frightened to speak. My heart hammered in my chest. Finally, I balled my fists and shook my head, clearing it. "Aye, and who the fuck are ye supposed to be?" I asked, matching the creature's bitchy tone with one of my own.

"Name's Cathal. Come with me if you want to live."

And, with that, the hound turned and began padding towards the ravine.

"Seriously?" I asked, scowling, anger rising. It struck me that—after being dragged from one realm to the other, not to mention strong-armed into following Manannan around like a lost puppy while he and my mother's ghost decided my fate—I'd just about had it with people ordering me about. And now I had a dog the size of a damn pony bossing me around? Fat fucking chance. "Oy! Cathy!" I yelled.

The hound's massive shoulders bunched, the muscles beneath that sleek fur rippling, his markings slightly less grey than they had been a moment before, closer now to white ash. He turned, then sat on his hind legs, glaring at me with those haunting, honey-colored eyes. "What did you call me?"

"What? Ye don't like nicknames?" I grinned, sensing his irritation. "Well, I don't like bein' called anyone's brat. So maybe we both try this again. Ye can start by tellin' me where we're goin', and I'll start by listenin'."

Cathal lifted those eyes to the skies above, the long line of his throat exposed as he huffed out what was either a bark or a sigh. "Mac Lir warned me you'd be a pain in the ass."

37

"Aye, well, he also said we'd be perfect for each other," I spat, my own irritation boiling to the surface. "So what does that say about ye?"

"It says I'm wasting my time," Cathal replied, rising to all fours. He licked his chops, stretched, and spun back around. "Good luck surviving the Otherworld, kid."

I ground my teeth, the faintest panic setting in as I watched Cathal leave me behind. In that moment, standing on an unfamiliar shore, I realized how utterly screwed I was, how completely I depended on having a guide. On knowing *anyone* here. A stranger in a strange land didn't even remotely cover how much of a foreigner I was, or how much danger that put me in. I was—for perhaps the first time since I watched my aunt die in my arms—totally powerless.

And I hated it.

I slid to my knees, hands brushing against sand, letting it slide between my fingers as I fought against this sudden feeling of impotence. For some reason, Manannan's words echoed in my head, something about purpose. My purpose. Now that I was kneeling in the sand, lost and alone, I realized I did have a purpose. That—since Dez's death—I'd found comfort in only one thought.

That I would never be powerless, ever again.

That was my purpose.

I closed my hands into fists, squeezing until my knuckles went white, then rose to my feet. Manannan had implored me not to forget, and now I knew why; giving up wasn't an option. Not anymore. If I ever wanted to get home, I needed to find my mother's realm, a celestial hallway full of windows that looked out into different spots in space and time. But I couldn't begin to guess how to find a place like that on my own. Hell, I wasn't even sure where *here* was. Which meant I needed to suck it up and quit bitching.

Although it didn't help that I was really, really hungry.

"Wait! Please!" I called, running after the hound.

Cathal cocked his head around, looking at me over one shoulder. Until now, I'd never have thought a dog could look smug. Apparently, I was wrong. "Change your mind?"

"Tell ye what, ye find me somethin' to eat and drink, and I'll try to be less of a pain in the ass. I'll even do me best not to call ye names. Do we have a deal?"

Cathal grunted, blowing small jets of steam through his flared nostrils that trickled up into the sky like smoke. "You know how to make a fire?"

I raised an eyebrow. "From scratch?"

"Yeah."

"Not really," I admitted. I'd picked up a host of random skills growing up, not to mention all the survival tricks Scathach had given me over the last few months, but when it came to fire the solution had always been to pack smart, not star on *Survivor: The Otherworld.*

Cathal resumed walking. "Well then, I hope you like your food raw."

"Mangy dog," I muttered under my breath.

"Brat," Cathal called back, ears twitching.

Yeah, we were getting along *great.*

The beginning of a beautiful friendship...as fucking if.

*T*ogether, Cathal and I hiked up the steep ravine, his size and speed making it difficult—though not impossible—to keep up. Part of me suspected he'd set a brutal pace just to piss me off, but I didn't complain; if we were going to do this, I couldn't go around second-guessing his every action. Of course, by the time we made it to the valley above, I was desperate for a pair of shoes, not to mention a glass of water. Fortunately, after a mile or so the ground leveled off, leading us into a lush, fertile valley rimmed by trees the size of redwoods, though they stood much closer together—a forest sporadically touched by sunlight, the canopy above providing plenty of shade from the soft afternoon light. Which, now that I thought about it, meant I'd been away from home for at least two days, maybe longer.

No wonder I was low-key dying of thirst.

"There's a spring in the forest up ahead," Cathal said, as if reading my mind. "Take one or two small sips from it, then we'll move on."

"Why sips?"

"Just trust me," Cathal growled.

"But I don't trust ye," I replied. "It's nothin' personal, mind ye. I can count on one hand the people I trust." Which wasn't a lie, though some might consider it a little sad. If Cathal thought so, however, he didn't say it. Instead, he slowed.

"The faster we get you out of here, the better," he explained. "Sips. Small bites. Eat and drink as little as you have to until we've left this place."

"And where are we exactly?" I asked, still churning over the idea that I should watch how much I consumed. Was it like some sort of poison? Would I get sick if I ate or drank too much in the Otherworld? It wouldn't have surprised me; last time I'd gone to Fae I'd encountered vampiric trees that exsanguinated the unwary.

Talk about climate change.

"This is the Land of Youth," Cathal replied.

I frowned. "Well, that doesn't sound so bad."

"And that's what makes it so dangerous."

"Come again?"

"Nevermind that. If we hurry, it shouldn't matter."

I opened my mouth, prepared to interrogate my guide further, when a horn blast erupted from somewhere within the trees—a deep, reverberating growl that sent birds soaring up into the air. An answering call echoed to our right, somewhere out among the large, unbroken plains beyond the valley. In moments, I could feel the faintest vibrations beneath my feet—the ground was shaking.

Cathal barked a series of curses. And I mean literally barked, the words too mangled to make out, though I could have sworn I heard a few colorful phrases I recognized in there somewhere. I noticed his hackles had risen, the fur between his shoulder blades standing straight up, the markings on his body glowing faintly—all of which made him seem even more intimidating, somehow. He swung his head around, surveying the landscape.

"What is it?" I asked.

"Company. Come on, we need to find a place to hide out until this is over." Cathal took off towards a small cluster of boulders nestled between the ravine and the valley, seemingly unconcerned whether I followed or not. Not that he needed to be; very little gets one moving faster than a minor earthquake beneath your feet and alarm horns going off above your head.

I bolted for the rocks and managed to squeeze between them just as the source of the quake—an absurdly large horde of riders on horseback—came pouring out along the forest edge, materializing so quickly it was like watching the tide come in. Many wore headbands to secure their shoulder-length hair, the various shades of brown and blonde only occasionally broken by black or red. They were all fair-skinned, dressed in embroidered tunics that left their arms bare, their richly colored breeches tucked into soft leather boots. They'd painted their skin blue in places, the designs flowing down their arms, designs that were recreated on their shields.

Once I realized they were facing the plain, I turned to study it myself, only to find an even larger army approaching. These warriors, however, were clad in so much fur it was hard to tell anything about them. Each warrior carried a spear twice as tall as I was, twice as thick as any I'd seen. From this distance they seemed like a forest themselves—a veritable sea of spears blanketed the horizon.

"What the hell is goin' on?" I asked, my voice a hushed whisper even though there was no reason to suspect anyone besides Cathal would hear me over the ruckus caused by the two armies and their warhorns.

"A battle. Be quiet and stay still. We'll leave when they're done."

"When they're done what? Fightin'?" I asked. A thought occurred to me and I had to glance back at the hound to confirm it, my eyes wide in disbelief. "We're just goin' to hide and *watch*?"

Cathal, who'd laid down and hidden himself behind a particularly large boulder, lifted his head to study me. "I'd take a nap, if you can. These things tend to last a while, and we still have a lot of ground to cover before nightfall." He flopped back down, long snout resting on his paws, and closed his eyes, though he wasn't fooling anyone; his ears still twitched with every neigh and whinny.

A nap.

Yeah, right.

9

*T*he cavalry—I couldn't think what else to call it—churned in loose, ever-widening circles until a dozen riders were within a stone's throw from where Cathal and I hid. Up close, I could see their clothes were finer than I'd thought at first, their arms and throats often either bare or decorated with copper bands. The paint on their bare skin seemed ritualistic, a series of blue, swirling patterns that reminded me faintly of animals. In fact, the three closest to us bore what looked like feathers down the lengths of their arms, as if—when they raised their arms —they'd have wings. Unlike so many of the others, however, these three seemed less eager for the fight than their fellows; they were silent, faces grim, watching that distant army approach with cautious eyes. Eyes that reminded me of mercenaries I'd met, or cops. Men and women who'd seen some shit and lived to tell about it—though at a cost.

Before I could study them further, however, the horns sounded once more. Almost immediately, the riders formed a loose line, falling into ranks, though without the precision you might expect. Still, there was a sort of discipline present in the way they prepared themselves, retrieving their spears and readying their shields.

"Why are they fightin'?" I whispered, glancing back at my canine companion, who didn't so much as crack open one eye.

"Doesn't matter."

I rolled my eyes. "Is that all ye lot ever say?"

"Oh? And just how many of the Cù-Sìth have you met?"

I glared at the hound. "Not your kind, I meant all of ye. Ye Other-worlders. It's like ye all enjoy bein' vague," I continued, "or is it just that ye don't *know* and ye don't want to admit it?"

Cathal yawned, his enormously long, pink tongue emerging like a snake before slithering back between those vicious teeth. "Pipe down."

An image of those teeth rending me apart made me shudder, but I wasn't about to back down. "Or what?" I hissed.

That made Cathal open one eye. He flicked his gaze towards me, face sour somehow. "Or I'll leave you to them." He turned that eye on the two armies, both of whom were moving inexorably towards each other. "Dagda only knows what they'd do to someone like you."

"Someone like me?" I asked, my own hackles rising.

Cathal closed his eyes once more, refusing to explain further. I sucked my teeth and turned, arms folded, to watch the battle—stewing all the while. At this point, I was beginning to suspect I was doomed no matter what happened; even if I survived the Otherworld, Manannan was probably going to hunt me down once he discovered I'd put his favorite pooch to sleep.

Fortunately, the battle got interesting long before I could dwell on the merits of puppycide. In fact, all thoughts of Cathal and his shitty attitude fled almost instantly the moment I spotted—out among those spear-wielding foot soldiers—someone I recognized. She wore thick, dark furs, including a black cape of what looked like raven feathers, but there was no mistaking that fiery red hair, nor the way she held herself, the way she studied the approaching horsemen—as if they were already doomed.

"Scathach?" I whispered.

"That's not possible," Cathal drawled.

But I didn't have time to ask what the hound meant by that.

Because I'd already abandoned our hiding place and sprinted onto the battlefield, waving my hands wildly in the air, screaming her name.

10

I knew I'd made a mistake the second I left the shelter of the rocks, but I didn't care. I was sick and tired of being led by the hand, and, while Scathach had always been a tough person to get along with, she was on the list of people I'd trust with my life. Hell, I *had* trusted her with my life. Frankly, no matter how highly recommended Cathal came, I *knew* that Scathach would get me the hell out of here. Of course, what she was doing here in the first place, not to mention what I was thinking diving headfirst into the middle of a freaking battle, well…that I couldn't tell you.

Just do it.

The voice crashed over me like a rogue wave, giving me a boost of adrenaline even as I begged my wild side not to use Nike slogans to pep me up in the future. Of course, I had to admit it wasn't the worst idea. I was in hostile territory in the middle of who-knew-where, trying to find the one person I could trust in the midst of what seemed like hundreds of blood-thirsty, well-trained warriors. The odds were definitely *not* in my favor, and the rational part of me knew it.

So, I simply turned off the rational part of my brain.

And let my wild side take the reins.

*W*e sprinted past the galloping horses of the nearest riders, laughing, the pure joy of moving among so many powerful beasts exhilarating and frightening all at the same time. A few horsemen called out to us in a familiar tongue, one we thought we almost understood, but then we were out of earshot.

Soon, we were ahead of the cavalry entirely, a lone runner approaching a very large army of fur-clad foot soldiers. We angled ourselves slightly, beelining for the woman we'd seen leading the army, scouring their ranks for her tell-tale red hair and that hauntingly beautiful face. The briefest, strangest thought—that these poor people must be ridiculously hot in all those furs—flashed through our head, but we shook it off. Clearly these warriors were from a colder climate, especially since they were approaching from the north. That's probably what had started this whole battle in the first place—limited resources.

Some people had, while others had not. None of that surprised us; that was the way of things, no matter where you were. Why would the Otherworld be any different? We let out a frustrated cry as we closed the distance, our prey no longer visible. Where had that woman gone? The one we were supposed to be looking for? We stopped and scoured the faces of the foot soldiers, but none were the warrior we sought. Damn, had we lost her?

Horses blew past us before we could find our answer, the force of it blowing our hair forward and rocking us onto our toes. We laughed, the sensation too odd not to enjoy. We laughed as the first spear struck the first horse. We laughed as the first rider went cartwheeling into the air to land in a broken pile on the ground, bleeding all over that once pristine grass. We laughed as the first footman took a hoof to the face, crumpling it like a soda can. We laughed as men and women died.

Because we were alive.

Finally.

*W*e shoved the man's face into the dirt even as he flailed, smashing it against the ground again and again until he went limp. We released his hair and sank back onto our heels, momentarily overcome with exhaustion. Around us lay the bodies of those who'd come to kill

45

us, thinking we were easy prey, their limbs twisted at odd angles, eyes open and staring. Now that we had a moment to ourselves, we realized the sun had nearly set and the sounds of battle had substantially diminished; it had been decided then. We wondered how long before the scavengers would arrive to pick clean the bodies and how many of them we'd have to kill before they left us alone.

But we never got the chance to find out. We rolled on instinct as a spear came flying from our right, narrowly dodging the projectile. Three men on horseback clomped towards us, the nearest having flung the spear. He looked surprised, the way so many of the others had before him. We laughed, welcoming that ecstatic surge of energy that came with putting our life on the line and waved at them—daring them to come closer. They obliged, urging their mounts forward.

We waited for them to close the distance as the others had, to get within our reach, but these men were smarter. They fanned out, coming at us from three directions. Not for the first time, we longed for a weapon of our own; we'd stolen several, but they were all broken or stuck inside someone, now. We searched the ground, but what we needed—one of those long spears— was nowhere to be found. There was a sword sticking out of a man's chest, but we couldn't use something like that to bring down men on horseback. Not unless we were prepared to cut out the horse's legs from under it, and for some reason, the notion of doing that bothered us more than anything we'd done so far.

We glanced back up to find the three men closing the distance between us. They were fast, and nimble; we looked for a path between them, a way to escape, but knew they'd cut off that route. Turn and run? But no, we knew that wouldn't work, either. They'd run us down, as tired as we were. Better to go down swinging, we decided.

We shook ourselves and rolled our shoulders, rocking on the balls of our feet. Soon, we told ourselves, eyeing the closest rider. Once he was close, we'd leap, then drag him off his horse as we had some of the others. If we could steal his horse, we might be able to get away. The odds were long, but we'd faced longer, hadn't we? Hadn't we?

For some reason, that thought struck me like a hammer.

Wait, why was I here? And where was here?

Too late, I realized now wasn't the ideal time to be asking myself questions; I watched in growing horror as a man on horseback galloped towards me, arm raised high as if he'd chop me in two, the sword in his hand already stained with blood. I flinched, shying away from the blade, too stunned to get out of the way.

But the blow never fell.

Instead, a monstrous black beast, its flanks covered in runes that glowed like hot coals, emerged from a fog of steam to rip the man right off his horse, dragging the unfortunate animal down in the process. The horse shrieked as it disappeared into that murky fogbank, the sounds of ripping and tearing within enough to give me goosebumps. I backed away, instincts screaming at me to get away from that creature—whatever it had been. It was something about those eyes, I recalled, shuddering. Those amber eyes, the kind that glow in the night, the kind that men built fires to avoid. Eyes that reminded me why we learned to fear the dark.

Cathal. The name sprung into my mind in a flash of insight, and I felt my memories tugging at me, trying to remind me who I was. What I was. But then, just as I was about to recall everything, I felt it: pain lancing across my back, pain like I'd never felt before. I felt my right side go numb almost instantly. Suddenly, I was on my knees, with no idea how I'd gotten there. A few feet ahead, another horseman rode past, his sword dripping blood.

My blood.

I collapsed to the ground. Grass. I could see tufts of grass. Looked like the sun had gone down almost completely, the horizon a pale shade of blue-grey. Distantly, I heard a howl piercing the air, though it seemed as if the sound were coming at me from down a long tunnel. Sadly, no matter how hard I tried, I couldn't seem to find the source. What poor creature had made that awful, broken noise? If only I could get up, maybe I could help, somehow. But no, I couldn't even move. Was I dreaming? Is that what this was, a dream? I felt so sleepy, all the sudden. So tired.

And so I shut my eyes.

And died.

11

I woke, screaming, to find someone's hand pressed against the small of my back, brushing up against the wound there—a line of pure, unadulterated pain radiating from my shoulder to my hip. I thrashed, trying to get away from the prison of my own body, willing to do anything to make it go away. The hand fell away and instantly three men were clustered in front of me, kneeling. I focused on their clean-shaven faces, anything to distract myself from the nerve-searing pain. As I studied their concerned expressions, a cool, rational part of me noted they were too alike not to be related; their noses were long and straight, their foreheads broad, their hair black and slightly curled despite differences in length. Brothers, if I had to guess. Feathered markings dominated the exposed skin of their arms and throats, markings I faintly recognized from…before.

"She isn't recovering," one said, though I wasn't sure how I understood him considering he was speaking a language I didn't know. I tried to concentrate on that mystery, but then a fresh wave of agony forced another scream from my lips, and I realized it didn't matter. I was dying; if the blood loss didn't get me, I knew the shock would, so why get myself worked up over something trivial? Why get myself worked up over anything, really?

The instant that thought crossed my mind, I stopped flailing. A deep, pervasive chill set in as I lay there on my stomach, though the longer I laid there, the more weightless I felt—as if I'd float away in only a few moments.

The pain faded, shoved out of my mind with the knowledge that soon it would all be over. Interestingly enough, now that I felt myself slipping away, I realized I was oddly fine with it. I had no last words. No final farewells.

Granted, I was fairly certain I had friends out there who'd mourn me—people whose faces I couldn't quite remember, but who I'd have liked to see one more time—but I also sensed I wouldn't be leaving behind anyone who wouldn't eventually recover. That I'd kept them all at arm's length, for one reason or another. Honestly, now that it was finally happening, it seemed as though I'd been waiting for this for a while now, as if I'd been going through the motions all this time, living just to live.

"Here, give her some water," another said.

The first nodded and took an offered skin, angling it so water spilled into my mouth from above, some dribbling down my chin to puddle against my cheek. At first, I considered turning my face away—why wouldn't they simply let me die in peace? But the instant the first drop touched my lips, I dismissed that idea entirely. In fact, I stopped thinking altogether.

The water tasted incredible. No, not tasted. Felt. It *felt* incredible. Part of that was the pain, which went from a distant, hellish ache my brain refused to acknowledge to nothing at all—as if it had never been there to begin with. But there was more to it than that; it felt as though all of me was mending, reknitting. Not just my body, but my *soul*. Like someone had given the whole puzzle that was me a shake and subsequently put all the pieces where they belonged. In the back of my mind, a warning—something about sips—registered vaguely, but I couldn't hear it over the sound of my blood pumping in my ears.

In seconds, I snatched the water skin out of the man's hand and rolled over, tilting it up, letting its contents spill into my mouth until I nearly choked, easing a thirst I hadn't realized was there until now. Once I'd drained its contents, I tongued the lip of the waterskin, savoring every last drop before tossing it aside. I lay there for a moment, just breathing, relishing the sensation of being alive. Eventually, I sat up of my own accord, shaking my head, trying to clear those alien thoughts from only a few minutes ago. Me, die? The thought alone made me want to laugh.

No one died in Tír na nÓg, the Land of Youth.

Everyone knew that.

"Not that I'm complainin', but what are ye boys doin' here, watchin' over me?" I asked. "And who are ye?" I looked at the three men in turn. A quick

49

glance at their weapons and clothes told me they were well-armed and fresh from a battle. Dangerous, perhaps, though I suppose if they'd wanted to hurt me, they'd had their chance.

"We were going to ask you the same thing," the man who'd offered me the waterskin said, bidding his brothers to rise. Judging from the way the other two deferred to him, I was willing to bet he was their leader. Probably the eldest, as well, given the faint crow's feet around his eyes and the grey starting at his temples.

"We saw you taking out warriors from both sides," the second brother added, his face a little leaner, but definitely younger. "Anyone who got close. We couldn't let you keep doing that."

I frowned, considering. I'd been fighting, then. That didn't surprise me, though it seemed odd I hadn't been more selective in my targets; fighting all comers wasn't exactly a good survival strategy. I turned to say something to that effect when I noticed the third brother, barely out of his teens, shifting nervously from one foot to another. His blade had fresh blood on it. The faintest memory stirred—a memory of his sword slashing across my back, of watching him ride past as I fell, of thinking I'd died.

"Ye did it then? Cut me from behind?" I asked, meeting the youth's troubled eyes.

"I gave the order," the leader said, deflecting my attention.

"It's alright," I replied, as I rose to my feet. I stretched, enjoying the languorous sensation of being alive, the sensation of being young and strong and capable. "It was a smart move," I admitted, grinning.

The youth brightened a little. "We didn't have much choice," he explained, guiltily. "Once we got closer, Bran said you were too dangerous to leave on the battlefield. Besides, after that hound appeared, we had to get to Finann."

Finann, who I took to be the middle brother, grimaced. Now that I knew what to look for, I could see evidence of a hound's attack; Finann's tunic had been torn to shreds and dried blood caked his upper body. The wounds —before they'd healed—must have been grisly. "Never seen anything like it," Finann said, shuddering.

"They're rare," Bran, the eldest, said. "The Cù-Sìth. I thought the last of their kind had died long ago." He drifted off, gazing out onto the plains— reflecting the light of the full moon above our heads—as if the hound were out there, somewhere, lurking.

Waiting for its moment to strike.

"Bran, what are we going to do with her?" Finann asked, filling the sudden silence.

I turned to find the middle brother studying me as though I were somehow more dangerous than the hound who'd attacked him. In a way, it was flattering, though I wasn't sure what I'd done to deserve it. What exactly had I done to those I'd defeated?

Bran answered before I could dwell too long on that question. "We'll take her to the King," he replied. "Tuathal will know what to do with her."

I grunted, not liking the sound of that one bit. "Oh? And I don't get a say in any of this, is that it?"

The youngest brother looked away, clearly still upset that he'd taken the coward's path by striking at me while my back was turned, no matter the circumstances. But Bran seemed unmoved. "If you tell me who you are and what you were doing attacking us," he said, "I'll consider it."

I opened my mouth to reply, but nothing came out. Who I was...what I was doing here...I should know those things, right? "I...don't know. I don't know who I am," I said, at last, staring down at my hands. "I don't know. Why don't I know?" A wave of panic washed over me, and, for a moment, the world spun. I felt dizzy, my knees weak. Fortunately, the youngest rushed forward, keeping me upright with a hand on my arm.

"Easy, I've got you," he said.

"Llew, be careful! It could be a trick," Finann cautioned. Ironically, in that moment—while the middle brother's cynicism made me think well of him—I really wished it *were* a trick, because the truth was so much worse by comparison.

"I don't think she's faking, Finann," Bran said, searching my stricken face. The elder brother moved to my side, supporting my other arm. "Come on. The King will know what to do."

For just an instant, a brief image of me standing over the three brothers, their bodies limp, flashed before my eyes. We could do it. Then they'd no longer be a threat to us. But I shook that off, repressing that urge completely; I wasn't about to assault men who'd helped me, no matter the cause. And so, instead, I let Llew and Bran guide me towards their gathered horses, praying all the while that Bran was right.

After all, that would at least mean someone knew what to do.

I quickly learned that—whoever I was—I knew jack shit about riding a horse. Bran had offered me his own mare, only to watch in genuine amusement as I tried to climb onto the thing's back. By the third attempt, all three brothers were watching me struggle, their heads all cocked, and arms folded, wearing nearly identical expressions.

"She looks like a child," Finann said.

"Even little ones know how to mount a horse," Bran replied.

"If ye two don't shut it," I said, gritting my teeth as I finally managed to swing one leg over the saddle, squeezing so tight with my thighs I thought they'd bruise, "I *will* come over there and make ye."

The two brothers exchanged glances.

"She's bluffing," Finann said.

"I'd say so."

"Doubt she'd even know how to get down." Finann headed for his own horse, his younger brother—clearly the nicest and least likely of the three to get punched in the face in the immediate future—trailing.

"Do you think we'll have a feast tonight?" Llew asked, changing the subject entirely.

I sighed and ignored them, doing my best to get situated. The saddle felt awkward, but once I had reins to hold onto, I felt at least secure enough to relax. Of course, the moment I did I felt the mare shift beneath me, shuffling nervously from side-to-side. Bran noticed and hurried over, running his hands along the mare's flanks, soothing her, whispering beneath his breath. The mare instantly calmed, though her tail still twitched. I breathed a sigh of relief as Bran stopped to study me, his raptorial gaze sweeping up and down my body.

"What?" I snapped, self-consciously.

"Your clothes," Bran replied, gesturing. I glanced down and realized I *was* wearing strange garments, the material both unfamiliar and somehow, well, wrong. Now that he'd brought them to my attention, I could only marvel at how restrictive they were, the pants and top unnaturally tight, not to mention the article covering my breasts—whatever it was bit uncomfortably into the skin of my rib cage.

"What about 'em?" I asked, turning away and covering myself defensively.

"It's nothing," Bran said, patting his horse's hindquarters. "Alright, let's go! The tribe will be on the move. Back to Caer Capall, before the Curaitl return." Bran walked to the spare mount Finann brought him, leaping onto his horse's back so gracefully I ended up gawking. He took the reins and used a rod with a sharp metal point to spur the horse into motion. My own mount, meanwhile, began following without so much as a jab from me. I may or may not have fallen forward, hanging onto the mare's neck for dear life, her ambling gait sending small shockwaves through my entire body.

"Who are the Curaitl?" I asked a few minutes later, recovered enough to sit upright despite the constant jerking. The others moved expertly in their saddles, finding the motion natural; Llew had insisted it'd get easier once we started moving faster—as if I'd survive that.

"The spear-wielders," Bran explained. "And we are the Tógálaí Capall. We're horse breeders, the finest in the Land of Youth. The Curaitl come from the north, mostly raiders who like to steal our cattle, especially before winter sets in."

"They weren't here to steal cattle," I guessed.

"No, this was a battle between our chieftain and their warmaiden."

"Warmaiden?"

"Aife the Fair," Finann called, clearly unashamed to be eavesdropping. "Exceptionally beautiful, from what I've heard."

I raised an eyebrow. "And why were ye all fightin'?"

"Our chieftain, Donall, wanted to propose," Bran replied, wryly.

"Come again?"

"He thought if he routed her army, she'd consider marrying him," Finann explained, shaking his head. "Lovesick fool promised her a hundred sows if she took the field."

"That sounds…" I drifted off.

"Ridiculous?" Bran nodded. "It was, but the King sanctioned it, all the same. Donall is his nephew, and Tuathal dotes on him. But, despite that, this was a good chance to test his mettle. Donall has always been more of a lover than a fighter. I think Tuathal saw this as an opportunity to see if that might change under different circumstances."

Finann scoffed. "And it wouldn't hurt to have Aife training our men instead of theirs, would it, Bran?"

"Tuathal rarely does anything without having multiple reasons, Finann. You should know that better than anyone." Bran glanced back at his brother, but Finann had fallen silent, expression closed off.

"So ye won, then?" I asked, hoping to break the sudden tension.

"Yes, though it cost us. We took the field, as well as several hostages, including the warmaiden's second-in-command. But from what I can tell, they made off with quite a few of our horses, which doesn't often happen. We'll have an exchange, eventually."

"People for horses?"

"And goods. For the more valuable hostages, they'll offer us supplies. Mostly furs from the large creatures that dwell in the north. For the safe return of our mounts, we'll give them cattle. It's how things are done." Bran shrugged, though I could see him watching me sidelong, perhaps wondering how I'd made it this far without knowing such obvious things. I wished I had an answer for him. Instead, I nodded, perceiving the sustainability of that way of life; the land provided Bran and his people with some resources, and the Curaitl with others. Rather than share, they warred with one another, turning it into a game, a competition that gave them purpose. It sounded, well…fun.

"So, does that make me a hostage, then?" I asked.

"I'm not sure what you are," Bran admitted. "A spy? But why would you have taken out so many of your own? And why would you be dressed so strangely?" The eldest brother shook his head. "The mystery you present is beyond me. I'll leave your fate to King Tuathal."

I really didn't like the sound of that but couldn't argue with Bran's logic.

For all I knew, I *could* be a spy. Or worse, an assassin. In the end, no matter what I was, and no matter how frustrating I found it to leave my destiny in the hands of someone else—even a king—I refused to blame Bran and his brothers for my fate. Although—as Bran urged the horses faster, my hips already aching—I realized I *would* gladly blame them for putting me on this damn horse.

I may not have known who I was, but at least I knew where I drew my lines.

*C*aer Capall—a fort made up of tiered, man-made hills, each of the three levels as tall as a man—was hosting one hell of a party. The festivities spilled out along the grassy knolls, with some revelers huddled together in pockets, singing and laughing and drinking. Others had already passed out where they lay. Guards stood watch on each of the levels, their backs to the torches which ringed the fort, overlooking the drunken shenanigans with the scowls of disapproving parents. Or maybe they were just pissed to be on guard duty. I considered asking the two who stopped us as we approached the sloped entrance that led to the top tier, but neither seemed interested in chatting with me; Bran was the focus of their attention.

"Donall was worried when you didn't immediately report back," the first guard said.

"The King said you must have gotten distracted," the other added, glancing past Bran to me, eyes speculative. I glowered at him until he looked away, coughing.

"Any sign of the Curaitl?" Bran asked.

"None. Why?"

Bran looked briefly troubled but shook his head. "It's nothing. Tell the guards not to join in tonight."

"Now Bran, you know—" the second guard began.

"Yes, I know. I know that once everyone is passed out, you all like to gather up what's left of the ale and split it between you for the night." He held up a hand. "Night watches are long, and a little ale never hurt anyone. But not tonight, understand?"

The two guards exchanged looks. "Alright, Bran. We'll pass the word along."

"Good. This one's with me." Bran jerked a thumb my way.

"Hostage?"

Bran glanced back at me, eyes narrowed. "Guest. For now, anyway."

"Best not let Donall see her, then," the second guard joked, craning his neck to stare up at me, pointing idly at my hair. "You know how he gets around the fiery ones. Even if she is a giant."

I leaned forward onto the pommel of my saddle, smiling sweetly at the man, though I kept my voice very low when I whispered to Bran out of the side of my mouth, "If anyone here tries anythin', this giant is goin' to fee-fi-fo fuck 'em up."

Bran raised both eyebrows at that, clearly puzzled, but turned back to the guards without a word. "I'll make sure she's treated as any *proper* guest in King Tuathal's house should be," he said, matter-of-factly.

The second guard averted his eyes and mumbled something. His companion merely nodded and waved us through. "Enjoy a flagon for us, would you?"

Finann gave a small salute as we passed. "Anything for you, lads," he quipped, merrily.

It wasn't until we'd ridden all the way to the top tier of the fort that I realized just how high up we actually were—the drunks at the base of the mounds barely larger than my thumb from this distance. It was impressive, and—for some reason—not what I'd expected. A fort should have stone walls, shouldn't it?

"You two," Bran said, interrupting my thoughts as he slipped from his horse, "head to the stables. Meet me at the hall when you're done." He held a hand out to me, helping me from the back of his mare. "As for you...no running, agreed?"

"Aye, whatever ye say," I replied, wincing almost immediately after putting my feet on the ground. "Wouldn't get very far anyway," I added, taking a few awkward, bow-legged steps—my inner thighs burned from the ride and made it hard to walk comfortably. Between that and my strange, blood-stained clothes, I imagined I'd make quite the spectacle when presenting myself in front of the king. But hey, at least this way they might take pity on me.

"Don't worry, *ceara*, you'll get used to it if you stick around," Finann called as he and Llew headed for the stables with the horses in tow. Llew waved at me, quiet as ever, though his smile was far more genuine than his older brother's.

"Ceara?" I echoed.

"He's teasing you. It means fiery." Bran eyed my hair. "It is a rather distinctive color."

I reached up and held a few locks out, watching as the firelight danced across the individual strands. Fiery, indeed. "D'ye not have many redheads here, then?"

"A few." Bran seemed about to say something else, but then snapped his mouth shut and turned away.

"What? What were ye about to say?"

Bran sighed. "There are a few. But rarely do they look so...unique. That's what I was going to say. Now come on. Tuathal will want a report." He marched off, forcing me to follow as best I could, marveling at the fact that he'd given me a compliment. I wasn't sure why, but it felt as though I hadn't received one of those in a while. I was...flattered. Maybe a little flustered, even.

Which is probably why, as we worked our way through the crowds of feasting drunkards—thicker on this level than they had been below—I kept quiet, unless you count hissing through my teeth every time someone bumped into me. That is until a lout with a flagon in hand tried to convince me to dance with him; he ended up on his knees, wailing at the pressure I was putting on his wrist.

"Sorry, not interested," I said, frowning. I released the man's wrist and stepped away, only to find Bran looming over my shoulder.

"This way," he said, tilting his head.

"Right."

After another twenty feet or so, he spoke again. "I shouldn't have left you alone. I'm sorry."

"It's alright," I replied. I realized that it hadn't bothered me at all, snatching that man's wrist when he'd ignored my initial protest, then twisting it back and up, knowing I could snap it if he tried to fight through the pain. If anything, it bothered me that I couldn't remember where I'd learned to do something like that; it'd sort of just happened. A knee-jerk reaction. "I handled it."

"I noticed." Bran slowed, then indicated a long, domed structure which dwarfed all the others. "The mead hall. That's where we'll find King Tuathal. Donall may be there, too, though I expect he'll be passed out by now." The eldest brother turned to stare at me. "I want your word that you'll harm no one inside."

I frowned.

"No one who doesn't offer you violence, first," Bran amended.

"And if I don't want to dance with someone?" I asked, wryly.

"I will announce you as Tuathal's guest. None would dare force you to do anything against your will, so long as you are under his protection. I give you my word."

Convenient, I supposed. But, in the back of my mind, something nagged at me. An instinct, maybe. Something. As I studied that distant hall, listening to the laughter and squeals around us, the faint hum of music coming from further within the camp, I felt something brush against my mind. A voice, maybe, urging me to take my chances and run while I still could. But of course, there was no turning back, now.

"What is it?" Bran asked, watching the emotions warring across my face.

"I may not know who I am," I replied. "But whoever I once was doesn't trust your word."

Bran's puzzled expression was clear, even by the dim firelight. "A man's word is the same as fact. Or truth. Once sworn, it cannot be unsworn."

"Just like that?"

Bran shrugged. "This is the Land of Youth. To break a promise here..." Bran shook his head.

"What?" I asked, curiosity piqued.

"To break a vow is to be exiled," Bran said, then shuddered. "No one would risk such a thing."

I sighed and began waddling towards the mead hall, suddenly eager; I could smell sizzling meat and felt my mouth water almost instantly, my stomach grumbling. "Then let's get this over with," I said, "and pray your king is as noble as ye t'ink he is." I glanced over to see Bran's eyes reflecting sudden doubt, but at last he nodded.

"As you say."

13

*T*he first impression I got from the mead hall was how hot and densely packed it was, despite its size; men and women crowded together along benches and tables that ran on either side of the building, clamoring at one another to be heard, raising toasts to punctuate every sentence, their exposed flesh lathered in a light sheen of sweat. I could see where the hall's design should have left a middle aisle free for people to walk up and down, but—as crowded as it was—the aisle had become more of a bustling bridge, encouraging travel from one table to the next. As I watched, more than a few men and women roamed, splashing ale as they bumped into each other, occasionally falling over into the laps of the seated to a mixture of cheers and catcalls. Basically, it was the sort of environment you either had to be drunk enough to enjoy, or sober enough to mock.

Sadly, it seemed we didn't have time for either.

Bran gestured for me to follow, clearly nonplussed by the rambunctiousness on display. Together, he and I weaved among the merrymakers, though the eldest brother kept checking on me as we went—worried I'd break someone's arm if they inadvertently bumped into me, perhaps. Frankly, it was a justifiable concern; I hadn't exactly intended to put that man on his knees before, and I wasn't entirely sure I'd be able to stop myself from doing it again.

Fortunately, we cleared a majority of the crowd without incident, a

SHAYNE SILVERS & CAMERON O'CONNELL

raised dais—our intended destination, it seemed—visible beyond the press of bodies. A little over a half dozen people milled about on the platform. Most struck me as what Bran might call chieftains, their bodies decorated in fine clothes, wrapped in the occasional fur, sporting silver collars and armbands. More than a few seemed to be nursing their flagons rather than tossing them back, surveying the festivities below wearing pleased expressions that never quite met their eyes.

Beyond these were two men who—as soon as I noticed them—captured my full attention. The first was, of course, the king. Tuathal, as Bran had named him, sat upon a tall throne wearing a black, bearskin cloak which was bound at his chest by a gold pin only a few shades more lustrous than his hair. A matching gold collar wrapped around his throat, followed by two gold armbands on his left bicep and a silver on his right. He wore no crown that I could see, but it made absolutely no difference because the truth was Tuathal radiated kingship. It practically oozed out of him, visible in the way he held himself, the way the others deferred to his every move, not to mention the way he looked upon his people—like a proud, doting parent.

And yet, the second figure seemed nobler still, somehow. Not as royal, perhaps, but just as deserving of attention. He was freakishly tall, enveloped in a thick cloak made of raven's feathers, and stood at the king's right hand like some sort of bodyguard, bending down from time to time to listen to whatever Tuathal had to say. For just an instant, he and I locked eyes, and a sense of foreboding flooded me. Something was wrong.

I yelled for Bran, hoping he might tell me what was about to happen, but never got the chance. Instead, the man walked out to the edge of the dais and raised his hands. A deafening cheer went up. Bran gestured again, indicating we should stop moving further.

"What is it?" I asked.

"Amergin. Our bard." He held a finger to his lips, and I realized everyone else had fallen silent, giving the bard their full and undivided attention.

"Tógálaí Capall!" Amergin called, his voice so rich it should have come with a warning label. "Tonight, you honor us."

Another cheer, this one somehow louder than the last.

"As a gift, I will let one of you choose tonight's song. Which tale will you have from me?" Amergin swept his arms out from beneath his cloak, revealing an intricately carved harp that drew a series of murmurs and excited chattering.

"The Children of Lir!" a woman called out.

Amergin smiled but said nothing.

"Fionn mac Cumhaill and the giant!"

"The Dagda's Harp!"

"The Tain Bo Cuailgne!"

"Deirdre of the Sorrows!"

"Tell us of Oisin, who left!" Bran yelled.

Amergin's eyes narrowed as he sought Bran out among the crowd, then widened upon seeing the two of us standing in the middle of the hall. I had to admit we were quite the sight—what with Bran still coated in warpaint and blood, not to mention how out of place I must have looked. Amergin held up a hand, and the varied suggestions fell away until all were silent once more. "The tale of Oisin the Forsaken, son of Fionn mac Cumhaill," he began, "is a tragic story. A cautionary tale. Heed it well."

Amergin cleared his throat and began to sing, accompanying himself on his hand-harp with the occasional flourish, though each strum seemed to come at just the right moment. "Oisin, cherished son and finest of the Fianna," he began, "longed for nothing more than to find the Land of Youth. Dreams of our fair lands and fairer people dominated his mind until it became his battle cry, his toast, and his prayer. Many tried to dissuade the warchief's son, to show him the folly of such ambition. For what could even a man as just as Oisin—warrior, bard, and poet—offer the Blessed People? And yet, he was not deterred. Such was the strength of his conviction, of his resolve, that even we in the Land of Youth heard tales of Fionn mac Cumhaill's bold son.

"Curious as to the nature of this man, one of the Blessed People, Niamh, Queen of the Southern Isles, rode across the seas, leaving the Otherworld for the realm of man on the back of her own steed, a horse raised by the Tógálaí Capall, a mount so swift he could gallop across the waves. And so it was Niamh came upon the young man and a host of his fellows. Shocked at her sudden appearance and stunned by her otherworldly beauty, the Fianna fell back as one—startled as many mortals are by the Blessed People.

"All but Oisin.

"The warchief's son approached the shore, drawn to Niamh like a moth to flame, and she saw in this youth and bearing all the potential of a king, despite his patchy beard and his rugged features. For, as you all know, even among mankind there are those who deserve our blessing, those who are called to live among us for their valor, for their achievements."

The bard spared a glance for Bran at this point before continuing, occasionally plucking the strings of his harp, his song ringing out among the ramparts of the mead hall. "And so it was that Niamh was invited to the hall of Fionn mac Cumhaill—white-haired leader of the Fianna and a legend in his own right—and there given welcome and praise, for none—not even the warchief—had seen a more beautiful woman. And yet still Fionn mac Cumhaill was saddened to learn of Niamh's most fervent desire: to be accompanied home by his most treasured son.

"But, as all fathers one day must, Fionn mac Cumhaill gave his son his blessing, saying only 'Return one day and tell me of your adventures, my son. Tell me of your dreams fulfilled and of the wonders you've seen.' And so Oisin, who had once rebelled against his father in the name of justice, swore to do as his father wished. At last, after several days of feasting, the Fianna rode out as one to bid the young warrior farewell, honoring the dreamer even as he and his fair lady rode off into the sea.

"Thus it transpired that Oisin, child of the Fianna, was carried to the Land of Youth and presented with a vision that defied even his wildest dreams—for the Land of Youth was more exquisite, more beautiful, than ever he could have imagined. Indeed, so lovely was the land that the instant the young man stepped upon the shore, he found its beauty transform his own flesh to match—the scars from all his battles fading within moments, his shattered nose reknitting, his teeth aligning, his skin smoothing and muscles firming. Vigor filled Oisin like an overflowing cup, and he seized Niamh in his arms. Together, they rejoiced in his arrival, their laughter ringing out upon the land like bells.

"Shortly after, Oisin and Niamh wed, becoming King and Queen of the Southern Isles. In time, it was judged that fairer, more just rulers the Land of Youth had never known. Such was Oisin's strength and skill with the blade that even the mightiest of the Blessed People dared not challenge him, and such was Niamh's beauty that all who looked upon her rejoiced to call her their sovereign. Indeed, for many years they ruled in total harmony, an example for all who would rule over others.

"And yet, Oisin had given a promise to return to his father and tell of his adventures, to describe this realm he'd come to call home. And, as is so often the case with truly honorable men, this promise lay heavy on Oisin's heart until one day the weight of it was too much for him to bear alone. Niamh, his beloved, tried to counsel her husband when he spoke of his oath, to warn him of the dangers should he return to his land, but Oisin knew he must fulfill his vow, or he would never be at peace.

"'Whatever you do,' Niamh warned, 'do not set foot once more upon the land of men. To do so would be to reject the gifts given to you by the Land of Youth, and you would be lost to me. Please, my love, you must return.'

"Oisin heartily agreed, impatient to pay homage to his father and his people so he might spend the rest of his days alongside his fair wife, free of burdens. Indeed, such was his eagerness that he rushed to the shore, leaping upon the horse raised by the Tógálaí Capall, sparing Niamh only the briefest of embraces before traveling to the realm of men.

"Here, but for the tales of man carried across the seas, our story would end. For Oisin was doomed never to return, though we knew it not." Amergin paused, eyes downcast, playing a sad melody that tugged at my heart, though I wasn't sure why.

"Once upon the shores of man," Amergin continued, "Oisin was greeted —not by the Fianna—but by the unfamiliar faces of much smaller, weaker men. Perturbed, Oisin rode on towards his father's lands, only to find one of these weaker men trapped beneath a rock which had tumbled from the cliff above, his fellows unable to move the boulder. And thus the fate of the honorable son of Fionn mac Cumhaill was sealed, for such was Oisin's strength that all he had to do was lean over and push the boulder aside, thereby honoring Niamh's warning. Except, as he bent down to push aside the boulder, Oisin's saddle broke beneath him, and the son of Fionn mac Cumhaill collapsed upon the ground.

"In moments, the once fair youth became an old, diminished man with many scars, his nose misshapen, teeth brittle, body frail and flawed. His horse, no longer recognizing his owner, returned to the sea, forcing Oisin to walk on unsteady, aged legs. Indeed, it took the son of Fionn mac Cumhaill many days to locate the remains of his ancestral home. The Fianna, you see, had long since disappeared, his father having died without ever having seen his son. For such was Oisin's obsession with the Land of Youth that he'd lost track of time, believing years to be mere months. It is said Oisin wandered the shores of man for years, hoping to see his beloved once more before he died, though this was not to be." Amergin struck a sharp, grieving note. "Thus ends the tale of Oisin, who reminds us all to cherish what we have gained, but never to forget what we have lost."

The bard fell silent and a hush settled over the room the way it might at a funeral after the final words have been spoken. I realized some of those gathered were weeping openly, and that—at some point—tears had spilled down my own cheeks. Indeed, I felt inexplicably sad, even drained. "What happened to Niamh?" I whispered to Bran.

"They say she waits for Oisin still, refusing to believe him lost," Bran replied. "Many have sought her hand since, but she declines them all." He glanced at me, noting my stricken expression. "It is a tragedy for a reason," he chided.

I socked him in the arm. "Then why d'ye suggest it?" I hissed.

Bran opened his mouth to reply, but Amergin's words interrupted him. "Tógálaí Capall! We have heard a tale of sorrow. Perhaps now it's time for a tale of joy! Shall I tell you all of Donall, nephew of King Tuathal, router of the Curaitl?!"

The cry that went up this time shook the rafters, and booze flew everywhere as men and women leapt to their feet, crowing. One of the chieftains, younger than the rest and obviously a little hesitant to bask in the spotlight, shuffled forward at Amergin's insistence. Donall, I gathered, grinned self-consciously, running a hand along the back of his neck. I could see instantly what Bran had meant; the young man was slender and beautiful, his lips full, eyes bright—but certainly no warrior.

Before I could say as much to Bran, however, I watched those lovely eyes widen, those pouty lips spread, as someone appeared at the entrance to the hall bearing a torch, waving it wildly back and forth. Everyone turned as one, their cheers fading as they, too, realized something was inexplicably wrong. I frowned, recognizing the newcomer as one of the guards who'd accosted us when we entered.

"My king," he yelled, voice straining, face lathered in sweat, "it's the Curaitl! They've come, using our very own horses, and have made it to the second step! Aife leads them!"

For an instant, no one spoke.

"Tógálaí Capall!" Amergin shouted, exchanging glances with King Tuathal, who had risen to stand beside his nephew, looking impossibly fierce even from this distance. Donall, I noticed, looked completely shell-shocked. The king placed a hand on his nephew's shoulder and nodded to his bard. "I say we turn this into an even greater tale!" Amergin continued. "Let us chase off the spear-wielders and regain Caer Capall!"

This time the cheers were bloodthirsty, full of rage and the promise of violence. I cringed at the sound, then watched in growing horror as flagons fell to the floor and the Tógálaí Capall charged the door, sprinting past Bran and I, the press of their bodies carrying me out in a wave. I fought and cursed, losing sight of Bran amidst the chaos, but soon I and the rest of the crowd had abandoned the mead hall altogether, listening to a night no longer full of laughter and music, but screams.

14

I scrambled to free myself from the horde of former revelers as they funneled out into the night, apparently very eager to join in the defense of their home. But even once they'd spread out, I still found myself carried along against my will towards the sounds of fighting. Their outraged screams were deafening, the air steaming from the heat of their bodies, and I knew without a doubt that—the moment I stopped moving—I'd be trampled beneath their feet.

At least until the Tógálaí Capall met some actual resistance, that is.

Up ahead, several of the horse breeders screamed and fell back as a small band of the Curaitl hit them from the side, wading into the throng like snakes, striking over and over again. They wore dark furs, their skin and the tips of their spears painted black, making them difficult to see by torch-light. Those around me shrank from the sight of their own people being so callously dispatched, their anger no match for the brutality of seeing their own slaughtered. They'd been encouraged to fight back by promises of glory and too much alcohol, but a mob is only as good as its odds of winning—and the Curaitl weren't taking prisoners.

Still, with the Tógálaí Capall's momentum suddenly slowed, I knew this would be my best chance to break free, so I elbowed my neighbors, vying for room. In the end, I had to push, shove, and pull a half dozen times each before I emerged on the far side of the crowd. I froze, only a foot perhaps from the edge of the top tier and its steep drop-off, and bore witness to the fight below.

To someone trained in the art of war, the battles that raged along Caer Capall's lower tiers might have been a wondrous thing to behold, but—to me—it looked like utter chaos. Horses milled about, screaming and unattended, along the base of the fort. The lowest step had already been overrun, and I knew there would be bodies sprawled out on the ground—not mere drunks, this time, but victims of the Curaitl's assault. The second tier was in better shape, but not by much; it seemed the Curaitl had broken through their defenses, though pitched battles were still taking place. Before I could study the aftermath further, however, I felt the crowd at my back shift as one, the nearest warrior nearly knocking me over the edge.

I spun to find more fur-clad spear wielders had ascended the final tier and were leveling their weapons at the Tógálaí Capall, many of whom were unarmed. Still, the horse breeders seemed to be holding their own; I watched as several leapt at the nearest spear wielder, getting inside the weapon's longer reach to drag down their prey. It was an ugly, grisly fight, but numbers were on their side.

Or that *was* the case.

Until the moment Aife the Fair, warmaiden of the Curaitl, arrived.

From where I stood, I could see the woman burst over the lip of the final slope, not even winded by the climb. True to Finann's assessment, she was indeed beautiful, though her features were more angular than feminine, all the more so with her red-gold hair pulled away from her face by a series of artful braids. She wore tan leathers and the skin of a white bear about her shoulders, the pelt already matted with blood, and wielded both sword and spear. Still caught between the crowd and the edge, all I could do was watch as she charged the Tógálaí Capall.

The first horse breeder who stepped close ended face down in the dirt without having so much as touched her, bleeding from a slash across his stomach. The second and third she simply knocked unconscious with the butt of her spear, slapping them both upside the head like errant children. The whole time her face remained remarkably impassive, almost as if she were going through the choreographed steps of a familiar dance. I quickly realized her fellow warriors fell into the gaps she left behind, securing more and more ground as she advanced, casually downing opponent after opponent. Soon they'd have a firm foothold on the top tier, and I sensed a rout was coming. But what should I do, if that happened? Flee? Fight? A horrifying howl split the night while I struggled with my decision, and I thought to spare a glance below, but something else got my attention first.

The ground was shaking.

I whirled to find Bran and his brothers leading a charge of perhaps a dozen armed guards on horseback. They galloped into the fray, taking the spear wielders by surprise, ripping into their midst and trampling over bodies. After that, it was total mayhem; Bran and his brothers moved as one, shielding one another from thrusts even as they mowed down their attackers, their mounts biting and kicking any who dared get too close. And yet, Aife and a small contingent of warriors continued their assault, working their way through the remaining Tógálaí Capall rather than doubling back to save their fellows. But that made no sense. Was she just hoping for maximum casualties, or did she have some other goal?

"You!" Aife screamed, jabbing her spear into the gut of a man maybe twenty feet from me, the tip of her sword aimed directly at my chest. Several members of the crowd stepped to the side instinctively, parting to make certain they weren't the intended target.

"Me?" I asked, placing a hand over my heart, surprised.

"Get her!" she called, gesturing to her warriors.

I watched three of the spear wielders hesitate and scour the area before advancing towards me, lashing out at those few who still stood in their way. Panic made my heart race. What had *I* done? I backed away, hands raised in supplication, until I could feel the emptiness behind me, my heel in midair. I gritted my teeth, realizing I had nowhere to run. Sure, I could throw myself over the edge, but the slope was steep enough I'd be lucky to survive the fall, let alone flee from there. Besides, for some reason, the image of me tumbling end-over-end in a bid to escape pissed me off. I felt something stir within me—a deep well of anger I hadn't realized existed. Overhead, a flock of birds soared past, their shrill voices joined in a harsh cacophony.

We would *not* retreat.

After all, that's not who we were.

We met the first warrior before he could so much as raise his spear, sweeping the weapon aside with our foot, then stepping in close to deliver a vicious throat punch. The bastard dropped to his knees, clutching at his crushed windpipe, spear forgotten.

Which was convenient, because we needed a spear.

We drove our knee into the man's face, then sidestepped, slipped our foot beneath the shaft of his fallen spear, and kicked it into the air with a practiced motion. From there, we snatched the spear from midair and flung it at our next attacker, the weapon taking her in the shoulder, missing her heart by inches. More's the pity.

The woman launched sideways from the force of the throw, momentarily out of the fight. Unfortunately, it seemed we'd lost the element of surprise; the final warrior came forward far more prepared for us, crouched low, jabbing with his spear. We danced away, warily, wishing not for the first time that we had some weapons of our own. Something that could strike from a distance, quick and often. But, since that wasn't an option, we decided we'd have to rely on something else: misdirection.

We glanced past the warrior between one strike and the next and opened our mouth in surprise, pointing as if something had stolen our attention. The warrior spun, completely taken in by the ploy, as we knew he would be. We tackled the moron, landing with our full weight on his back, a hand locked in his hair, and began bashing his head into the ground. He scrambled for his weapon, but we swatted it away, snarling. Again and again, we slammed the man's face into the dirt, screaming in outrage. How dare they attack *us*?

Which is likely why we didn't see the woman we'd wounded until it was too late; she stabbed us through the chest with her own weapon, her strike weaker than it might have been, but still with more than enough force to drive us to the ground. She pinned us there with all her weight, grunting with the effort. The pain was excruciating, but we knew we couldn't let her win; we lashed out with one foot, catching her knee at an odd angle, and she collapsed with a shriek. We tried to get up, to finish what we'd started, but we couldn't. We couldn't breathe.

A lung, a distant part of us realized.

She'd pierced my lung.

Alarm set in, and I squirmed, my heart thundering in my chest. The edges of my vision blackened. I rolled, unable to do anything else, and watched as Bran and his brothers chased off the spear wielders in the distance, forcing them to the tier below, successfully repelling the invaders.

It seemed Aife had come to the same conclusion; the warmaiden signaled the retreat among her remaining warriors, angling towards the opening my three assailants had secured when they'd come after me. My vision tunneled further until all I could see was the warmaiden's legs as she approached, her spear and sword caked in blood, firelight dancing over her skin.

Her shadow fell over me as I blacked out.

15

My guard trekked alongside me, a coiled rope wound about her waist which ended at my bound wrists. Blair—as she'd introduced herself on the first morning of our march—had a heart-shaped face, much more attractive now than I remembered, though I doubt anyone looks their best when in ridiculous amounts of pain. The shoulder wound I'd given her, like my own chest wound, had healed days ago—not that she seemed inclined to forgive and forget. If anything, Blair seemed to despise me more now than when I'd first woken up in Aife's camp on a makeshift cot of mounded furs, my ankle tied to a post.

Confused and disoriented, I'd asked all sorts of questions, but Blair and her people hadn't been inclined to answer any of them. Instead, they'd referred me to their leader, saying, "We don't know, ask Lady Aife." Of course, Lady Aife had been far too busy to see me that morning. Or, indeed, any morning since.

We'd traveled dozens of miles since then, the air growing crisper with every step until at last Blair had taken pity on me and given me a tattered fur of my own, as well as a pair of fur-lined boots. I'd been given water and a little food, but my stomach still ached. Though I'd hoped otherwise, I hadn't regained my memory over the intervening days. In fact, the longer we marched, the more I seemed to forget. Had even Caer Capall been a dream? What of Bran and his brothers? Were they out there, even now, searching for me? Or had I simply made them up, a fantasy to latch onto while Aife and her spear wielders carried me off?

"There it is again," Blair muttered.

"What?" I asked, startled by the woman's voice; Blair had rarely spoke unless spoken to, and even then all that came out of her mouth had been some variant of "keep moving."

Blair gave me a withering look, but finally jerked a thumb to our right, where a series of rocky hillsides dominated the landscape. The rest of Aife's forces were largely on our left or in front—a long line of warriors moving at a fair clip towards the distant peaks of northern mountains. Lately, I'd begun praying we'd reach our destination long before I discovered just how tall those mountains really were; I wasn't the least bit interested in losing any of my appendages to frostbite. "What about 'em?" I asked, eyeing the rugged landscape she'd indicated.

"Look!" Blair urged, giving me a shove.

I stumbled a little, caught off guard, but did catch something out of the corner of my eye in the process. I squinted, studying the space between two boulders where I thought I'd seen…something. "What *was* that?"

"A horse, probably," Blair replied, though she sounded unsure. "Must have followed us from the fort. Maybe it thinks we have food to spare." Blair shrugged and returned her attention to the march, using her spear like a staff to navigate the uneven landscape. I trailed after her, aware she'd use the butt-end of that spear on me if I held her up but continued to glance back at the hills. I didn't say it but somehow, I knew that what Blair had seen—what I had caught a glimpse of—hadn't been a horse.

Not unless there were horses around here which looked like feral dogs.

"How much further?" I asked.

"You ask that at least ten times a day. Tell me, *strainséir*," Blair snapped, using her preferred term for me, a word that I'd learned meant foreigner, "do you get as tired of the sound of your own voice as I do?"

"Not really," I replied, pursing my lips thoughtfully. "But I'll tell ye what, let me carry your spear for a while, and I'll gladly watch over ye while ye take a much-needed nap. What d'ye say?"

"Why would you do that?" Blair asked, suspiciously.

It took me a moment to realize Blair hadn't caught on to what I'd been implying. That, in her mind, I really *was* offering to guard her while she slept. "Ye lot really struggle with sarcasm, don't ye?"

"You mean lies."

I shrugged, the difference negligible to me. The warrior I'd tricked during the battle, a thin, bald man named Rhys, had been even more critical of my deceptive tactics; I'd spent the better part of ten minutes retching after the blow he'd landed to my stomach on our first day's march. Of course, it'd been at least partially satisfying watching Blair clout him over the head with a rock for having attacked a defenseless prisoner.

"I don't understand you, *strainséir.*"

"Ceara," I insisted, using the name Finann had given me on the night of Aife's raid. Three days later and I had only barely pieced together what the warmaiden had intended—a strategic strike into the heart of the Tógálaí Capall's territory, proving herself and her warriors the greater threat and essentially rebuffing Donall's proposal. Personally, I thought it all seemed a little extreme when a simple "no" might have sufficed. That was until Rhys had inadvertently revealed the real reason Aife had fought her way to the top of Caer Capall: to capture me.

Blair spat to one side. "That is not your name."

"It was given to me, and it's not like I have another."

"Well you cannot have this one, either. Pick something else."

"Why?" I reached up, using what little slack I had, and grabbed a fistful of my own hair. "It's accurate, isn't it?" I asked, waving it about.

Blair's eyes widened. "Red?" She barked a laugh, then pointed to a piece of cloth tied to the end of her spear. "That is red. The color. But Ceara, the name, means *spear.*" She shook her weapon in front of my eyes, defiantly. "When you woke and told us your name, we thought you were mocking us," Blair admitted, searching my face.

I frowned, realizing my mistake. Finann hadn't given me a name, he'd been teasing me. Like ribbing a fair-skinned person for being pale. Of course, this wasn't the first social gaffe I'd committed among the Curaitl; the more I interacted with them, the more apparent the gaps between us became, even if we did technically speak the same language. Indeed, the miscues and blunders seemed to go both ways—my every joke taken seriously, my occasional gesture viewed with open hostility.

"I didn't know," I admitted. "I'm sorry."

Blair's eyes narrowed. "It is hard to tell when you are lying."

"That's how ye know someone's good at it," I replied, without thinking.

The shaft of Blair's spear hit me across the knuckles. I screamed, the pain immediate and sharp, and sank to my knees clutching my throbbing hand. Blair jerked me to my feet, putting that lovely face mere inches from my own, eyes searching. "From now on, if I catch you in a lie, I will do this. You have been given to me until we reach the pass. By the time we arrive, I will have broken you of this habit. It is far kinder than what will happen to you if you lie to Lady Aife, or to others among us who do not appreciate being made to look foolish. Do you understand?"

I fought back tears, biting my lip so hard I knew it'd bruise, all while suppressing the sudden urge to choke the woman to death using her own spear as above us, a crow cawed, accompanied by the sound of wings flapping. We could do it, we knew. We'd never make it far dragging her corpse along for the ride, but we could at least hurt her.

But wait…that's what had gotten me here in the first place, hadn't it?

In fact, it seemed like every time I lashed out without thinking, losing myself to bloodshed and violence, I'd ended in a worse situation than before. And so I rejected the voice inside my head, ground my teeth through the pain, and fought to stand under my own power. Once on my feet, I met Blair's eyes, and what she saw behind mine made her flinch.

"I reject your kindness," I said, voice thready with pain, but menacing, nonetheless. "Know this: if ye ever touch me like that again, I swear I will tear out your eyes and keep them as trophies, leavin' ye to wander this world blind for the rest of your long and miserable life."

Blair took a step back, face pale. "To swear such a thing…" she whispered.

I frowned, surprised by her reaction. Too late, I remembered Bran's warning and the horror that had lurked behind his eyes. To break a promise in the Land of Youth was to invite exile, he'd said. Which meant I'd just triple-dog dared Blair right out of the gate. And yet, there was no going back on it, now; the best I could do was hope the threat was enough. "I may lie when it suits me," I said, still cradling my injured hand, "but I keep me word, too, Blair. Remember that."

16

*B*lair kept her hands off me for the remainder of that day and the next, though she did keep an eye on me at all times, walking slightly behind rather than alongside. We hardly spoke, and I could sense her disdain for me festering into hate. Frankly, I was beginning to resent her, too. Of course, it didn't help that I hadn't so much as caught a glimpse of Aife in four days, which meant I still had no idea why I'd been singled out and captured. As far as I could tell, neither did anyone else; the Curaitl who would talk to me seemed genuinely baffled to find a bound woman among them, even if I was a foreigner and a former enemy. Indeed, it occurred to me that I'd seen no other prisoners taken at all, though Aife surely would have been able to capture some of Tuathal's warriors if she'd been so inclined. It made no sense.

What was so special about me?

Maybe I'd get my answer once we reached the pass, I thought. That, or they'd throw me in a cell and toss away the key. Either way, at least I'd be done with this infernal walking.

"I informed Lady Aife of what you swore to do to me if I struck you again," Blair said. I turned and found her eyeing the mountains ahead. They'd grown much larger in the last couple days, and I was beginning to suspect my prayers weren't being answered. *Could* you lose fingers in the Land of Youth, I wondered?

"Tattletale," I muttered.

"What's that?"

I frowned, unable to explain. "Nothin', nevermind. So, what did your warmaiden say?"

Blair made a sour face. "That I probably shouldn't hit you, then."

I raised my eyebrows at that. "Sounds like a smart woman."

"Lady Aife is a genius," Blair replied, her eyes going soft and docile for just a moment, the full curve of her lips exposed by her gentle smile. The woman really was quite lovely, I decided, when she wasn't being bitchy or assaulting me.

"Aye, makin' off with Tuathal's horses, then usin' 'em to sneak past his defenses," I said, nodding. "All very clever."

"Why do you always sound like you have something else to say?" Blair asked, mouth pursed.

"No, no, it's a brilliant plan. Except there's still one t'ing I don't get," I added, raising a finger, "why bother with me? Gettin' your hostages back, that I get. Provin' a point to Donall. Puttin' the fear of the Curaitl into the Tógálaí Capall. All that makes sense. But why am I the only one ye took back with ye? Why *me*?"

Blair stopped walking, forcing me to halt as well. She cocked her head slightly, then reached out, quick as a viper, and sliced through the ropes on my wrist with a knife I hadn't even noticed her holding. I hissed, surprised, and probed at the skin of my wrists, which were blistered and red from days of chafing.

"Why d'ye do that?" I asked.

"So it's true," she whispered, ignoring my question.

"What's true?"

"That you aren't one of us. One of the Blessed People." She pointed at my aching wrists, which I quickly hid behind my back out of reflex. "None of us would bear those marks. And yet, what else could you be?" Blair mused, still staring at the space where my hands once were, eyes unfocused. "You can't be from the realm of man. You just can't. That's been closed to our kind for so long no one thinks it still exists. You even survived your wounds. But then, what are you?" This time the question had heat to it. Blair searched my face as if willing me to tell her the truth, for once.

If only I could.

"Ye want to know what I am?" I replied, sighing. "I'm tired." I turned and made to follow the train of people headed into the mountains, unwilling to make a break for it even with my restraints removed, but a hand locked on my shoulder, drawing me back. "Look! I don't know who I am, alright?!" I shouted, eyes pinched shut in frustration. "The last t'ing I remember was that battle and drinkin' from Bran's waterskin and listenin' to a sad song, and gettin' in a fight I didn't even want! Just let me be!" I jerked away, suddenly on the edge of hysteria. But then, maybe I'd already crossed that line; alone and cold and surrounded by enemies without even my own memories to keep me company, maybe I'd been pushed past the brink.

"If that is what you wish," a woman's voice—melodious and yet somehow steely—said, "then you may go. Wander the land with the blessing of the Curaitl." I turned and found Aife standing there in all her glory, no longer coated in blood, but wearing a pristine cloak of pale-yellow fur that covered everything but her pale, angular face and the brilliant waves of her unbound hair.

"If you choose that path, however," she continued, "I expect you will not survive long. Winter is but days away, and even those who cannot die can suffer." She studied me, Blair by her side—the woman's head bowed so low she might as well have been checking on the state of her boots. "But, if what you say is true, then you are welcome among us."

"But, but," I stammered, "I don't understand. Why? I mean why now? And why take me at all?" Another question rose, one I hadn't even considered until this very moment, standing mere feet away from the woman who'd taken me prisoner. "Why shouldn't we try to kill ye right now?"

Aife held a hand out to still Blair, who'd already leveled her spear as if to attack me. "Because," Aife replied calmly, "I believed you to be something you are not. You are free to kill me, if you think it wise. Or," she cocked her head, "you could ask me for the one thing you want most in the world right now."

That thought stopped me cold, the momentary urge to lash out immediately quelled. What *did* I want most? Freedom? They'd already undone my restraints and told me I could leave under my own power. From a people so forthright they couldn't grasp sarcasm, that boded well. But no, freedom wasn't enough. What I wanted, more than anything else, was answers.

"And you shall receive them," Aife said, as if reading my mind. "In time. But first, I think, rest. And, perhaps, food."

My stomach lurched with the mere thought, and the hunger I'd been staving off for so long seemed to hit me all at once; a tidal wave of nausea that made me a little faint. I wobbled a little, then nodded. "Aye, food."

Aife clapped my shoulder, once, and I nearly toppled beneath the strength of that one blow. "Excellent," she said, her smile wide and inviting. "Come, while I tell you of the Curaitl."

I nodded absentmindedly, catching Blair's remarkably inquisitive expression out of the corner of my eye; I had a feeling she and I were far from done. But I couldn't focus on that, now, because Aife was already talking, leading me by the arm towards the mountains as if we'd been friends all along.

"It began long ago, you see, when my sister and I were still young. She was a fierce, hard thing, even then, whereas I had always been the gentler one. And yet, we fell in love with the same man. Which meant, when the war came..."

I planted the spear between my opponent's feet and jerked left, then right, forcing him off balance with each blow, exposing his improper stance. He cursed, suddenly bow-legged, as I ducked a shoulder and rammed him to the dirt. The poor bastard landed with a crunch, the cold ground a little less solid than it had been when winter hit in force months ago, but still plenty firm enough to knock the wind out of him on impact. I flipped the spear and angled it under his throat, the tip flush against his jugular. Or it would have been, had we been using real weapons as opposed to practice staffs.

"Ye overcommitted with that last strike," I said. "Should've—"

"Retreated," Tristan interjected, grimacing. "I know, I know."

"Too bad ye never retreat."

Tristan rolled his eyes but flashed me a grin. "Are you going to help me up, or is this some sort of punishment?" He cocked his head a little, glancing past the line of my staff to stare up at me. "Because I've had worse views."

Suddenly it was my turn to roll my eyes, but I gave him the laugh the comment deserved as I reached for the man's hand, hefting him to his feet. Tristan was a slim-waisted, broad-shouldered, square-jawed hunk who outweighed me by at least fifty pounds, but—after training half a day every day for the past few months—the effort cost me almost nothing. "Next time —" I began.

"Staggered stance," Tristan said, nodding.

"Footwork is important," I leaned on my staff for support, relishing in the afterglow of a good practice bout. "But it's more than that. Ye have to stop relyin' on your strength." I tapped his chest. "Technique. Don't try so hard to overpower everyone."

"As if he could!" a voice called. We turned to find Rhys and three of his cronies watching us from outside the practice ring. Tristan stiffened beside me as their laughter spilled out into the courtyard. Two of the men mimed his fall, exaggerating the motion to the point of ridicule.

Tristan made to step forward, but I held out an arm. "Oh? And would ye prefer to try your luck, Rhys?" I called. "Assumin' you're more prepared than ye were last time I beat ye."

Rhys purpled but didn't take the bait. "We'll meet each other in the ring soon, Ceara. Your tricks won't save you, then," he said, then spat into the dirt before gesturing to the men at his back. "Let's go."

The men fell into step behind their leader, though those who trailed flung a variety of rude gestures in our direction, just in case it wasn't clear how much they despised us. Or, well, me at least. "I'm sorry, Tristan," I said. "He wouldn't have said anythin' if I weren't here."

"Yeah, Rhys sure does hate you," Tristan replied.

I glanced over at him. "Ye don't have to look so pleased about it," I chided.

"Oh, I'm not. Rhys isn't worth the cattle shit he used to shovel." Tristan stretched, relishing in the play of midday sunlight on his clean-shaven face—the only time of day we ever saw sunlight in the North Pass. "I'm just glad I'll get to watch you put him on his ass in front of everyone, soon."

I frowned. "There's no guarantee he and I will even be paired up," I reminded him. "From what Lady Aife said, there'll be contestants from all across the Land of Youth."

Tristan waved that away. "The Curaitl always advance further than most. Mostly it's the way the tournament is set up. No horses, no bows. Gives us and a few others an advantage. Besides, while Rhys is clearly an idiot, he's a capable enough fighter."

"And who's to say I'll stick around?"

Tristan clapped me on the shoulder, flashing me a wide, guileless smile I'd come to associate with the man. "We both know you're going to do well,

Ceara. As far as I can tell, the only person who stands a chance against you with a spear at this point is Lady Aife."

I grunted. "She's a demon."

"A what?"

I blinked, then shook my head. "I meant she's a force of nature. Like a blizzard. Or a wildfire."

Tristan nodded thoughtfully. "Yes, I suppose she is. But she doesn't have your reach." He glanced up, meeting my eyes the way so many among the Curaitl were forced to—from below. "She has to work to get in past your guard, and even that has become a challenge for her, lately. I've never seen her break a sweat beating anyone until you came."

I shifted, uncomfortable with the praise, and shrugged. "Aye, well, she's a good teacher. And I have good sparrin' partners," I added, smirking.

Tristan belted out a laugh. "Yes, we all love being your plaything." He winked, then wandered off with a wave. "Anyway, I have to get back. Make sure you get some rest and say hi to your lover for me!"

I glanced up at the sun overhead, eyes wide, realizing what time it was with a start. "Shit!" I cursed, hurrying to the nearby water trough. I began splashing the chilly liquid all over my face and rubbing it over my chest and arms. A shudder ran through me as a gust of spring wind blew through the practice arena. For just a moment I felt a wave of dizziness pass through me, my vision blurry, as a voice called out to me. A name. Something about a name. But I shook it off a moment later, took a deep breath, and continued washing; I knew better than to show up at home smelling of sweat, no matter the excuse.

The things we do for love.

𝓘 hurried through the village, hoping to skirt the edges of the midday foot traffic, but I'd forgotten all about the Beltane feast; the market was clogged with people gathering odds and ends or simply gabbing amongst themselves. I craned my neck, hoping to find a way through, but a hand appeared in front of my face at almost that exact moment. Startled, I glanced down, only to find a young girl grinning up at me.

"Imogen," I said, ruefully. "What is it, now?"

The girl huffed, folding her arms over her chest. "Well, now I don't even want to ask you," she said, pouting.

"And yet I'd bet me boots you'll ask me anyway," I replied, tousling the girl's russet-colored hair, a drabber shade than her mother's, but no less red by the Curaitl's standards.

Imogen slapped my hand away, tidying up the bird's nest I'd created, scowling. "You're just like mother sometimes, you know that?"

"I'll take that as a compliment, if ye don't mind."

Imogen rolled her eyes. "So, are you going to help me, or what?"

"Depends on what ye want. I'm runnin' late, as it is."

"That's alright, you don't have to help me, now."

"Oh?"

"Tonight," she affirmed, grinning impishly. "I want to steal Tristan's armband. But it has to be a secret. He can't know you helped me, or it won't count." The girl—who I realized wasn't quite as young as I'd thought if she was already plotting to find herself a lover—shifted her weight nervously from side to side.

"And why would ye want to do that?" I asked, cocking an eyebrow.

Imogen blushed. "I...well, he's..."

I laughed and ducked down, putting my face but a few inches from her own. "And are ye sure he wants ye to steal it?"

For just an instant, doubt flickered across the young woman's face. But when she finally met my eyes, there was a fierceness to her gaze that reminded me all too much of Lady Aife—a certainty bordering on stubbornness. "No, but—"

I pressed my forehead against hers, the gentlest of headbutts. "Well, I am. He'll be a lucky man to have ye, Imogen." I flashed her a reassuring smile, winked, and rose to my full height. "D'ye at least have a plan?"

Imogen beamed up at me, bouncing a little on her toes. "I do!"

"Find me at the feast tonight, and we can go over it, then."

Imogen clapped, nodded, and bolted off into the market throng, threading through the crowd like a knife through butter. I sighed, then glanced back up at the sky, cringing; I was going to be so late. Still, I could admit it had been worth it to see Imogen so ridiculously happy.

Not right, not right, not right!

I spun, wondering who was speaking...but there was no one. Or, rather, there were dozens of people within hearing distance, but none who matched that voice. No one was that agitated. I reached up to work at the bridge of my nose to relieve the sudden pressure, massaging my sinuses, and prayed I wasn't going crazy.

I kept distractions to a minimum from then on, slipping through the crowd as best I could, though I occasionally bumped into a friendly face and felt obligated to exchange a greeting or two; despite my less than cordial interactions with Rhys and his men, many of the Curaitl had welcomed me with open arms, offering to teach me the ways of their people so I might contribute to their society. Indeed, where once I'd found uncertainty and even hostility, I now found warmth and companionship. Part of that, of course, was Lady Aife's blessing; the Curaitl practically worshipped the woman. Another was my apparent skill with the spear, a talent so revered by the Curaitl that even cattle shits like Rhys were afforded a certain degree of respect. And then there was the fact that I was seeing—indeed, living with—one of their own.

I finally skidded to a stop outside our hut, breathing labored from having run all the way home from the market. I squinted against the dwindling sunlight, spotted the figure leaning against the doorway, and held out my hands in surrender.

"You're late," Blair said.

"What can I say? I got distracted," I replied, hanging my head.

Blair flicked her eyes to the sky in exasperation, but couldn't hold back a smile, which was probably the closest thing to forgiveness I'd get from her. "Come in, then. You best take off your clothes and clean yourself up," she added as I rushed past, "you smell like sweat."

It turned out I wasn't expected to peel off my clothes by myself; Blair ducked inside right behind me and latched her arms around my waist before I could take another step, pulling me close, her face pressed against my shoulder. I could feel her body spooned against mine, soft and hard in equal parts. "Did you win?" she asked.

I turned in Blair's embrace, reaching out to wind my fingers through her blonde, curly hair, the two of us shifting our weight just so—a slow dance to music no one else could hear. Blair stared up at me, and, not for the first time, I was struck by the odd sensation of holding someone shorter than me. It had happened often at first, but I certainly didn't mind it nearly as much now as I once had. Love is like that sometimes—so overwhelming that even that voice in the back of your mind that won't shut up, that can't help but notice flaws, falls silent. Besides, her eyes were certainly worth bending my neck for; a brown so pale they flashed gold in sunlight, rimmed by dark lashes. I sometimes seemed to lose myself in them—failing to listen to whole conversations in the process. My mind utterly blank for one blessed moment. Personally, I thought it was romantic. Blair—who admittedly always ended up having to tell her story a second time—disagreed.

"I fought Tristan."

Blair laughed, then bent forward, brushing her lips over the hollow of my throat. "As if it matters who you fight, these days." She glanced back up, smirking. "But at least Tristan takes it well when you put him on his back."

I raised an eyebrow. "Oh? And ye don't?"

Blair's expression grew rueful as she slid her hands beneath my leathers, fingers exploring the flatness of my stomach, so much firmer now than it had been when I arrived. Not that Blair—who was at least as fit as I was, if considerably curvier—seemed to mind. "You owe me for being late, you know," she whispered, standing on her tiptoes to run her teeth along my throat, her tongue dancing lightly over my skin.

"I owe ye for a lot of t'ings," I admitted, tugging on her hair, just a little. Blair made a soft noise and pressed herself firmly against me, putting as little space between us as physically possible.

"Then pay up," she growled.

And so I did.

18

$\mathcal{W}$e lay coiled in each other's arms, the shadows outside deepening, which meant it wouldn't be long before Blair returned to work; she and Tristan were both members of Lady Aife's household guard, trading off with a few others to watch over the warmaiden and her family. Still, I wasn't going to complain; there was something about her eventual departure that always drew us closer as night fell—our conversations more meaningful, our actions more tender. Absence makes the heart grow fonder—one of the few phrases I occasionally recalled from my old life.

Blair absentmindedly ran her hands up and down my naked back, letting them trail along the curve of my hip as they descended. "Are you ready for the tournament?" she asked.

I frowned, my own arms wound around her shoulders. "Why?" I asked. Blair shrugged, but I noticed the tension singing through her body and knew the question hadn't been a casual one. "What is it?"

Blair sighed, her breath brushing across my exposed chest, making parts of my body tighten in response. She held me closer, giggling, and shook her head. "It's nothing."

"Blair…" I growled.

"It was nothing, really. It was just something Rhys said. He was being… well, Rhys."

I nodded, relaxing somewhat. "What did he say?"

"He…he said if he wins the tournament, he'll ask that you be banished for his boon." Blair spit all this out quickly, as if dreading how I'd react. She shook her head. "I know he doesn't stand a chance of winning, it's only—"

I placed a finger against Blair's lips. "It's alright," I said, smiling, though—on the inside—a part of me was seething. Taunting us was one thing, but trying to get to us through Blair? "We'll deal with him."

"We?"

I hesitated, then nodded. "Aye. I'll talk to Lady Aife. See if there's anythin' she and I can do. Rhys is a proud man," I added, thoughtfully, "if all he wants is attention, maybe she can give it to him." Then, for some reason, I bridled at my own words—as if giving Rhys that much credit had somehow subconsciously offended part of me. Indeed, I was struck by a sudden urge to cut him down, to eliminate him before he became a problem. It was a very callous, but very practical solution.

And it scared me a little.

"That's a good idea," Blair replied, grinning. She nibbled on the end of the finger I'd left hovering by her mouth, stealing back my attention. "I have to leave soon," she murmured, searching my face.

I laughed. "And I still owe ye, is that it?"

"No, I think it's the other way around, this time," Blair replied, sinking lower along the line of my body, hands no longer restricted to my back alone.

"Well, if ye insist…"

19

The Beltane feast took place beneath the stars, though the smoke drifting lazily up from our fires concealed the night sky. The market square had been commandeered for the occasion, vendor stalls converted to serving platforms—dishes of all sorts had been put on display, mostly a variety of prepared meats, their contents still sizzling. I was somewhat surprised to find casks of ale had been dispersed among the long tables taken from the mead hall, anchoring either end for easy access, at Lady Aife's request. She and a handful of her finest warriors—Tristan and Rhys among them—occupied a table of their own at the head of the event, a massive, roaring bonfire burning behind them. Though I couldn't make them out from where I stood, I knew Blair and a few other guards were out there, prowling the shadows, keeping an eye out for anything irregular, anything that might ruin the festivities.

Which, tonight, included us.

"Ye want to take it *when?*" I asked, studying Imogen's earnest face.

"When he's peeing."

I shook my head, struggling to remember why I'd agreed to do this. "That's a terrible idea."

"No, it's not," Imogen argued, voice petulant. "If he's peeing, that means he'll be drunk, and away from everyone else."

"Oh? And is that usually how this sort of t'ing gets done?"

"Well, no," she admitted. "Usually we'd wait for the man to take a bath and steal his clothes. But Tristan bathes with his arm rings on."

"Does he now?"

Imogen blushed. "Look, I just need you to distract him."

"Distract him how?"

"I don't know," she replied testily, gripping the loose folds of her dress so tight her knuckles had turned white. "Hit him over the head or something."

I gaped at the young woman. "Let me get this straight. Ye want me to knock your potential beloved unconscious while he's pissin' so ye can steal his armband and proclaim your intentions?"

Imogen frowned, bit her lip, but finally nodded. "Yes."

"Absolutely not."

"Wait, why?!"

"Because," I said, flicking the girl's ear for emphasis, "if Tristan wakes up with his pants around his ankles and his armband missin', you'll have completely embarrassed the man. Not exactly an auspicious beginnin' to a relationship. Besides, the whole point of this is to be clever. Not cruel."

Imogen rubbed gingerly at her ear, staring at the ground, disheartened. "You're right. I'm being silly. Let's just forget it, alright?"

I flicked her other ear.

"Ow! Why'd you do that?"

I pointed, ignoring her question. "What size is that servin' girl's dress, d'ye t'ink?"

Imogen glared at me, but finally turned to look. "Aisling? She and I used to spar together until last year. We're about the same..." Imogen drifted off. "Wait, what are you—"

"Maybe if we dirty up your hair," I interrupted, holding her red locks up to the firelight.

"Hold on, I—"

"You'll have to move differently. Like she does. See how she sways when she walks, turnin' this way and that with her hips? None of that struttin' nonsense ye do."

"I do *not* strut!"

I pressed a finger to the young woman's lips. "Imogen," I said, meeting her eyes, no longer playful or teasing in the least. "D'ye really want to give up? Or are ye willin' to try somethin' bold, even if it means gettin' caught and lookin' like a fool? Because that's what it may come to."

Imogen reached up to take my finger from her lips. "You're serious."

I nodded and searched the shadows for a figure in the dark. "Sometimes love is the most humiliatin' t'ing there is. It's awful, needin' someone so much that you're willin' to give up parts of yourself. But, if ye aren't willin' to take that risk, ye may not deserve it."

"You really are an outsider, aren't you?"

I planted both hands on her shoulders, shook her a little, and grinned. "Maybe. But this outsider has a plan that just might work."

Imogen shifted nervously from side to side for a moment, but eventually let out a small groan of frustration. "Alright, fine, tell me."

"Well, first you're goin' to have to talk Aisling into givin' ye her dress..."

I took my own seat at Lady Aife's table just as the Beltane feast truly began. As I settled in, a procession of perhaps a half-dozen cloaked men and women—the sum total of the Curaitl's druid population—weaved through the tables towards the bonfire, chanting as they approached our table. The druids, it was said, were mystical practitioners who dedicated their lives to the Tuatha de Danann, though all paid particular homage to the Dagda, the greatest and noblest of their gods. Indeed, I'd learned Beltane was as much a religious holiday as it was a celebration of winter's end—a time-honored tradition designed to venerate the coming summer and its bounty, neither of which would be possible were it not for the intercession of the gods.

Once they were arrayed before us, Lady Aife rose to her feet and held her arms wide, her gold armbands glinting with reflected firelight. "Curaitl!" she cried, her melodious voice carrying remarkably well throughout the market square. "Douse the lights!"

In an instant, all flames except that of the bonfire were extinguished, the torches and braziers put out so quickly I actually felt a thrill of panic—as if someone had thrust a hand over my eyes. Fortunately, once my eyes adjusted, I realized it wasn't as bad as all that; I could still see the druids as they filed out on either side of our table, working their way towards the bonfire at our backs, their chant uninterrupted. As I watched, each of the druids produced a torch and pressed it to the flames, though when they withdrew them, I was surprised to see the cloth-wrapped ends burning with an inexplicably bright, otherworldly light. As one, they returned to stand before us, their torches casting uneven shadows upon the ground that I could have sworn were facing the wrong way.

"Go forth and rekindle our fires," Lady Aife said, arms raised once more. "Together, the Curaitl will welcome the coming season! And," she added, folding her arms across her chest, "if it's not too much trouble, maybe you could put a good word in for those who will be participating in the coming tournament."

One of the druids stepped forward, reached up, and pulled his hood back, revealing a stately face covered in fine, faintly blue tattoos which spun around his mouth and eyes like whirlpools. "Let all who bathe in this fire," he said, lifting his torch, "know the warmth found in the heart of the gods for the Curaitl." He grinned, then, surprising me with the mischievous glint in his eyes. "And know we'll do what we can to ensure victory, my Lady. It never hurts to ask, right?"

Lady Aife barked a laugh, then turned to those of us at her table, snatching up her mug in the process. "To the Curaitl!" She tossed back her mug, and I—like everyone else in the market square—followed suit. The ale was faintly bitter, but refreshing, and a great cheer went through the crowd as Lady Aife returned to her seat, speech apparently concluded.

Meanwhile, I quaffed my drink before slamming it onto the table. "More ale!" I called, waving. Tristan, who sat only a few seats down, leaned forward until he could see me, his eyebrows raised in surprise; he knew I rarely, if ever, drank. It wasn't that I minded the taste of alcohol so much as it was the way I behaved when I'd had one too many—not to mention that damned voice.

"You and Blair planning to celebrate something tonight?" he teased.

I ignored him, gesturing to the nearby serving girl. She swayed towards me, working her way down the table, snatching up mugs and filling them as she went. Her hair was a muddy brown, her dress a little too big on her, but no one seemed to notice or care. Besides, with all the torches and braziers yet to be lit, it was hard to tell even that much.

"More ale?" Imogen, disguised as the serving girl Aisling, asked. Her voice was a bit higher-pitched than I'd have liked, but at least she sounded nothing like herself.

"Aye, and pour some for the homely one over there," I said, pointing at Tristan.

"Oh no," he insisted, "I haven't even finished this one."

"Ah. Well, never ye mind, then," I replied, patting the serving girl's hand. "I was just tryin' to let the poor man beat me at *somethin'* today, that's all."

Tristan grunted. "Oh, is that how it is?" he asked, and I realized he was chuckling, shoulders bobbing up and down. He held up a hand and tossed back his own mug, wiping the froth off his chin with a flourish. "Bring it on, then." He held up his freshly drained mug.

The serving girl flashed me a shy smile and began to close the distance between us, our plan going remarkably well; all Imogen had to do now was trip and spill her pitcher on Tristan. Then, together, she and I intended to slip off his armband in the confusion, and replace it with a cheap, bronze replacement he'd wear until Imogen revealed herself in front of everyone, dressed in her own clothes, cleaned up. It wasn't the most elaborate plan, or perhaps even the most brilliant, but I had a feeling it would all work itself out.

Or, it would have, anyway.

If not for Rhys.

"You're in the way," the bastard said, planting himself firmly between Imogen and her target, having apparently risen from his own seat at the end of the table for some reason. "Go down below and serve the others." He snatched the pitcher out of her hands. "We warriors can pour for ourselves."

Imogen turned to look over her shoulder at me, eyes wide. I jerked my head, realizing it would cause too big a stir for her—a mere serving girl—to argue with one of the Curaitl's champions; she'd be found out in no time. Better that she retreat while she still could. Fortunately, Imogen seemed to come to the same conclusion; she gave the faintest bow and spun, returning to the crowds below, back stiff, sway utterly forgotten.

"You didn't have to be so rude, Rhys," Tristan said, taking his eyes away from the serving girl to stare up at the man.

"She didn't belong up here," Rhys said, sniffing suspiciously at the pitcher.

Tristan frowned, realizing Rhys was probably right; Lady Aife's household servants were typically the only ones allowed among us during large events like these—a security precaution few could argue with. Indeed, convincing Lady Aife's steward that he should let Imogen and I enact our plan had been, until now, the biggest obstacle we'd had to overcome.

"She probably just wanted to meet someone worthwhile," I said, offhandedly, deciding not to stray too far from the truth. "Girls her age are romantic like that, hoping to attract the eye of a true warrior. It's too bad she ran into ye first, eh, Rhys?"

Rhys slammed the pitcher on the table, loomed over my shoulder, and glared down at me. "Any woman would be lucky to share my bed," he growled, then straightened. "After all, Blair never complained," he added.

I scowled, craning my neck to look up at the bastard. "What d'ye say?"

"You really are a moron, Rhys," Tristan muttered.

"What?" Rhys turned to face the other man. "Surely Blair shares such things with her *lover?*"

I glanced back and forth between the two men, but it was Tristan's face that told me what I wanted to know: Rhys wasn't lying. I turned from them both, momentarily disgusted by the mere idea of Rhys and Blair together, but it was the sudden jealousy which made me want to hit something. The images that flashed through my mind.

Images I knew would haunt me later.

I clenched my teeth, knowing I was being ridiculous. No, Blair *hadn't* told me. But who was I to judge? It wasn't like I had no past of my own to share. Why would Blair bring up her former lovers, when I couldn't so much as remember mine? But then, how was I supposed to tell her I sometimes woke up in the middle of the night with the sensory memory of a man's full lips pressed against my mouth, his tongue dancing over mine, his very touch feverishly hot, like a brand against my skin?

And yet...and yet I *hated* Rhys for mocking me like this, for having known her body, even for an instant. The very idea that he'd held her in his arms, that he might know where and how she liked to be touched, made me want to destroy something beautiful.

Irrational? Absolutely.

But so what?

"Rhys, you should go sit down," Tristan urged, having moved to stand next to the man.

"Why?" Rhys planted his hands on his hips. This close, I could see the bastard's general appeal: he was handsome in a rugged sort of way, well-built and fair-skinned. And yet the crooked tilt of his lips, the faint tightness around his eyes, made something cruel out of all that potential. Something wounded and nasty.

"It's alright, Tristan," I replied, sounding far calmer than I felt. "I'll go."

"She'll never be one of us, you know," Rhys said. The words seemed directed at Tristan, but his eyes were all for me, and I knew in that moment that the man was itching for a fight, that he'd come over here to specifically provoke me. "We can't even be sure what she is," he added.

"She's a warrior, like us. A spear wielder—" Tristan began.

"Is she, though?" Rhys mocked a pouting face, then shook his head, disgusted. "Tell me, do you know why Lady Aife wanted her? Why we attacked Caer Capall that night?"

Tristan and I both stared at the man, speechless. Personally, I'd wondered that for a long time, though it'd seemed less and less important as my time with the Curaitl went on; whenever I'd thought to ask Lady Aife, she'd insisted it had been a mistake on her part, a response so out of character for her that I'd never thought to pry further. Eventually, I'd stopped caring enough to ask. But, now that Rhys had brought it back up, I felt the stirrings of something. Curiosity, maybe...or perhaps panic.

"'She fights like my sister'. That's what Lady Aife said," Rhys continued, without waiting for either of us to respond. "Blair and I were guarding Lady Aife when we saw her fight. Lady Aife made us stop to watch. She was a *savage*, Tristan. She fought without honor, striking down anyone who got close, as if her only goal was to survive."

I frowned, trying to recall the battle Rhys was talking about and my reason for being there, but couldn't. It was, like the rest of my past, locked away in a murky, insubstantial place with no windows or doors. And yet, to remind Lady Aife of her sister—by all accounts a fierce warrior Lady Aife both clearly despised and respected—came as quite the shock.

Rhys was nodding, noting my dumbfounded expression. "You're no spear wielder. You're a spy, sleeping with one of our own while you plot our destruction and undermine our way of life. Ceara, I name you *ghiall*."

A collective gasp went up from those sitting around us, many of whom had been listening at least surreptitiously. Tristan actually placed a restraining hand on Rhys' chest, his other held out to stop anyone else from moving. Indeed, by this point we'd drawn the attention of the whole table, Lady Aife included.

"What's going on down there?" she called.

When no one immediately replied, I cleared my throat. "Well, that depends," I yelled back.

"On?" Lady Aife sounded amused.

"On what a *ghiall* is," I replied, trying to match her light, good-natured tone.

Anything to diffuse the tension.

And yet, the instant I spoke the word, the few remaining conversations ceased. In seconds, Lady Aife's guards, Blair included, seemed to materialize out of thin air alongside their warmaiden, weapons drawn. Bewildered, I studied the various faces I'd come to know over the last few months, wondering what social miscue I'd committed this time. But then it wasn't *my* fault, was it? It'd been Rhys who used the word.

And yet, why did I have the sinking sensation that I was the one about to suffer?

"Where did you hear that word, Ceara?" Lady Aife asked, approaching us, her entourage in tow.

"Rhys used it," Tristan explained, words strained as though he were speaking through clenched teeth. "To describe her."

Blair drew everyone's attention with a startled noise, shock and despair warring across her face, her duties as a silent-but-deadly bodyguard momentarily forgotten. "Oh, Rhys. How could you?" she asked, staring at her former lover.

"Rhys," Lady Aife said, her voice as cold and brittle as it had been the night she came for me, "you should not have done that."

"It is my right, warmaiden," Rhys replied, shrugging off Tristan's hand, though he seemed intent on ignoring Blair. "You have given her our blessing, but at what cost?" He shook his head. "I'm not the only Curaitl who does not trust her, my Lady. I am, however, the only one willing to defy you to say so. She is *ghiall*. She is our enemy."

Lady Aife halted, eyes narrowed, lips a thin line. "So be it."

I glanced back and forth between the two, but neither seemed willing to blink first, so it ended up being me who stood and stepped between them. "Can someone tell me what's goin' on?" I asked.

"I have challenged you in front of the Curaitl," Rhys replied.

"Challenged me to what, exactly?"

"A fight to see who the gods favor," Lady Aife replied. "And who they do not."

I raised an eyebrow at that. "Oh, right."

Wait, what?

20

*B*lair hurriedly explained the shit storm I'd inadvertently walked into while she escorted me back to our hut. According to her, by calling me a *ghiall*, Rhys had labeled me an enemy, not just of the Curaitl, but of the Blessed People. From what I gathered, the term was archaic, a curse reserved only for the most despicable, traitorous person one could imagine. Meaning it was, loosely put, the most offensive thing you could say to someone. So offensive, in fact, that it required a duel to settle whether or not it applied—another archaic practice.

"And winners get what, exactly?" I asked, plopping down on the edge of our bed so I could trade in my sandals for boots.

"They get to stay," Blair replied.

"In the village?"

"In the Land of Youth."

I froze, leather straps slipping from my fingers, and stared up at the woman I'd given my heart to. "Ye can't be serious."

Blair nodded, her face stricken, lips pressed together so tight it was as if she were holding back tears. I looked away, fumbling with my boots, momentarily numbed by the idea that the loser of this duel would be banished to the Blighted Lands—a landscape apparently so unlike the Land of Youth that it might as well have been the seeds from which our nightmares grew.

Of course, it wasn't the Blighted Lands I cared about.

"Who are ye more afraid to see go?" I asked, shattering the sudden silence.

"What? Ceara...how could you even ask that?"

I finished tying my boots, stood, and met her eyes. I saw pain in them but didn't look away; part of this was her fault, and we both knew it. I used to think Rhys had always despised me, that he'd taken his defeat at Caer Capall too personally, but was that really all there was to it? Somehow, I doubted it.

I shook my head. "Nevermind." I took a long look around the room—our room. At the cloaks hanging from a set of cattle horns on the wall, the mass of fur blankets Blair insisted she needed to stay warm at night, the cradle she'd carved for our spears. I marveled at all those telltale signs of cohabitation, of sharing a life with someone, and felt it all slipping away. "I t'ink ye should go," I said, turning to face the wall as I undid the brooch holding my dress in place at the shoulder, preparing to change.

"But—"

"Please, just go," I said, voice tight with emotion, clutching at the material across my chest to keep it from falling off. For some reason, I really didn't want Blair to see me naked right now; I felt vulnerable enough as it was.

Honestly, part of me wished I could turn and take her in my arms, hold her close and tell her none of this was her fault, or mine. That Rhys was to blame. That what was about to happen had been a long time coming. But I couldn't. Because I still wasn't sure how much of what had happened was Rhys hating me, and how much of it was Rhys still loving her—and he did still love her. Why else would he have told her what he intended to do if he won the tournament? What else had he said, I wondered, when they were alone together?

When had they been alone together?

And for how long?

I grabbed my hair and tugged with my free hand, frustration and jealousy and anguish hitting me one after the other until all I wanted to do was scream to stop from drowning. And, in the back of my head, that damn voice clamoring, repeating the same phrase over and over again.

Let it go. We have a job to do.

"I don't know what I'd do with myself if you left," Blair said, and I glanced back over my shoulder to find her still hovering in the doorway, tears spilling down her cheeks. "Win. Win for me. And for us." And, with that, she left.

For us.

*B*y the time I returned to the market square, the druids had reignited all the braziers, though the flames now spit and fizzled with that harsh, brilliant white light that still seemed discordant and wrong to me somehow, no matter what the Curaitl claimed about purification and blessings. I stalked towards the gathered masses in a black leather cuirass, dark wool pants, and boots, crow feathers tied into my hair—an outfit meant for mourning, dismissive of the bright, clashing colors of which the Blessed People were so fond. Personally, I thought it fitting; once an outsider, always an outsider, right? As such, I made a point of ignoring the crowd's murmurs and perturbed glances, content to let the Curaitl part swiftly before me.

Distantly, the sound of drums began, beating low and deep and steady like the heart of some primordial beast. I marched to it, letting the percussive rhythm seep into my bones, letting it stoke that simmering rage I'd held locked away for so long—a rage that had never seemed to belong to me, until now.

I found Lady Aife and Rhys waiting for me in the center of the square. The warmaiden had changed, donning gear of her own, wrapped in the cloak of a white bear, cheeks and chin painted red, her sword and spear in either hand. She crossed them as I approached, a sign of respect. I raised my own spear in response, but my attention was all for Rhys; the man wore a pair of vibrant checkered trousers, naked from the waist up, even his feet bare, and held two javelins in either hand, rather than the more traditional, heavier spear.

"Curaitl," Lady Aife began, "tonight we are gathered to bear witness to the whims of fate. By our laws, after tonight, only one of these two champions will remain among us. Only one can claim victory. Will it be Rhys Two Tusks?"

A small cheer went up, mostly from the men gathered behind Rhys, full of catcalls and bawdy language. Rhys raised his javelins, crowing, the veins in his neck straining. I noticed he'd smothered his hair in lime and spiked it, the result a blond mass that rose from his scalp like a corona.

"Or will it be Ceara Battle-Forged?" Lady Aife asked once the cries died down, using the name she'd given me when I'd first begun training with her —a reminder of how she'd found me as well as who I'd become since.

The cheers for me were few and far between, though—of the faces gathered around me—I realized few, if any, bore any animosity. If anything, everyone appeared as though they were already grieving, their festivities cut short by the knowledge that the loser of this fight would not only be exiled but forgotten. Ripped away from tales, their name unspoken, their legacy tarnished beyond redemption. To be banished was the Land of Youth's ultimate punishment—a fate far worse than death.

"Is there no other way?" I asked, so softly only Lady Aife would hear.

"No," she replied. "I've spoken to him, but his mind is made up."

I sighed, leaned on my spear, and began shifting my weight from side to side, warming up my legs and hips as Lady Aife raised her sword. True to his namesake, Rhys leveled his javelins low and wide, like the twin tusks of a boar. I kept warming up, rolling my neck and shoulders.

"Are both contenders ready?" Lady Aife asked.

"Of course I am," Rhys growled.

I nodded. "Whenever ye are."

Lady Aife swung her sword down. "Begin!"

Rhys made the first move, closing the distance between us so fast Lady Aife barely had time to get out of the way. It was a good strategy; the element of surprise often proved the difference between a win and a loss in a fight between skilled opponents. But, unfortunately for Rhys, I wasn't surprised in the least; I'd sparred with Rhys several times in the past, and— despite the fact he'd never taken me on with his weapons of choice—I knew his habits. I knew, for example, that the man enjoyed dominating a fight, winning so quickly and decisively that his opponents never again challenged his skill or his authority. Which meant I knew he'd come right at me.

Which is why, the instant he charged, I already had my spear in the air.

My spear took Rhys in the shoulder, just beneath his clavicle, his heart saved only because he'd dropped into a lower crouch than I'd expected. Still, the bastard staggered back in surprise, dropping one of his javelins, clutching at the haft of wood jutting from his body. The crowd, meanwhile, was similarly stunned. After all, they'd expected a fight, not an execution.

But I wasn't here to play by their rules.

Not anymore.

Rhys fell to one knee as he endeavored to tear the spear free, watching me the entire time—aware that, if I made a move now, he'd be at a disadvantage. But I knew better; even wounded, Rhys could put up a fight. So, I let him remove the spear. I even watched impassively as he pried the spear tip free from his wound, blood pouring down his naked flesh, eyes fluttering from the pain.

"You bitch," he muttered as he fumbled about for his discarded javelin, refusing to take his eyes off me. But even the lighter, smaller weapon proved too heavy for his wounded side to hold; it fell from his fingertips twice before he gave up on it, rising with only the single javelin in hand. "What if you'd missed?" he bellowed, casting his gaze over the crowd. "What if she'd hit one of you, by accident?"

It was a good question.

"That was a risk I was willin' to take," I replied. I pointedly ignored the mutters of the crowd, giving Rhys the full weight of my attention. "Ye see, I thought this place was to become me home. That I was welcome here. That I had friends. And yet, when ye called me *ghiall*, none of the Curaitl spoke up on me behalf." I held up a hand at the sudden clamor. "Some of ye may have urged Rhys not to go so far, but not one of ye denied his claims. Not. One." I let the pain of that betrayal show on my face, allowed them all to see what I'd been feeling ever since Blair left me alone in our hut: the bitterness that came with finding out how naive I'd been to put my faith in strangers. That disembodied voice that haunted me, that sense of *wrongness*, grew stronger by the moment, as if—by defying these people, by choosing to distance myself from them—I was behaving more and more like myself.

But was that really a good thing?

"Because they know the truth!" Rhys asserted, planting the butt end of his javelin in the dirt.

"Aye? And what truth is that?" I asked, sounding tired even to myself. "That I am an outsider? That I will never be one of ye?"

"That you're a poison!" Rhys spat. "That you taint us all!" He stalked the edges of the crowd, angling towards me. "Everyone speaks of it. How you try to change the way we live. How you urged us to store our food differently. To breed our animals. To hunt—not as the gods would—but as cowards, with traps." Rhys jabbed at me, still too far away for the strike to do any damage, but menacingly, nonetheless. "You would make of our people something we are not meant to be."

I frowned, backing away, struck by the idea that what Rhys was saying might be true. As I danced away from the man, I glanced at the expressions on the faces milled around us and realized that it was. That—by trying to help and be a part of their community—I'd incidentally criticized their way of life. That I'd introduced alien concepts to their world, concepts I couldn't even entirely grasp myself half the time. I hesitated, dropping my guard for an instant.

What if Rhys was right?

What if I didn't belong in the Land of Youth?

"Ceara saved my son," a woman called, the crowd peeling away to reveal a familiar face—a mother I'd met a few weeks back after a hunt. "He was trapped in one of the caves, and she showed the others how to get to him safely, though everyone said it couldn't be done."

"She helped us design and build a better fence," another added, this time a gruff older man who, along with a handful of others, had been tasked with keeping the cattle secure despite the various predators that wandered the mountains.

In moments, a slew of others began to speak, each of them reminded of a time I'd either helped, or at least tried to help, them. Most were amusing tales of how I'd floundered, but some featured me as a hero, as a savior. With each passing moment, I felt that voice in the back of my mind recede, quieted like a shushed child, almost as if it, too, were listening. All the while, Rhys glared at his peers, growing angrier by the moment, until at last one voice broke above all the others.

"She makes me feel safe," Blair said, moving to stand just outside the circle, the hubbub around her dying away. "And loved. She's kind, and thoughtful, and clever. She is not our enemy, Rhys, she's—"

"Enough!" Rhys roared. "Don't you all see? *This* is why she must not be allowed to stay. What will the other tribes think of us when they discover how we've changed? What will the *gods* think of us?"

"The gods," the druid with the face tattoos said, stepping forward into the circle with Lady Aife at his side, "do not rule here as they once did. They, themselves, chose to walk a different path long ago. It would be wise, Rhys Two Tusks, to revoke your challenge. Choose a new direction, as they did."

Rhys snarled, hefting his javelin, his shoulder wound still bleeding. But then he straightened, surveying the crowd as though gauging their reaction, face impassive. "Very well," he replied, shoulders slumped. "I can see that you are all against me." I felt a slight amount of tension ease out of my body as he spoke, praying this nightmare was finally over, slightly overwhelmed by the knowledge that the Curaitl had accepted me despite my foolish attempts to change them.

And that's when he attacked.

"No!" I screamed, diving to put myself between Rhys and Blair.

His javelin took me in the stomach, piercing my gut, the pain not even registering at first. In fact, I was so shocked all I could do was stare at the thing, my hands wrapped around the shaft to keep it from going any further. Rhys, meanwhile, held the other end, putting all his weight into the thrust he'd intended for Blair. He yanked, tearing it free from both my stomach and my hands, then thrust again, taking me in the shoulder this time.

"Weak," Rhys said, working the javelin's point deeper into the meat of my shoulder until all I could do was scream. I heard a commotion behind me and glanced over my shoulder to see Tristan holding Blair back, the bigger man explaining that she wasn't allowed to interfere, though his eyes danced with hate and the promise of violence as he glared at Rhys.

"She wouldn't have been injured permanently," Rhys said, withdrawing the javelin. He lashed out, kicking me in the chest. I fell onto my back, groaning, trying to fight through the pain to stand. "And yet, I knew you'd try to stop me," Rhys added, studying me from above. "See? You still think like an outsider."

"Ceara!" Blair screamed. "Get up!"

Rhys grimaced and drew back for another strike, though I expected this one to be more fatal—an end to our match, once and for all. And yet, with Blair's voice still echoing in my ears, I realized I didn't want to lose. That I didn't deserve to be forsaken. Not now. Not when I'd finally found someone to care for, found a place to belong. It wasn't fair.

It wasn't *fair*.

Suddenly, it felt as though wings were beating against my skin, the sensation so visceral I hugged myself, pinching my eyes shut, and screamed. In that instant, our outrage poured out into the night like a living thing, a dark swarm that swept through the pulsing white lights around us like an errant wind until those once ethereal flames bled to a familiar orange. In the space between heartbeats, our skin pulsed with that otherworldly light, flesh glowing with power stolen from the druidic ritual. Power that raged within us, so much so that Rhys' strike seemed to descend in slow motion, his javelin inching towards our heart.

Moving instinctually, we rose to a sitting position, angled away from the blow, snatched the shaft of his weapon, and snapped the thing in two. Then, with a lightning quick thrust of our own, we buried the splintered end into the soft flesh of Rhys' exposed throat.

The crowd gasped as Rhys fell onto all fours across our lap, blood spilling, the hot liquid seeping into our wool breeches. We shoved him off us and rolled over onto our knees, perched over the man, admiring the way he struggled to breathe past the metal lodged in his windpipe. We reached out and withdrew the splintered end, slowly, feeling only relief.

We had won, and he had not.

It was enough.

"You are all fools," Rhys hissed, somehow managing to draw enough breath to speak, even as blood bubbled up from his lips, his throat little more than a gaping wound.

"Perhaps," Lady Aife said, kneeling beside her fallen warrior, though her eyes were locked on ours. We backed away, sensing something from her body language, her attention, that we did not like. "But," she said, turning her attention to the wounded man, "sometimes it is better to be foolish than it is to be alone. I don't envy you that discovery, my friend." The warmaiden passed a hand over Rhys' scalp, brushing her hands along the spikes of his hair, sighed once, and rose.

"Curaitl! Fate has spoken. Rhys Two Tusks, once a champion among us, has lost the right to call himself Blessed. He has lost the right to his own name. The right to his own past. The right to peace. Tonight, he leaves this place, never to return."

Inexplicably, Rhys managed to find his feet, though it seemed almost as though something else—some force not of this world—had pulled him upright, as if he were some sort of puppet being held up by invisible strings. Blood marred his body, some dry and flaky, but most still fresh and wet. The wounded man made as if to speak, to plead his case, but nothing came out. Indeed, aside from his panicked eyes, it became quite obvious he wasn't in control of his own body; he began to shamble awkwardly towards the village gates. The Curaitl, as one, turned their backs on the man, parting enough to let him pass, but otherwise pretending he didn't exist, facing out into the night. Only we and Lady Aife watched the man who had once been Rhys Two Tusks fade from view, swallowed by darkness.

"It is done," Lady Aife called after Rhys was no longer in sight. "The gods..." she trailed off, staring at us with the same intensity that had chased us away only a few moments before, "The gods have spoken. No longer an outsider, the Curaitl welcome you as one of their own, Ceara Light-Eater!"

And yet, the instant our new name was bestowed upon us, we knew there was something wrong about it. Something incomplete, like a half-remembered dream. Indeed, it seemed to be only a small piece of a much longer name. Which meant the rest had to be out there, didn't it?

Somewhere out there...

21

he cheers, when they went up this time, were universal and loud enough that it made us jump. We shied away from the deafening noise, noting our faintly glowing body, our wounds already closing, and wondered if we should make a run for it. If we should leave these people and their strange traditions behind, carve out a new path for ourselves in this unfamiliar world full of inexplicably beautiful, immortal people. Until, that is, a woman from among the crowd rushed us, tackling us from behind.

We snarled and spun as we fell, determined to pin our attacker to the ground. But the vision of her beneath us, her slight, muscular body riddled with tension, brought back the faintest memory. We studied the woman, but it was the scent of her hair as it brushed our face—the barest hint of clay and leather tanning oil—which brought me back. I stared down into Blair's tear-filled eyes and released her wrists, tracing the curve of her cheek with my blood-stained, but otherwise ordinary fingers. "It's alright," I said as I drew her into an awkward hug. "I'm alright."

"I was so worried," she admitted, face tucked into my shoulder, squeezing me so hard it hurt to breathe. When at last she seemed to realize I wasn't going anywhere, she let go. "Don't you ever do that to me, again, alright?"

"Me? It was—"

Blair pressed a hand over my mouth, already shaking her head. "You must not speak his name. He's been cast out." Blair looked away for a moment, guilt flickering across her face.

I nodded and peeled her hand away "Fine. I promise not to get in another fight like this one ever again, if I can avoid it. How's that?"

Blair burrowed her face into my shoulder once more, and I felt her nod. I stroked a hand through her hair, feeling oddly numb. Had I really considered running away only a moment ago? What, or who, did that voice belong to? Before I could dwell on that, however, a polite cough forced me to look up.

"Is this a bad time?" Tristan asked.

I scowled up at him, then at Imogen, who practically stood in his shadow. "If I said yes, would ye leave?" I asked, drawing Blair around to see the two, gesturing in their direction. It was only then that I noticed Imogen's arm wound through Tristan's much larger limb, the line of her body pressed possessively against his.

"What are you doing here?" Blair asked, glowering at the man.

"I've come to pay my respects," Tristan replied, face unusually somber. "Hail, Ceara Light-Eater."

"Hail, Tristan," I replied, matching his tone. The two of us stayed like that for a moment, gazes locked, until at last his smile flickered to life once more.

He shook his head. "The answer is no," he said. "Not until I have apologized."

"For trying to stop me?" Blair interjected.

Tristan shook his head. "If you had stepped in, others would have done the same. It would have been a bloodbath." He switched his attention from Blair to me. "I *am* glad you won, though I wish it had not come to this. No matter what I thought of the man, exile is not a fate I would wish on anyone."

"Neither would I, but—" I began.

He waved that away. "There's no point talking about that anymore. I simply wanted to apologize for not saying more in your defense, that's all. You deserved better from someone who calls you a friend."

"Are ye sure that's what ye want?" I asked.

"If you'll have me," Tristan replied, bowing slightly.

"And me too," Imogen chimed in.

I scrutinized the two of them, focusing on their linked arms and the easy way they stood together until, at last, I saw it. "Hold on, is that what I t'ink it is?" I asked, gesturing at the silver band wrapped around Imogen's throat.

"That depends on what you think it is," Imogen replied, blushing.

"It seems," Tristan said, gazing fondly at the young woman, "a woman with all sorts of strange notions got it into this one's head to be exceedingly sneaky."

"Oh, did she? Well, then, ye should probably thank her."

Blair glanced back and forth between Tristan and me. "Is someone going to fill me in?"

"Ceara has been conspiring with Imogen here to steal my armband," Tristan replied, matter-of-factly.

"Ceara!" Blair hissed. "You're not supposed to interfere like that. Courtship rituals are between the would-be couples. No outside help."

"Oy! I didn't have anythin' to do with it," I insisted, holding up both hands. "Besides, as I recall, ye didn't exactly play by the rules with me, either, ye hypocrite."

Now it was Blair's turn to blush. "That was different."

Tristan nudged Imogen, grinning. "Ooh, this is a good story."

Blair scrambled to her feet, reached back, and socked Tristan in the arm. Hard. The big man winced, his skin already reddening from the blow, but his grin hardly faded. "No hard feelings?" he asked.

"As long as you never get between me and Ceara ever again," Blair replied. "And," she added, jabbing him in the chest with one finger, voice a low whisper, "don't you dare tell anyone about that."

"Speakin' of *that*," I said, rising gingerly to my feet, "care to tell us how ye came by his armband, Imogen?"

The young woman smiled, her eyes twinkling with mischief. "Do you remember what you said about waiting to steal it until he was preoccupied with something else? Well, I was in the crowd waiting for the fight to start when Tristan found me." Imogen reached up and absent-mindedly ran a hand through her grungy hair.

"I wanted to know why she'd tried impersonating a serving girl," Tristan explained.

"You did what?" Blair asked.

"Hush," I said, patting Blair's arm, "I'll explain it all later. So, what d'ye tell 'em?"

"The truth, sort of." Imogen cleared her throat.

"She told me you two were planning to take something that didn't belong to you." Tristan nudged the young woman again, smirking. "She said it was your idea."

"Imogen!"

"Well it was your plan!"

"Ceara!" Blair chastised, mirroring my tone.

I ducked my head a little. "Allegedly."

"Anyway," Imogen said, trying her best not to look guilty, "we waited together for the fight to start. But then, when everyone was telling stories about you, I realized Tristan wasn't paying me any attention, so..." Imogen drifted off. "I mean, it's not like I wasn't worried about you, too, but...well..."

"Ye saw your openin', is that it?" I asked, smirking.

"The little thief pretended she was upset and grabbed my arm," Tristan replied, totally deadpan. "I was too busy trying to think of what I should say to realize I was being robbed." Tristan chuckled and kissed the top of the young woman's head.

"Well, isn't this an interesting development?"

Tristan's eyes widened to the size of serving platters, and suddenly he and Imogen were several feet apart, the latter hugging herself. Tristan had thrust both hands behind his back, doing his best to look innocent as Imogen's mother sauntered up to them, her white cloak brushing against Blair and me in the process.

"Explain," Lady Aife commanded.

Tristan opened his mouth to speak, but Imogen beat him to it. The young woman glared defiantly at her mother, jaw jutting forward, though I noticed she kept subconsciously playing with the silver band around her throat. "It was my choice, mother," she said.

Lady Aife looked amused. "And did you think I'd have no say?"

"But you did!" Imogen insisted. "It was Tristan you picked to train me when I came of age, remember?"

"Yes, I remember."

"Well, then, it's at least partially your fault I love him," Imogen asserted. Realizing what she'd said, the young woman turned to Tristan, her face as red as the flesh of the richest apple. "I mean—"

"That's enough, Imogen. I—"

"I love her, too, warmaiden," Tristan interrupted. The four of us turned to study the man, though it seemed the warrior only had eyes for the thief who'd stolen his armband. Indeed, despite Lady Aife's commanding—and perhaps borderline terrifying—presence, we may not as well have even been there.

"Oh, that's adorable," Blair said in a hushed voice, nudging me, waggling her eyebrows.

"It really is," I acknowledged.

"Is that so, Tristan?" Lady Aife asked, ignoring us.

"It is." The warrior grinned. "She's fierce and determined. Too conniving by half, but then Dagda knows, I'm far too trusting. Perhaps we'll even each other out." Tristan flicked his eyes back to the warmaiden. "With your blessing, of course."

Lady Aife barked a laugh, waving both hands. "Oh, you have it," she said, ignoring the shock displayed on her daughter's face. "Truthfully, this was what I'd hoped for all along. I just didn't think I'd succeed." The warmaiden leaned over to Blair and me, one hand perched on the side of her mouth. "Imogen never does what I want her to do, you know," she whispered, conspiratorially.

"Mother, that's not true!"

Lady Aife winked, then turned back to the would-be lovers. "Well, in any case, I am happy for you both. Oh, but Tristan," Lady Aife crooked a finger until the man bent an ear. This time when she whispered, her words didn't carry in the least.

Tristan straightened a second later, face ashen. "As you command, my Lady."

"Good. Now!" Lady Aife said, clapping her hands. "It's time I see to the people."

With a start, I noticed the crowd had largely dispersed throughout the market square, though everyone remained, standing in their own clusters, many of them staring openly at the five of us. No, not at us. At me.

"And you," Lady Aife said, resting a hand on my shoulder. "Be careful not to reveal any more of yourself here. I have spoken to the druids, and they won't interfere, but that is the most I can do for you." Then, with that very mysterious statement still hanging in the air, the warmaiden left, beckoning to the nearest swarm of Curaitl.

"What's she talkin' about?" I asked. "Why would the druids care about me?"

"Because," Blair said, wrapping an arm around my waist to pull me close, "they think you're a goddess."

"But I—"

Blair pressed her finger to my lips. "It doesn't matter." She flashed me a brilliant smile and pressed her lips to mine, sliding her finger out of the way in the process.

And I let her.

Because some questions can wait.

And some kisses can't.

22

*T*he following morning's sendoff was somewhat more lackluster than it might have been otherwise, what with the turbulence of the Beltane feast and the copious consumption of ale that had followed. Still, the Curaitl gathered as one at the gates to wish us a safe journey and good luck at the tournament, many offering tokens of support. Of course, I doubted anyone received a symbol of affection quite as—well, affectionate —as Tristan; Imogen had sucked on his face so long and hard before we departed, I was pretty sure the man's lips would still be bruised by the time we made it to the Southern Isles.

Frankly, I was simply glad to have the man along, puffy lips and all. Originally, there had been six of us participating, none of whom had Tristan's gift for lightening the mood. The others had included Rhys, Lady Aife, and two of her household guard—Liam and Anna. But now, with Rhys gone, it seemed we suddenly had room for one more fighter.

The next woman up, as it were.

"I hate riding by carriage," Blair groused, sitting with her face cradled in her hands, taking every bump in the road as a personal affront.

"It's really more of a wagon," Tristan replied. "A covered wagon. Which would make us cargo, wouldn't it? Tell you what, just think of yourself as a box," he suggested.

"How is that supposed to help?"

"Ever met a box with an attitude problem?" Tristan shrugged. "Be the box, Blair."

Blair flicked her eyes to me, scowling "Do you think Lady Aife would be upset if Tristan didn't survive this trip?"

"It's not her I'd worry about," I replied.

"Then who?"

"D'ye want to be the one to explain to Imogen why her lover hasn't returned?" I replied, cocking an eyebrow even as another sudden jerk sent us all flying. I cursed, wishing not for the first time that the Curaitl had absconded with more of Tuathal's well-trained horses. Maybe then we wouldn't have had to ride in the back of a makeshift wagon, thrown about like ragdolls every time we hit a bump in the road.

"Point taken," Blair replied, rubbing at her lower back.

"You two are just cranky," Tristan said, grinning from ear to ear as we bounced yet again, my shoulder colliding with the side of the wagon. "This isn't so bad. Reminds me of a boat at sea."

Something about his comment tickled my mind, but I couldn't quite place it. Like fumbling for a word or walking into a room and forgetting why you were there. "We're not cranky," I asserted a moment later, frustrated, "*you're* just in too good a mood."

Tristan waved that away. "I spent the night with a beautiful woman in my arms, that's all." He leered at us. "Shouldn't we *all* be in a good mood?"

"That's it, I'm throwing him off the first cliff we see," Blair muttered.

Tristan barked a laugh, but wisely said nothing else; even he knew when to stop pressing buttons. Still, he wasn't wrong, and it could have been worse—we could have been dragged along by a train of plodding cattle, forced to practically crawl our way across the Land of Youth. Instead, Lady Aife had managed to tame two aurochs—freakishly large bulls which stood a few hands taller than I was, and were as thickly muscled as any thoroughbred. I'd spent the better part of that morning marveling at the specimens from the back of the wagon; the damn things made only slightly less frightening by the fact that they were so damn docile.

"Not that you should think of them that way," Tristan had explained as we'd loaded the wagon with supplies. "In the wild, those things have been known to gore horses and trample people."

Looking at them, I could believe it; nothing got that big with horns that long without being dangerous. "They look nervous," I'd mentioned offhandedly, noting the way they kept shuffling from side to side, like horses about to bolt.

"It's that thing that's out there," Tristan had replied.

"What t'ing?"

But of course that's when Imogen had showed up, and I hadn't thought to follow up with him regarding what "thing" he'd been referring to. I had asked a few of the others precisely *how* Lady Aife had managed to tame the aurochs, though—curious to know how she'd gone about it. Sadly, everyone I spoke to had proven far less knowledgeable on that subject.

Big surprise.

"How long is this supposed to take?" I asked, doing my best not to sound as petulant as I felt.

Tristan and Blair exchanged considering glances, as if neither had thought to ask. Tristan shrugged. "I assume we'll get there when we get there," he said.

I groaned but didn't bother pressing; with Lady Aife and her two guards up front driving the would-be carriage, the best I could hope to do was wait until we stopped to ask. "Alright, run me through it, again," I said, giving Tristan a come-at-me gesture.

"Why? We've been over this a dozen times."

"Humor me," I replied. The truth was, ever since my fight with Rhys, I'd had trouble remembering certain things. Nothing major, but little things, like which side of the bed I liked to sleep on, or whether I liked eggs for breakfast more than porridge. Indeed, it felt almost as though I'd taken a handful of such memories and thrown them to the wind.

"Alright," Tristan replied, though this time when he and Blair exchanged looks, I could tell there was more to it. "Tournament rules. Single elimination bouts. Six people maximum per nation competing, excluding the nation who hosts."

"That's new. Why aren't they allowed to compete?" Blair asked.

"Something about home-field advantage, I expect," I chimed in.

Tristan gave me an odd look but nodded. "The home nation has to be the judge in case any final decisions have to be made. This way they're less partial. At least in theory."

"In theory?" I asked.

"Some nations find it hard to be objective," Tristan replied, smirking. "When the Tógálaí Capall hosted, for example, we found ourselves eliminated as a nation by the end of the first round."

"Even Lady Aife?" I asked, surprised.

"A technicality," Tristan explained. "They said she refused to bow to the judge and accept his authority, which meant she had to forfeit."

"Well, did she refuse?"

"Of course, but since when does Lady Aife bow for anyone, much less a filthy horse wrangler?"

Blair and Tristan laughed, the joke clearly lost on me. But then I hadn't been raised with the Tógálaí Capall as my neighbors, constantly picking on each other for millennia—maybe it was one of those "you had to be there" things.

"So, the rules?" I asked, when they were done.

"Fight until someone surrenders or until the other person is declared beaten by the judge. You may bring any weapons you wish, except a bow. Oh, and no animals—even if you trained it." Tristan shuddered, though he kept whatever memory that had provoked to himself.

"Why not a bow?" I asked, frowning. Now that he'd mentioned it, I realized I'd have loved to have a long-range weapon available for fights like these. I mean, sure, the spear was great, but once you threw it, the weapon lost most of its value. Arrows, on the other hand, were much more appealing—quantity over quality for the win.

"The bow is a coward's weapon," Blair said, distastefully.

No, it's a hunter's weapon.

"It complicates things," Tristan said, bringing me back to the moment before I could wonder where that thought had come from—or why it had sounded so vehement. "Especially depending on the arena. Too large, and the warrior with the bow will have a definite advantage. Too small, and the melee fighter will likely cut them down before they can draw. Besides, there were too many accidents. Injured spectators and what not."

"And which sorts of arenas will we have?" I asked.

"We're headed to the Southern Isles. Their lands aren't particularly spacious," Tristan noted, "but the Southerners are very good builders. I imagine they'll have come up with something."

*T*urned out Tristan was right; the Southerners had built a series of artificial islands connected to the shore by a series of bridges, the entire archipelago visible from the city itself. And city it was—nothing like the fort I'd first seen after the battle on the plains, or even the village tucked away between the mountains we'd left behind. No, Oileán Baile—as it was called—was a sprawling thing, practically bursting with life, its people dressed in flowing, multi-colored robes and light breeches, their skin darkly tanned. The air smelled alternatively of cooked fish, spices, and brine. In fact, it was so large we had to park our wagons outside the city limits and proceed on foot.

Together, the six of us worked our way through the milling populace, passing structures carved from sandstone and quartz that shimmered in the sunlight. I found myself admiring the easy, almost lackadaisical attitudes of the Islanders; compared to the industrious Curaitl, the Southerners seemed downright slovenly. But then, they weren't fighting to keep warm in the winter, to feed themselves despite a scarce supply of available meat and vegetation. Here, where trade was prevalent, the Islanders had a surplus of food, their diets rich and varied, their homes built to withstand even the wildest storms. Indeed, even their clothes reflected opulence and splendor: every garment we saw was immaculately tailored, each armband and torc carved, not forged—multi-faceted stone as opposed to precious metals.

"Stop dawdling," Lady Aife insisted, picking up her pace. "And you, quit drooling," she chastised me.

I gave her a wry smile. "I'd have to close me eyes, first."

"Then shut them, and let Blair guide you around. At least that way I'll know you won't wander off."

Blair snatched up my hand. "Don't worry, she isn't going anywhere."

I rolled my eyes but found myself grinning all the same. "It *is* beautiful here, though, aye? Surely I'm not the only one who's noticed."

Tristan grunted as a young couple bumped into him, the girl squealing in delight, the boy spouting Islander gibberish that might have been poetry. "Oh no, we've just all been here before, that's all."

Lady Aife nodded. "The Southern Isles are like pure gold. Lovely to look at, but soft enough to sink your teeth into." She eyed that same couple with a degree of hostility that spoke volumes about her thoughts on how romance should be conducted. "The only reason no one invades is because they have established themselves as a neutral nation."

"That," Tristan said, "and because everyone wants to marry their Queen."

"Oh right, I've heard this story," I interjected, only just now recalling the tale of Oisín and Niamh that I'd heard the night of the Curaitl's raid. I shook my head at the memory. "It was awful. Those two bein' parted like that, I mean."

Blair squeezed my hand, reassuringly.

"That story is not a tragedy," Lady Aife said. "It's a lesson. A bedtime story with teeth."

"How so?" I asked, frowning.

The warmaiden shot a glance back at me. "It warns us not to make promises we cannot keep. Now come on, the nations are meeting above." She pointed at a flight of stairs carved into the mountain upon which so much of the city was built, a flight that went so high the steps actually faded from view before I could see the end of them.

"We're walkin' up *those*?" I asked, mouth ajar. "What's the plan, to exhaust us before the tournament even starts?"

"Actually, that's not a bad idea," Lady Aife replied, thoughtfully. "I'd never given it much thought before, but it's true that by the time all the nations gather up top, we're often too tired to squabble." She barked a laugh. "Trust Niamh to think of such things."

Then, without another word, the warmaiden took off, bustling up the stairs as if a pack of hounds were on her heels, her fur cloak fluttering out behind her like a cape. Liam and Anna quickly joined her. I shared a glance with Blair and Tristan, both of whom seemed unsurprised.

"She doesn't expect us to keep up with her, does she?" I asked, hopeful.

"Last time we were here on a diplomatic mission," Tristan said, "The one who finished last had to shop for souvenirs."

I frowned. "What kind of punishment is that?"

"Lady Aife likes to see that everyone in the village gets a little something," Blair added for clarification. I simply stared at them for a moment, processing. Then, without warning, I took off at a full sprint, ignoring their startled yells and laughter.

*T*he three of us arrived mere minutes behind Lady Aife, each of us dripping with sweat, our furs tucked over one arm, though only Tristan had opted to go about shirtless. I'd be lying if I said I hadn't seriously considered it. But for all I knew, that would have started a riot in the streets, and—since I wasn't interested in adding Ceara Bare-Breasts to my growing list of titles—I'd decided to hold off.

We found Lady Aife waiting for us at the top, her breathing smooth and even, grinning as if she'd just won a fight, the sheen of sweat coating her face making her look lovelier, somehow. "I'm surprised you three ran the stairs," she admitted. "You know I would've been happy to wait."

I shot Tristan and Blair very, very dirty looks.

Tristan was the first to wave away her comment. "We just wanted to show you how well-prepared we are," he replied, though it took him three tries to get it all out between his heavy breathing.

"If those stairs exhausted them," a man's voice interrupted, "I can't wait to see how they fare against our warriors."

As one, the six of us turned to see a giant of a man approaching, the small crowd gathered in the courtyard parting quickly before him. Impossibly tall, though lean-muscled, his thick black hair had been shaved to the skin on either side of his scalp, leaving one long braid to fall down past his shoulders. Like us, he carried no weapons, though with men his size the threat of physical violence is rarely relegated to whether or not they're armed.

Fortunately, the man didn't seem inclined to toss any of us down the stairs.

"Boru!" Lady Aife cried, throwing her arms wide. "How are the Hill Tribes?"

The giant belted out a laugh, teeth flashing bright from within his bushy beard. "You know they don't like being called that," he replied, lifting the warmaiden in a crushing hug that would have left me gasping for air.

Lady Aife grunted and slid smoothly out of his hold. "Not my fault they all choose to live on hills," she replied, planting her hands on her hips.

"Sassy as ever, I see." The giant flicked his eyes over to us, then widened upon seeing me. "Oh, you've found yourself another fiery one! And of a proper height, as well!"

"Ceara Light-Eater," Lady Aife acknowledged, gesturing for me to step forward.

"Light-Eater, eh?" The title seemed to surprise the big man. "Best keep her out of sight," Boru said, conspiratorially, one hand perched on the side of his mouth. "Wouldn't want Gormflaith getting jealous."

"Is that right?" a woman asked, striding up alongside the man, standing perhaps an inch or two shorter than me, though it was hard to tell. She, too, had red hair, though it was a scarlet shade just shy of brown. Like so many of the Blessed People, she was beautiful, though it was a stately, natural beauty—the kind you find with women who age so gracefully they hardly seem to age at all.

Boru winced as she reached out and tugged on his braid, though his ensuing wink suggested he knew she'd been able to hear him. "I'm Gormflaith, this oaf's wife," the woman said, dipping her head towards me. "A bit of friendly advice? If he so much as utters a compliment in your direction, I suggest you run away."

"Oh?" I replied, eyebrows raised. "Is he so bad as all that, then?"

Gormflaith tugged on the braid again. "The man has had three wives besides me, so yes, I'd say so."

"But none were as passionate as you, my dear!" Boru cried. "Nor so violent," he added, with another wink.

Blair slid her arm through mine. "I wouldn't worry about it," she said.

Gormflaith nodded, seemingly mollified. "There, husband," she said, "yet another woman who would rather the company of her own gender than bother with yours."

Boru barked a laugh. "Far be it for me to complain! Dagda knows I prefer them, myself!"

Another tug, not so gentle this time.

A bell chimed overhead, drowning out Boru's ensuing curse. He rubbed absent-mindedly at his scalp, then scooped his wife up in his arms, carrying her easily despite her height and complaints. "We'll see you inside, Aife!" he called.

The warmaiden waved, then gestured for us to follow. "It's time. Remember, be silent, but watchful. There will be new warriors since the last tournament. Observe them."

The others nodded and fell into step behind her, though I trailed for a moment, marveling at the view below now that I had the chance. Breathtaking, I decided, a delighted laugh bubbling up from my throat before I could help it.

"Ceara, you coming?" Blair asked.

I nodded. "Aye, right behind ye."

23

$\mathcal{T}$he venue for our little get-together was a round amphitheater already bustling with representatives from the twelve nations, at least nine of which I knew almost nothing about aside from what I'd heard in passing. As Lady Aife insisted, I began scrutinizing the various tribes—noting the diverse wardrobes and styles, most appearing to be climate-derived—only to land eyes upon someone I recognized. Several someones, in fact.

"It's you!" Llew said, pointing from across the room. His brothers turned, spotting me at the same time, and gaped. Bran, naturally, recovered first. He studied me, eyeing my furs, scowling, then whispered something to his brothers. Finann jerked a nod and faced the other direction, though it took Llew a few seconds longer, his expression akin to a kicked dog's.

I frowned, confused by their reaction. But then it hit me: they must be under the impression that I actually was a spy all along. That perhaps I'd even been in cahoots with the Curaitl, plotting to raid Caer Capall all along. Looking at it objectively, I could see how Bran had come to that conclusion; I *was* dressed in their furs, fighting as one of the Curaitl in the tournament. Still, for some reason, it stung. But, before I could head over and explain myself, the bells chimed once more, though the reverberations lasted much longer now that we were indoors.

A moment later, a woman glided through the double doors. Dressed in the same fashion as her own people, though perhaps more prudently, Queen Niamh was a vision in silver, her body lithe and darkly tanned, contrasting fiercely with her chestnut-colored hair. She wore a crown of iridescent scales which glimmered and changed colors in the light, flashing pink, then blue. The room fell silent almost immediately, and those few who'd been sitting rose swiftly to their feet.

"Welcome, Blessed People," she said, her voice oddly striking—the sort of voice that makes you look up from whatever you're doing when you hear it.

Everyone bowed in response, and I rushed to do the same. She laughed, brightly, and curtsied. "It is good to see you all," she said, then proceeded to name all twelve tribes, one after the other. As each nation was mentioned, the tribe's representative—their leader in most cases—took a step forward. Of course, I recognized three of them from my time in the Land of Youth: Boru, Tuathal, and Lady Aife. The others varied in size and gender, though only a few made an impression, and none so much as Queen Niamh, herself.

"You will all find lodgings throughout the city," the Queen continued, "though not too close to invite neighborly visits, I should think."

Laughter rose up from among the assembly.

"As tradition dictates, the rules shall be posted for all to see before tomorrow's bouts," she went on, smirking. "The winner shall, as always, receive guest rite and be given leave to roam the tribes freely. And, of course, be given one boon of their choice if it is within the power of those gathered here."

Excited murmurs went up at that, though they quieted swiftly as Niamh made to speak again. "I expect this need not be said, but I will tolerate no misconduct during the duration of the tournament. If someone wrongs you, please do not take matters into your own hands. Report it to us and know that justice shall be swift and severe." Queen Niamh ran her eyes over us all, and I saw in them an intensity that made me shiver. "Remember, you are my guests. Please, be welcome here." She smiled wide and dipped her head, arms akimbo.

Those of us gathered bowed again, though conversations were already bubbling up around us as Queen Niamh left the chamber. Lady Aife grunted. "Glad that's over with," she muttered, then turned to us. "Well?" she asked.

"Tuathal's brought the brothers," Liam replied, thoughtfully. "We'll have our hands full if Bran decides to go all out with that claymore of his."

"Boru's only got two of his people with him, but both are as big as he is," Anna noted. "They were awful quick to get to their feet when the Queen arrived, though. Faster than they look."

Lady Aife turned to me expectantly. I cleared my throat. "Um, well, I can see why Queen Niamh keeps gettin' marriage proposals?" I offered.

Blair socked me in the arm.

"Not from me!" I insisted. "Just in general, sheesh."

Lady Aife frowned, her disappointment clear, then turned to the others, listening to their reports. I sighed. At last, she gestured for me to lean in, though it was clear she expected to be overheard. "Ceara, do you see that warrior over there? The one in the black cloak?"

I eyed the man, though there wasn't much to see; the warrior's hood was raised, a two-toned cloak obscuring the majority of his body even when he moved. "Aye, I see him."

"Her," Lady Aife corrected. "She's new. One of the Moor Tribe. Now, what if I were to tell you that she's able to use both hands, prefers a trident and net as her weapons of choice, and likes to drag out her matches?"

We all turned to stare at the warmaiden, though only I wore an incredulous expression. "Well, if I didn't know ye, I'd say ye were makin' shit up," I replied, at last.

Lady Aife held up one finger. "She bowed holding her cloak with both hands, when usually you'd do so either with the right or left." Another finger. "Her right hand is calloused on the outside as well as the inside, both of which are consistent with a net. The trident is a common pairing, and when she moved down the aisle she led with her right foot. Net first, trident second. Right hand, left hand."

"And what about draggin' out her matches?"

"An educated guess. Anyone who fights with a net is patient. The goal is to catch you, then stab you, not charge in blind." Lady Aife shrugged.

I blinked at her a few times, then finally nodded. "Alright, I see your point. I need to be more observant."

"That's not my point at all, Ceara," Lady Aife replied, testily. "My point is that I noticed all that about a woman wearing a cloak. Now tell me, how much do you think the others know about you, by now?" Lady Aife gestured, and I took a long look around the room, realizing as I did that more than a few tribe members were staring at us, though most eyes were specifically on me—the newcomer.

Well, shit.

2 4

I eyed the swarthy competitor across from me as he stretched and hopped up and down, completely unperturbed by the constant bob of the man-made island—as if it were perfectly natural to fight on a churning surface. But then, as one of the seafaring tribes, I suppose that made sense. I, meanwhile, had to make peace with the fact that—if a rogue wave hit mid-fight—my next attack would likely involve projectile vomiting all over the bastard.

Not the worst plan, but by far the most humiliating.

I frowned, shaking my head to clear it, and resolved to focus on something other than the terrain; it was just past dawn on our second day in Oileán Baile, the horizon still blushing purple, the crisp sea air making it damn near chilly despite the warm climate. I held my spear loose in one hand, letting the wind caress my palms to keep them from getting sweaty.

"Contenders! Are you ready?" the judge called.

The fisherman raised his sword, a hooked thing that reminded me more of a climbing tool than a weapon. I mimicked him, lifting my spear, its haft decorated with the crow feathers I'd worn when I fought Rhys—a memento of victory, I'd explained to Blair when she'd asked, though in truth I wasn't sure why I'd done it; it wasn't like me to take trophies.

Before I could dwell further on the subject, however, the fight began.

The fisherman came at me low, practically scuttling across the wooden slats of the artificial island as though it were the deck of a roiling ship, hooked sword drawn back as if planning to thrust rather than hack. And thrust he did; he extended his sword, the blade pointed directly at one of my legs. Except the strike was almost comically early; even a novice would have time to get out of the way. But this tournament wasn't full of novices, which is why I realized he wasn't trying to stab me at all—not with a sword like that. Instead, it seemed he planned to use his blade like a fishing hook, hoping to impale me from behind as he withdrew.

But I wasn't about to get caught that easy—pun intended. Rather than wait for his blade to pass me by, I sidled to my left and lashed out with a kick, my foot connecting with the man's hand, his thrust swept harmlessly wide. The kick didn't have much power behind it, but it was enough to deflect the man's attack, which was the only opening I needed; I lunged forward, executing a thrust of my own, and skewered the man's thigh. He wailed and crumpled, dropping his blade in the process, which was enough for the referee.

"Winner, Ceara Light-Eater!"

I rose, prying my spear free, surprised at how quickly the bout had ended. The fisherman rolled onto his back, clutching his wounded leg, cursing as blood began seeping from the wound. I dropped to a knee beside him, fetching a strip of cloth I carried for such emergencies, and held it out. "Move your hand."

The fisherman's eyes widened, but he did as I asked, watching in mild fascination as I tied a tourniquet above the wound, cutting off the blood supply. "Thought I might have you if I went fast," he admitted while I worked. "Should have known you'd see me coming."

"That should help until you make it to the healers," I said, dipping my bloody hands between the island's slats, letting the sea clean them.

"Thank you, lady."

"Least I could do after I stabbed ye," I replied, grinning. I offered the fisherman a hand, though he clearly hadn't expected me to; his eyes were skeptical as he gained his feet, though he limped on his one leg. "It was a good strategy," I admitted, clapping him on the shoulder. "But ye left yourself too open for a counterattack. Next time, I'd feint with the first strike, then go for another, but aim high the second time. Hook the back of their necks while they're busy thinkin' about their feet."

The man grunted, shaking his head. "To think I'd see the day when one of the Curaitl offered advice on how to win a tournament!" He laughed, gripped my arm, squeezed, and began hobbling away. "I'll be rooting for you, Ceara Light-Eater!"

I frowned after him, wondering what he'd meant by that.

Turned out he wasn't the only opponent I'd surprise.

Over the next several hours, I competed in two more duels, each of which ended decisively with a single blow. Both opponents, like the fisherman, seemed more than content with losing—as if it were to be expected when facing one of the Curaitl. Maybe Tristan had been right to assume Rhys and I would fight each other, I realized. Indeed, few of the tribes seemed to relish fighting for its own sake as the spear wielders did. I even witnessed two bouts decided by an immediate surrender by one of the participants.

"Artists and musicians," Blair explained. "They send representatives, but they rarely fight. Most come to watch the warriors and find inspiration." She shrugged. "It's all a bit frivolous, but few complain. It's a free match, after all. Besides, it's always nice having someone sing a song in your honor."

I nodded, deciding that made quite a bit of sense. I'd seen a bard at work already, obviously, and such men would need to come from somewhere. Why not a tribe of bards, as there were tribes of warriors? In fact, it seemed obvious to me now that those representing the arts would be in attendance, even if they refused to duel; unlike Blair, I found nothing frivolous in their actions at all. Sadly, it seemed not all of us were destined to enjoy the luxury of skipping a match.

Because the next announced fight was between Tristan and Finann.

ristan bunched his shoulders and twisted back and forth at the waist, his spear perched against the stone wall that wound along the sea's edge, occasionally raising either foot in a stomping motion—anything to stay limber. "Come to wish me luck?" he asked as I sidled next to him.

I didn't answer immediately, but instead studied the three brothers lounging on an array of boxes by the docks. Like Tristan, Finann had opted to wait by the boats rather than risk showing up late and forfeiting by default. As for the other two, my guess was they were here for moral support. That, or like many siblings who end up spending too much time together, they simply had nowhere else they'd rather be. Llew, I'd learned from Blair, had already lost to one of Boru's giants, though it had been a closer match than she'd expected. The other two had summarily dispatched their opponents, one of which included poor Anna, and already there were rumors that Tuathal's men were targeting the Curaitl—payback for personal grievances.

"Mind your feet," I replied.

Tristan grunted, then reached for me as I shuffled past him. "Hey, where are you going?"

I ducked beneath his outstretched arm, dipped past the dockhands and sailors, and danced around the fishermen and their nets until at last I stood before the Crows—their title among the Curaitl. When I'd asked why, Tristan had muttered something about always finding them standing over fallen bodies on the battlefield.

Not unimpressive, as titles went.

Finann noticed me drawing close first, tapping shoulders as I approached. "Ceara Light-Eater," he said, once I was in earshot, voice laden with spite. "To what do we owe the pleasure?"

"I thought I owed ye an explanation." I stopped a few feet away, the weight of their combined stares enough to keep me from standing within reach.

Better to be safe than strangled.

"Oh, I think your name is explanation enough," Finann replied. "Ceara Light-Eater. So you're what, the Curaitl's spear in the night?"

I couldn't help but laugh at his translation. The brothers bristled, but I was already holding a hand out to stay them. "No, ye idgit. Ceara is the name I gave the Curaitl when ye took me. I didn't realize the name and the word were different." I shook my hair out in front of my face like a dog might. "Fiery, remember?"

"And Light-Eater?" Llew asked, his voice as timid, as soft, as I remembered.

"Recent development," I replied. "Bit of a long story. But it has nothin' to do with bein' a spy."

Bran grunted. "Couldn't find you after the attack."

"The crowd overwhelmed me," I explained. "I saw ye take Caer Capall back, but I was stuck on the other side of the hilltop fightin' Lady Aife and her guards. They're the ones who took me."

"Why would she have wanted you, unless you were her spy?" Finann asked, incredulous.

"She took it personally when I attacked her people on the battlefield before ye lot found me," I lied, though it was close enough to the truth that it really didn't make a difference; I still hadn't talked to Lady Aife about what Rhys claimed. It had proven harder than I thought, considering I couldn't mention the man's name, but there was more to it than that. For some reason, every time I thought about what he'd said, every time I thought about what I'd done to make my skin glow, every time someone called me "Light-Eater," I felt a twinge of...something. Guilt, maybe? That feeling you get when you have something you know you should be doing, but you can't quite remember what it was. And so you move on, though the nagging feeling never really goes away.

"I wonder why she'd do that?" Bran said, sarcasm obvious, bringing me back to the conversation at hand.

"So you weren't sent to spy on us?" Llew asked, hopeful.

I shook my head.

"Then why are you here?" Finann asked, skeptically.

"She was recruited," Bran replied, answering for me. He cocked his head, studying my leathers, the spear in my hand, eyes lingering on the crow feathers. "You any good with that thing?"

"Now why would I go and tell ye somethin' like that?" I asked, grinning. "Tell ye what, though, either of ye are welcome to find out for yourselves. Unless Finann here loses to Tristan in the next hour or so."

Finann bared his teeth at me, but I could tell he'd returned to his usual, teasing self—his suspicion allayed, at least for now. "You think your man has what it takes to beat me?"

"I wouldn't know," I admitted, honestly. "The only fightin' I've seen ye do is for your life against a dog."

Finann grimaced. "I'm never going to live that down, am I?"

I raised an eyebrow. "Live what down?"

"No one believed us. Especially not when Finann said the hound was on fire," Llew said, patting his brother's back. And yet, the moment Llew spoke, I pictured—not a hound on fire—but a beast with glowing runes etched into its fur. It was as if I could feel the heat radiating off the creature's body, like standing too close to a campfire.

Finann snorted. "Not to mention it was the size of a damn horse."

"Why not?" I asked, blinking away what must have been my imagination, ignoring the middle brother's comment as I rubbed my arms, my skin pebbled with goosebumps.

"They didn't want to believe a Hound of Ulster still existed here," Bran replied, leaning back against one of the boxes, watching waves lap against the docks. "That's all it was."

"Ye called it that before," I remarked, recalling the peculiar name. "But what are they?"

"They're pups Cú Chulainn raised before he died," Bran explained. "A specific breed of Cu-Sith. A Faerie dog."

I frowned, blanking entirely on both the name and the terms Bran had used. Knowledge I'd had before, maybe? Either way, I wasn't going to make Bran break things down further. "And what's wrong with 'em, then?"

"It's said they serve the gods," he replied. "The Tuatha de Danann. A Hound sighting, no matter how rare, is far too close to a god sighting for comfort."

"But…wouldn't that be a good t'ing?" I asked, thinking back to the feast of Beltane and the druidic ritual, to the reverence they'd put on display as they lit their torches. All three brothers were shaking their heads, however. In fact, their expressions were so grim I almost considered retracting my question.

"It's said that—if the gods ever return—it means the Land of Youth is going to war. That we'll return to the lands of men to fight and die, led by Lugh Long-Arm, his father Nuada, and the greatest of the Tuatha de Danann." Bran sighed. "And yet, many of the Blessed People have chosen to live their lives in defiance of that prophecy."

"What he means is, maybe the gods should go fight their own damn war," Finann said. "Dagda knows some of us have seen enough battles to last a lifetime. Besides, why would anyone want to leave this place?" He held out both arms and twisted back and forth as if to showcase the entire landscape.

I took a slow look around, admiring the glorious morning light as it drifted over the wooden slats of the dock, the briny smell of the sea wafting in the air, the soothing sound of the surf harmonizing with the cries of birds. I took a deep breath, acknowledging how *right* it felt here. How whole and perfect.

"No clue," I admitted, thinking of Blair, of the budding relationship between Imogen and Tristan, of the bustling Curaitl with their easy greetings, of the stillness that pervaded the mountain pass in the heart of winter —a stillness I could feel in my bones, urging me to embrace the purity of the moment. "I love it here."

"As do we," Finann replied, mirroring my expression. He grunted, hopped to his feet, and brushed at his breeches. "Now, if you'll all excuse me, I'm off to kick some spear wielding ass." He grinned, clapping me on the shoulder. "Glad you weren't a spy, after all, *ceara.*"

I rolled my eyes. "I'd say good luck, but I'm sure ye don't need it."

"You could give me a kiss?" Finann teased. "I'm sure that would do wonders."

"Ceara, is this man bothering you?" Tristan asked, apparently having caught the tail end of our conversation. I whirled to find him standing only a dozen feet away, head tilted, expression wry. Glancing back and forth between the two combatants, I realized they were surprisingly similar men. Teasing, easy-going, with a hard edge that showed under pressure.

And, what's more, I considered them both friends.

I sauntered up to Finann and kissed him on the cheek. Then—before Tristan could so much as make a startled noise—I strode over and planted one on his, as well. "Good luck, boyos. Don't break each other, alright?"

I waved as I departed, ignoring their bewildered expressions, though I knew their eyes followed me the whole way.

$\mathcal{W}$hile Finann and Tristan busied themselves by squaring off on their island, I decided to find Blair and drag her through the city. She'd been eliminated after her third bout by Lady Aife—an unfortunate pairing by anyone's standards—which meant she'd had plenty of time on her hands since. I'd even changed into a dress Blair had bought me at one of the city's bazaars, a low slung number that hugged my waist while leaving my shoulders and upper back bare.

My next fight, meanwhile, hadn't yet been announced—not that I was particularly concerned. If anything, I found the duels a little, to use Blair's word, frivolous. An excuse to test one's abilities, sure, but the whole thing lacked the camaraderie that usually came with sparring alongside one's peers. That, and I was beginning to realize I simply didn't have much interest in fighting. The bloodshed, the screams, the violence—the more I engaged in it, the more repulsed I became.

And why shouldn't I be? I had a woman I loved in easy reach, a strenuous but fulfilling lifestyle, a growing group of friends, and—with Rhys in exile—no true enemies. With all that in mind, I angled towards the tavern Blair preferred, wondering idly whether or not Lady Aife would let me bow out of the tournament early and spend the rest of our time here touring the Southern Isles. It was probably a long shot, but I'd at least risk asking if it meant avoiding further butchery. Besides, I had everything I wanted already —who needed a travel writ or some boon?

That was the last thought I had before the blade took me in the back.

he blade—and I'd been struck by enough of them by now to know that's what it was—pierced deep into my side, grating agonizingly along the crest of my hip bone, tearing through muscle and flesh to end lodged along my spine, and then back out again with the same savage quickness. I collapsed almost immediately after the attacker withdrew the blade, a throbbing, burning pain like I'd never felt before driving me to my knees, my legs caught in the folds of my dress, making it hard to move. Still, I tried to turn and locate my assailant, but something connected with the side of my head before I could so much as raise my eyes from the ground. A fist, maybe. Or a boot. Either way, I was too dazed, my view too blurry, to make anything out beyond a slight, cloaked figure holding an oddly-shaped knife before the blow landed and I slumped to all fours.

"The Queen sends her regards," a child's voice whispered into my ear. I jerked away, but I was too nauseous, the pain too intense, to move that quickly, and I ended up retching onto the stone. Someone nearby must have finally noticed what was happening, because I heard them scream for help, drawing a small crowd of gawkers. I could see their feet gathered around me through my tears, and I felt oddly embarrassed to have puked in front of so many people. I wanted to look up, to reassure them and say I was alright, but I couldn't; my was body so tense, so traumatized, it refused to budge.

"Clear the way!"

Another pair of boots, though these were closer, so close that the pool of my vomit lapped against them. So gross. And yet even my revulsion felt like a distant thing—a luxury I couldn't afford. The boots quickly gave way to a face, one I thought I knew, as the man knelt down. A man with a hawkish nose and steady eyes. He was speaking, but I couldn't catch the words. I blinked, or thought I blinked, except it's not a blink if you can't open your eyes, is it?

Someone shook me.

"Ceara!" the man screamed.

"Bran?" I asked, eyes fluttering open, able to speak somehow past chattering teeth. I was so damn cold, and I'd fallen onto my side, at some point. The crowd had gotten larger. But Bran didn't answer me. Instead, a woman thrust him back, and suddenly there was Blair, her mouth slack, eyes horrified, squatting beside me. She spun on her heels. "What did you do to her?!" she shrieked.

"Not...him..." I croaked, trying to sit up. Of course, I had no idea whether or not she heard me, because—halfway up—my body gave out, my head striking the stone floor as I collapsed. Ironically, it didn't even seem to hurt. In fact, I felt a comforting warmth spread through me. I swirled into unconsciousness, the tormented groans of the damned hounding me towards sweet oblivion. Distantly, someone screamed, although it sounded inhuman somehow...a howl, maybe? Either way, that was the sound which chased me down a dark, dark tunnel with no end.

27

I woke to the smell of sulfur and brimstone—not exactly reassuring scents. Of course, no smell could have terrified me more than the sight of the hulking, bestial creature looming over me. With eyes like pools of liquid amber, the druidic marks on its snout literally burning from within like hot coals, and teeth as long as my fingers, the hound was a reflection of a horrific nightmare. And not just any nightmare. My nightmare. I'd woken in a cold sweat more than once remembering that shadowy figure as it padded behind the curve of a distant hillside, though in the dream it had emerged to chase me across the plains—always chasing, but never catching, its breath hot on my heels, teeth snapping mere inches from my back.

"No, no no..." I tried to scramble away, but even that slight movement tugged at something near the base of my spine, a ripping sensation that threatened to make me sick. I screamed, clawing at the dirt, unable to decide which was worse: my pain, or being torn to shreds by a colossal hound.

"Stop moving, or it'll get worse."

The voice was deep, so much so that—as close as the hound was to me when he spoke—I could feel it in my chest. But no, that wasn't simply his voice, I realized. It was his paw; he'd pinned me in place to stop me from struggling further.

Or to stop me from getting away.

"Please, let me go," I whispered, sounding frail and broken, my voice hoarse from screaming.

"Once the fire is ready," the hound replied, mouth moving slow and uneven, the words spilling from a throat that should have been unable to form them. He raised his gigantic head, ears cocked, nose twitching. "They're coming for you. We'll have to hurry."

"Who?" I asked. "What am I doin' here?" Memories began to assault me one after the other, though they were disjointed. Blair screaming. Boots in a vibrant liquid. Pain lancing through me from behind. Pain from above. A howl...a howl. "Wait, was that ye? The one howlin'?"

The hound glanced down at me. "I've been keeping an eye on you all this time. Seemed like a waste to let you die in the street." He shook his shaggy head, ears flopping in the process. "Your friends didn't like me dragging you off."

"Are they alright?" I asked, trying to sit up.

He pressed down harder on my ribcage. "I left them alive, if that's what you mean. They've been tracking us since this morning."

"Where are we? Why'd ye take me?" A dozen other questions flew through my mind, so many I couldn't keep up with them all. Who had attacked me? And why? What did the hound mean he'd been watching me "all this time"?

"Because you're dying," he replied, gruffly.

"That's impossible," I said, shaking my head. "No one—"

"Dies in the Land of Youth?" he interjected, lowering his snout, eyes locked on mine, the markings flashing brighter for just a moment, tendrils of steam slipping out to caress his jowls. "Except you aren't *from* the Land of Youth, are you, Morrigan's daughter?"

I frowned, fighting past my terror to meet that glare. "What d'ye mean?"

He snorted and rose, withdrawing his paw. "Humans are the worst. Tell me, what did I say when you first got here? Small sips, tiny bites. Small sips. Tiny bites."

The hound disappeared from sight, though I could still hear him moving about, grumbling under his breath, though it sounded remarkably like panting from where I lay. Now that his gargantuan muzzle wasn't obscuring my view, I could see the night stars overhead. I could also tell there was a fire burning nearby; smoke billowed towards the sky, and I felt a faint heat caressing my left side. I considered rising, but the memory of how much pain it had caused when I tried to escape was too fresh. Besides, it didn't seem like the hound had any interest in eating me as I was. Maybe that's what the fire was for?

The thought made my stomach churn.

"Then you go and chug a whole waterskin and lose yourself," the hound growled, shuffling closer. "Not to mention all the feasts you've attended since. And Manannan wonders why I hate humans."

"I don't know what you're talkin' about," I admitted, unable to follow the hound's train of thought—to me it sounded increasingly like the ramblings of a crazy person. "But...what is it you're plannin' to do to me?"

"Save your life, apparently."

"Me life?"

"You're dying, remember? By the Dagda, your species' frail minds never cease to amaze me." The hound reappeared above me, though upside down this time, his chest and throat more prominent than his face. "You were stabbed. Remember that part?"

I nodded, though my attention was all for the hound's massive, muscular chest and neck; it reminded me faintly of the aurochs Lady Aife had tamed —as if he'd been designed to prowl a world that no longer existed.

"Whoever stabbed you used a blade from the human realm," he continued, his voice patronizing, as if he were speaking to a child. "I'm not sure how they smuggled it in, but the wound is festering. It's killing you."

"The human realm? But that's closed..." And yet, something—a gut feeling perhaps—told me otherwise. What had Bran said when we'd first met? Something about my existence being impossible? I couldn't remember.

"To the Blessed People, yes. But not to you."

"Why not me?"

The hound huffed, almost a sigh. "Couldn't Manannan have sent me someone with a lick of sense?" He padded away again. "What do they call you, now, anyway?"

"Ceara," I replied, too dazed by everything that was happening to ask about the person he kept mentioning, though the name did sound somewhat familiar. Part of the druid chants, maybe? "Ceara Light-Eater."

The hound stilled, the night falling silent except for the crackle of flames. "I've heard that name. They chant it in the city, sometimes. The tribe with the spears has mentioned it, too, on their hunts."

"You *have* been watching me…"

"Not close enough, it seems. I had to keep my distance, especially once you were taken to the mountains. The Blessed People aren't fond of my kind. They'd hunt me down if they knew I was out there, as they once did my brothers and sisters."

I nodded, recalling my earlier conversation with Bran and his brothers. "They fear the return of their gods."

The hound yipped a few times, and I realized he was laughing. "If only they knew what they were harboring this whole time, they'd have sliced your throat a long time ago."

"What do ye mean?" I asked, though I feared I already knew the answer. That I'd known it all along. The voice in the back of my head was silent, but I could feel it there all the same, practically purring with pride. "You're sayin' I'm what, a goddess?"

"Not yet," the hound replied. "But you'll have to become one, and soon."

"Why?"

"Because your mother's dying, and now, so are you."

"My mother?"

But the hound didn't answer. "The fire's ready," he said, instead. He approached, slid his muzzle under my shoulder, and shoved me onto my side. The pain was excruciating, like having my spine yanked out from the base of my back. "Stop squealing," he demanded. "This will help."

While I lay there whimpering, I felt him move away. I realized I was lying in sand—coarse grains pressed against my face. I strained to listen and recognized the sucking refrain of the surf as it beat along the shore. A beach, then. But I didn't have time to wonder where we were any longer; I sensed heat approaching my exposed back. Too much heat.

"What are ye doin'?" I demanded.

"Cleansing the wound," the hound replied, though his words were garbled, guttural. Then, without warning, he pressed that wicked, searing heat against my wound.

The last thing I remembered was the stench of sizzling flesh.

I'd have preferred sulfur and brimstone.

There are times in a person's life when they have cause to sit back and reflect on the decisions they've made, the people they've wronged, the path they've taken. Usually those moments are provoked by some life-altering event, or a seminal conversation, or perhaps a drug-induced epiphany. Either way, the result is a gut check which pokes at our misconceptions, makes us question our sense of reality.

This was nothing like that.

This was like someone tossing a Molotov cocktail onto my gasoline-riddled limbic system. This was electroshock therapy delivered in a bathtub full of eels. This—waking up with not one, not two, but three voices screaming in my head at once—was the closest thing to hell I could ever have imagined.

Hands snatched me up the instant I awoke, pinning me to a breast that felt familiar and unfamiliar at the same time. Earnest faces studied mine, their expressions haggard and pained, bathed in the light of a nearby camp-fire. Three of them—*the Crows*—squared off against a hound the size of a horse.

Cathal.

The name rose unbidden, as did the memory of our first meeting on the beach—of a beast rising from the sand like a poster-pooch from *The Land of the Lost*. From there, a slew of other memories cluttered my mind, a puzzle with pieces I couldn't begin to place, with edges that made no sense. I shook my head, mumbling something unintelligible, unable to form coherent words. The arms wrapped around me clutched tighter. Too tight. I struggled to get away, though it hurt; my lower back was on fire, the pain a dull ache that wouldn't go away no matter how I twisted or turned.

"It's alright, Ceara," a woman whispered into my hair. "It's me. It's Blair."

Blair. More memories. A woman lying naked on the bed, the smooth curve of her back exposed as she slept, her body taking up our side of the bed. Her brilliant smile when we'd first kissed her, our argument too heated for anything else, how she'd snatched at our clothes as if she'd tear them off us. Our clothes. But not my clothes. Not my side of the bed.

Hell, not my bed.

"I'm not Ceara," I said. My voice was raspy, my throat raw from overuse.

The arms around me stilled as Blair froze. Eyes swiveled to me—even those of the three brothers. Bran, Finann, and Llew. The Crows. Ceara's memories of them flooded my consciousness: the rough stubble of Finann's cheek beneath our lips, the gentle guiding gesture Llew made when escorting us to a waiting horse, and Bran watching us...always watching.

The remaining two took a moment longer to place. Scathach I recognized first, the redhead wrapped in a white fur cloak, studying the flames of a nearby fire, using the tip of her spear to scoot a lump of smoking wood across the sand. But there was something about the way she moved, the way she held herself, that reminded me of someone else.

"What's wrong with her?" the last figure asked. Tristan. That was his name, though his name proved hardest to recall; his face looked damaged, his eye swollen, lips puffy, almost unrecognizable. His arm was in a sling. He'd lost a fight, it seemed.

Probably lost his footing.

I lurched out of Blair's arms, pressing my hands to my ears, the clamoring voice in my head too much to bear. Scathach—no, Lady Aife, I realized—shooed Blair away, leaving me to kneel alone in the sand. More memories threatened to come roaring back. I could hear her, hear them— there were two voices whispering in my mind now—vying for control, demanding my attention.

"Make 'em stop," I begged. "Oh God, make 'em stop."

Lady Aife jerked back as if I'd slapped her, face stricken.

"I told you," Cathal grumbled. "She's not of this world."

139

"But how?" Lady Aife asked. "I thought...I thought that—"

"That you'd stumbled on a goddess reborn?" Cathal was shaking his shaggy head, and I realized he was sitting upright like a trained poodle, looking as non-threatening as possible. "Not exactly. Besides, I'd have thought you and your sister would have learned your lesson by now."

"Scathach has nothing to do with this, pup," Lady Aife growled.

Cathal snorted. "Why do you think she ran out onto that battlefield? She thought *you* were *her*."

"Wait, she's—" I began.

"You and I aren't speaking right now," Cathal barked, glaring at me. "If you'd listened to me in the first place, none of this would have happened. Now, let the adults talk."

I snapped my mouth shut, struck by another wave of recollections. Cathal's warnings. His advice. How I'd thrown it all away, irrationally, believing I'd find Scathach on the battlefield and that she would protect me.

Foolish. Reckless. Childish.

Ceara's words, chastising me inside my own head. I ground my teeth, trying to drown out her thoughts with my own. But another slithered in—the same voice I'd listened to when I'd stepped out onto that battlefield. A voice which longed to fight and fly and...yeah that, too.

A voice we couldn't ignore.

Somewhere, a bird's shrill caw split the night air.

We lowered our hands and surveyed the beach, sensing the tension riding the air, the potential for violence. Swords and spears were already drawn. It wouldn't take much. A little distraction, and we could make a break for it. We shifted our weight, sliding one foot forward, prepared to make a move, to steal a weapon from the wounded one—Tristan.

"Don't," a man said. We turned to find a tall, cloaked figure with a slender blade pressed against our throat. We froze, acknowledging the dead look in his eyes; this one would kill us without remorse.

"Amergin—" Bran began.

"Bard," Cathal growled, cutting off the elder brother, "what do you think you're doing?"

"She's possessed by the battle *awen*," the bard replied. "Can't you see it?"

Cathal sniffed the air, then cursed. "No, but I should have."

"Battle what?" Tristan asked.

"It's rare. In Fae they speak of it as one's wild side," the bard replied. "In

the mortal realm, I believe it's known as one's id—though their under-
standing of it is simplistic at best. Regardless, her impulses are ruling her,
right now. She's lost control of herself."

"How do we get Ceara back?" Blair asked, hand covering her mouth,
eyes wide.

"You misunderstand me. The woman you knew as Ceara Light-Eater is
no more," Amergin replied.

"But you said she's possessed, which means—"

"The 'she' I was referring to is not Ceara. Hound," Amergin's eyes flicked
to Cathal, though his sword never for a second wavered, "do you know her
true name?"

Cathal dipped his head. "She's called Quinn MacKenna, Morrigan's
daughter."

The bard's sword twitched, and we felt blood running in tiny rivulets
down our throat. "That's not possible," he said, softly.

"Times change," Cathal replied, sardonically.

"Then the *awen*—"

"Inherited," Cathal said, cutting the bard off. "She's yet to master it,
though, it seems."

"I still don't understand," Blair interrupted, stepping close, kneeling to
meet our eyes. "Ceara..." she reached out, sliding her fingers across our
face.

My face.

"No," I growled. "Not Ceara."

She yanked her hand back as if I'd snapped at it. The sword at my throat
fell away almost instantly, which was good; I wasn't about to let the bastard
cut me a second time. And yet the tension I'd felt earlier not only remained,
it seemed to have gotten worse.

"Is it true?" Bran asked, planting a sword nearly as tall as he was into the
sand, no longer remotely focused on Cathal. "What the hound said, I mean.
Are you the Morrigan's daughter?"

"That's what they keep tellin' me," I replied, rising gingerly to my feet. I
brushed the sand off my...dress. Jesus Christ, I was wearing a dress! For
some reason, both voices—until now still lingering somewhere in the
darker confines of my brain—fell immediately silent, my disdain too
powerful for either to overcome. I groaned, fighting the urge to tear my
hair out.

"What's wrong?" Blair asked, kneeling before me with one arm raised.

I gestured at my body. "I do *not* wear dresses," I hissed. "*That's* what's wrong."

The woman's eyes filled with tears. "Oh, Ceara—"

"That's not me name!" I shrieked, turning away from the raw need, the vulnerability, in the woman's face. "And what the hell are ye three doin'?" I yelled, pointing at the brothers, all of whom had dropped to a knee with their heads bowed.

Cathal swiveled his head back and forth, then yipped once. "These are the Crows, aren't they?"

"Yes," Lady Aife replied. She'd taken a seat by the fire, far from the piece of wood she'd been playing with earlier, clutching her legs to her chest like a lost child. The bard had joined her, though he remained standing. "Her power must have called to them."

"Wait, what nonsense are ye on about, now?" I asked.

"We used to be your mother's soldiers, my Queen," Bran replied.

"Her bodyguards," Cathal corrected. "And occasional lovers, from what I recall."

Bran shrugged. "We served."

"Well, I'm officially grossed out. Anyone else?" I threw up my hands, letting my frustration show, trying my best not to think about the fact that my mother had traipsed about with three men-at-arms who doubled as bedtime snacks.

"Why is she here?" the bard asked Cathal, ignoring my outburst.

"I'm escorting her to the Hall of Lives," Cathal replied. "Her mother... needs her. And now it seems she needs her mother."

"What d'ye mean?" I asked.

"He means you've been hurt," Lady Aife replied. "Wounded." She pointed at my waist, and as soon as I turned my attention to it, I knew exactly what she meant. I remembered, the pain hitting me like a phantom blow.

"Someone stabbed me..."

"Do you know who?" Tristan asked. I turned back to find him holding Blair up, letting her lean into his chest as she sobbed, quietly.

I frowned, trying to think, but it was hard; it felt like the last few hours—the last few months—were part dream, part reality. Hazy and hard to define, like childhood memories that may or may not have been real. "'The Queen sends her regards,'" I repeated, at last.

Lady Aife's head shot up. "Queen Niamh? But...that doesn't make any sense."

"The reason doesn't matter," Cathal insisted. "She'll survive, but only if I take her to her mother."

"Then we shall accompany you," Bran said.

Cathal growled, hackles rising, the ashy grey markings decorating his fur emitting a gentle glow. "No, you won't. If you want to chase after your goddess, be my guest. But I only agreed to escort one human. One."

"We won't be a burden," Llew interjected, speaking for the first time since I'd come to.

"All humans are burdens," Cathal spat.

"Oy, Cathy!" I yelled, drawing the hound's attention. "How long do we have?" I left the rest of the question unspoken. Not how long did I have, but how long did *we*—my mother's ghost and I—have. After all, I'd been lost for months inside this realm. If time had been running short before, I could only imagine how little of it we had now.

"Days, at most."

I hung my head, cursing. "Then we'd better get goin', before it's too late."

The hound met my eyes and nodded imperceptibly, his druidic marks fading once more. "I'll keep a closer eye on you this time."

"Aye, I'm sorry about that," I replied.

"My Queen," Bran said, rising to his feet, "will you allow us to join you?"

I glanced at each of the brothers in turn, studying the resolve on their faces. "No," I said, at last. They hung their heads. "I'm sorry, but I don't know ye. This woman, Ceara, her memories..." I drifted off. "I can't trust me own judgment. Cathal is me guide, and I've decided to let him call the shots from now on. If he says we go alone, we go alone."

"And me?"

I felt my shoulders tense involuntarily at the desperation in Blair's voice. I didn't turn; I didn't want to see the crushing disappointment in the woman's face. I honestly still wasn't sure how I felt about my memories of her, of our time together. Besides, if I couldn't trust my perception of the brothers, how was I supposed to trust my feelings for Blair?

"Look at me...Quinn."

I winced but did as she asked. It was worse than I imagined; she no longer looked sad but determined. It was the face of an overzealous worshipper hoping to convert a non-believer—she was fixated on bringing back her lover, even if it meant following me to the ends of this—and perhaps another—world.

"No," I said.

Her eyes tightened. "I know she's in there."

I sighed, exhaustion setting in, the pain in my lower back cresting. "And so what if she is?"

"I forbid you to leave," Blair replied, matter-of-factly, as if that were the logical response.

I laughed, but it was a sad, tired laugh. "I don't t'ink ye have a choice."

"Oh, but I do."

Before I could reply to that, Blair lashed out, jabbing the butt of her spear into my stomach. I bent over, out of breath, and finally dropped to my knees. When I looked up, I found the brothers shielding me, facing off against the Curaitl.

"Don't make me hurt you again, spear wielder," Finann threatened, sword leveled at Tristan.

"Stop!" I yelled, though it was a struggle to breath. I dry heaved for a moment, then got back to my feet, cradling my injured gut.

I shoved past the brothers to find Blair crying in the sand, her spear lying discarded beside her. "Now you have to do what you swore you'd do," she said, her voice soft and broken.

"What's she talking about?" Cathal asked. He and the bard stood away from the others, though he'd risen menacingly onto all fours.

This time both voices in my head spoke at once, and the memory they shared was a joint thing—Ceara's vow, spoken out of anger. A promise that made Ceara feel so guilty she'd sought out the woman she'd threatened often, hoping to make up for her breach of etiquette.

So often they'd fallen for each other.

"If you remember," Blair insisted, "that means she's still in there. Which means, if you leave me behind, you know what will happen."

She'll never forgive us.

I gritted my teeth, shaking my head, anger rising. "What have ye done, Blair?"

Blair rubbed an arm across her eyes, smearing her cheeks with sand in the process. "I told you I didn't know what I'd do if you left. Well, now you know," she replied, bitterly.

"Quinn..." Cathal growled.

"She wants me to blind her," I said, glaring at the woman. "I swore, if she ever hurt me on purpose, ever again, I'd take her eyes." As one, the others looked at me, their faces equally horrified—even the bard seemed appalled.

Only Cathal looked away.

"Then take her eyes. But hurry up, we have places to be."

"Cathal!" I swung around to square off with the mangy bastard, but the second I saw his face I knew what he meant; his lips twitched, teeth bared. He didn't like this anymore than I did, but then he had a job to do—a human to escort, regardless of how long it took, or who had to be blinded along the way.

"Do it," Blair said, rising to her feet. "In a world without Ceara, I may as well be blind."

"Blair—" Lady Aife began.

"No!" Blair whirled to face the warmaiden. "You don't get to lecture me about this. Not you."

Lady Aife's face flushed uncharacteristically red, looking even more like her daughter's in that instant than I'd ever thought possible. And, for some reason, that triggered something else inside me. Inside us. I turned to Blair, studying her as Ceara would have, noting her beauty, yes, but also her flaws. Her eagerness to follow orders, to fight, to believe the best in people even when they didn't deserve it.

"I won't do it," I said, softly.

"You must!" Blair screamed, kicking up sand. "Do it!"

"No, Blair," I said, the expression on my face stilling her. "No, I have another choice."

"Ceara?"

I shook my head. "No, it's still me." But the truth was more complicated than that; I'd experienced the emotions of that strange, loving woman—just for an instant—long enough to know I could never hurt Blair like that. Not her. "And *I* have another choice."

Cathal whipped his head around. "You can't be serious."

"Can I reach the Hall of Lives from there?" I asked.

Cathal's markings lit up, steam spewing from his body. "Cross the Blighted Lands in a few *days*?! Are you insane?"

"Can it be done?"

Cathal howled, a sound so brutal it made all of us cringe, the patterns splashed along his body going from red to blue, like the inner core of a candle flame. By the time he was done, we were surrounded by a light fog. "I *hate* humans," he said, finally, chest heaving.

"I didn't say ye had to—"

"Of course I'm coming, you idiot! I'm your guide. As if there's a guarantee you'll even survive the Blighted Lands in the shape you're in!" He stalked towards me, eyes glowing through the mist. "If I have to drag you by the throat with my teeth, I'll deliver you. Do you understand me?"

"I...I didn't mean..." Blair stammered, only this time it was Lady Aife who took her into her arms, brushing her head soothingly.

"Go," she said, glaring at me. "Go, and do not return. You are a stranger among the Curaitl, and no longer welcome among my people."

I winced; for some reason, that had hurt a hell of a lot more than I thought it would. "Come on, Cathy," I said, trying to keep the regret out of my voice. "We've clearly overstayed our welcome."

"Don't call me Cathy, brat."

I didn't bother responding. But then, I wasn't sure I had anything else I could say; I was too close to tears to force anything witty, and too damn tired to complain. At this point, I was willing to chalk it up to experience—yet another failed relationship to contemplate. The only difference this time around was that the hyperbolic "I wish I could just die" mentality that usually follows a breakup would likely end up being more literal.

Here Lies Quinn MacKenna.

She Never Could Get It Right.

29

The bard, Amergin, left the Curaitl and the Crows to talk amongst themselves, trailing instead after Cathal and me. I briefly considered telling the guy to back off but wasn't in the mood to bark at anyone; I'd had my fill of being the bad girl for a little while. Instead, I drifted behind until I was even with the bard. I realized I recognized him, though it took me longer to place him than I would have liked. Ceara's memories—the tall man strumming and plucking his lyre as he wove a tragedy, the fervent gleam in his eyes as he urged his people to war—flashing behind my eyelids like snippets of a film.

To say it was jarring would be an understatement.

Would it continue like this, I wondered? Ceara's memories, her emotions, overwhelming me at the most inopportune moments? It occurred to me that, aside from these flashes, I knew very little about the woman I'd become over the last few months, a woman who'd taken a lover and found a home among a village of primitive strangers. To be honest, I still wasn't sure how I felt about any of this, let alone about who I'd evolved into among the Otherworlders—the "Blessed People" who dwelt here.

"Are they all heroes, then?" I asked the bard, absentmindedly.

"Excuse me?"

"The Blessed People. Lady Aife. Bran. Tristan." I waffled a hand in his direction. "Even Amergin has a familiar ring to it," I admitted, recalling tales of the last race to conquer Ireland and the warrior poet who'd led them against the Tuatha de Danann.

But the bard was shaking his head. "Some are, as you say, heroes. Legends. Figures from myths. Figures from the past. Kings and warriors. Bards and artists." Amergin shrugged. "But most lose track of these things, their memories, much as you did. They become something other than whom they once were, even if parts remain."

"But not all do," I challenged, quizzically.

"Not all, no. The individuals you might call rulers, typically, are the rare few who never forgot their old lives. Those who recognize themselves in the old stories. And, in a few cases, those who tell those stories to begin with."

I shook my head, trying to process that. A world full of champions, of larger-than-life personalities, of...well, immortals. "So, what? This is like, heaven? Their reward?"

"Heaven..." the bard drifted off, considering the notion. He frowned. "Perhaps."

I cocked an eyebrow at his sudden caginess. "Perhaps?"

"This place is a prison," Cathal muttered, far enough ahead of us that I could barely make out his comment.

"A what?" I called.

Amergin shot the hound a dirty look. "It is *not* a prison."

Cathal kept padding forward, though it seemed almost as if he shrugged mid-stride, shoulder blade bunching for just a moment. "Have it your way."

"What did he mean?" I asked, looking to the bard for clarification.

"I meant," Cathal said, before the bard could reply, "that everyone here is living under false pretenses. But maybe the bard's right. Maybe prison isn't the right word." He swung that massive muzzle around towards me, rage simmering just beneath the surface as he spoke. "This place is a garrison."

"A what?"

"That's enough, Hound," Amergin interjected.

Cathal halted, turning in a lumbering circle until he stood facing the bard, the edges of the surf lapping against the shore like a death knell, a bell tolling away Amergin's last moments. "Are you telling me what to do, bard?"

Amergin blanched, but bravely—or perhaps stupidly—held his ground. "No. I merely wish you wouldn't say such things." He glanced back the way we'd come, scrutinizing that distant campfire and the shadowy figures crouched before it.

Cathal tracked the bard's stare and snarled. "You prefer to maintain the lie, is that it? That this is paradise, and not a staging ground for the war to come?"

"There is no such thing as paradise," Amergin replied, sounding tired. He turned his attention to the hound. "Not one without a purpose, at any rate."

I frowned at that. "What's that supposed to mean?"

"It means no version of the afterlife exists outside of time," Amergin explained. "Even Heaven is attuned to a ticking clock. Judgment Day. Ragnarok. The Sermon of the Seven Suns." The bard ran a thin-fingered hand through his hair, mussing it up in the process, clearly agitated. "Paradise *cannot* be infinite, or you'd call it Hell."

Cathal swiveled and resumed walking, his markings flaring red for just an instant. The two of us trailed after him while I considered everything Amergin was telling me. I had to admit, the bard had a point. Even in scripture, the End of Days coincided with a huge battle between good and evil. Or perhaps not good and evil itself, but the *forces* of good and evil. The troops had to come from somewhere, after all.

"Wait, you're sayin' the Blessed People really are livin' here until their gods call on 'em to fight?" I asked, everything finally falling into place at once. "Isn't that a bit...manipulative?" I struggled to think of a better word. "Or, well, wrong?"

Amergin chuckled. "Since when are gods exclusively benevolent?"

I thought about that and had to admit the bard was right; just about every myth or parable I'd come across in every religion featured capricious, self-serving gods. Sure, they helped mortals from time to time, but their assistance always came with an expectation, or at the culmination of some awful trial. Even Abraham's God had demanded sacrifice, and Noah's Ark hadn't exactly been built in a day. "I don't like it," I admitted.

Cathal grunted his agreement.

"That's why I wanted to speak with you, before you left," Amergin replied, adamantly.

"Oh?"

"Yes." The bard halted, looking away towards the sea, expression unreadable. "What the Tuatha de Danann have created here...this world...it cannot go on as it is."

I frowned. "Why not?"

"You have seen for yourself why not. Or your Other self has, at least."

"Me Other self?"

"The woman you became. Ceara. *She* is your Other self. The woman you might have been, had you been raised among us." He waved that away before I could ask the dozen or so questions his explanation raised. "But that's not important. Simply think back to the tournament, to your time in the Southern Isles."

I grimaced but did as he asked. "What about it?"

"Didn't the whole event strike you as odd? Forced, even?"

I nodded, murky memories resurfacing under Amergin's gaze. "I remember thinkin' there was little point, if that's what ye mean?"

"Exactly." The bard's chin bobbed up and down enthusiastically. "The leaders, those of us who know the truth, who know this realm's intended purpose, continue to bring together our best warriors to test each other's mettle. We even recruit our most skilled artists to glorify their accomplishments. But we have been at peace too long. Too few are compelled to wage war. And why should they? Not when—"

"When love is already in our grasp," I interrupted, reminded of Ceara's final thoughts before being stabbed, of her eagerness to explore this great, wide world—to spend her days and nights by Blair's side for an eternity.

A pang of regret accompanied the thought.

"Exactly!" Amergin exclaimed.

"What would you have her do about it?" Cathal asked, glancing over his shoulder at the bard with one ear cocked, the other drooping.

"I don't know," Amergin admitted, shaking his head. "But if she is who you say she is, maybe she could speak with her mother. Warn her. Entreat her."

"You want me to ask her to, what, make your people more bloodthirsty?" I asked, raising an eyebrow.

"Perhaps." Amergin sighed. "That, or give us someone, something, to fight. To fight for. Peace is often considered a warrior's reward, but the truth is peace has become our penance. I ask that you at least talk to your mother. For all we know, she and the rest of the Tuatha de Danann have forgotten all about us." He studied Cathal, then me. "Until tonight, I believed they'd abandoned us. That we were alone."

"And what's wrong with being alone?" Cathal asked, bitterly.

"Ye *are* alone," I replied with certainty. Amergin stiffened, but I continued as if I hadn't noticed, refusing to elaborate. "So, let me get this straight. Ye believe we all need a purpose, and ye t'ink the Otherworlders have forgotten theirs?"

Amergin nodded.

I hesitated, thinking back to my time as Ceara. "I'll speak to the Morrigan on your behalf," I said, finally.

"Thank you, I—"

"But I doubt you'll like what I have to say," I interrupted, recalling Finann's casual, practically blasphemous dismissal of the gods and their machinations. "Tell me, the Tógálaí Capall and the Curaitl. Is that rivalry real? Or an arrangement between Tuathal and Lady Aife to keep their people occupied?"

Amergin coughed, guilt written all over his otherwise noble face. "They needed someone to hate," he murmured. "They'd forgotten how."

I felt Ceara's sorrow and found myself sighing. "Hate," I said, voicing her thoughts, "was never the point."

"What's that supposed to mean?"

I wished I could explain it to him, that I could put into words the satisfaction Ceara had felt in Blair's arms, the exhilaration she'd felt sparring with her friends, the depth of her jealousy when she thought it all might be taken away. "I'll speak to the Morrigan. But I cannot condone what ye and your fellow rulers have done."

Amergin's forehead creased. "What we've done?"

"Aye," I replied, considering the man. "I t'ink ye lot are the problem. Ye remember the mortal world, which makes ye outsiders, same as I am." I found myself cringing at the idea that Rhys might actually have had a point, all along. "Ye kept hate alive."

"We—"

"Our ride's here," Cathal rumbled, interrupting the bard before he could splutter his defense. The hound was eyeing me consideringly, as if I'd finally said something he didn't absolutely despise. I turned away from the hound's scrutiny to watch the lone, empty boat glide across the waves. Another gift from Manannan, perhaps? Or the standard ferry between the Land of Youth and the Blighted Lands? I had no idea. I jerked my chin in acknowledgment and approached the shore, ignoring the bard's irate expression.

"We only did as the gods would have had us do," Amergin grumbled, finally, before stomping back the way we'd come.

"That's part of the problem," I murmured, staring out at the moonlit water, waiting to begin the next, potentially fatal leg of my journey. But already my mind had wandered further ahead, anticipating a turbulent heart-to-heart between mother and daughter.

Assuming neither of us died, first.

30

*T*he boat, which I'd assumed would be large enough for Cathal and I to fit comfortably, was a tad more cramped than I'd have liked; Cathal's hot, moist breath spilled onto my shoulders as we sailed across an otherwise quiet sea. Still, after the turbulence of the last several hours, I wasn't necessarily complaining. A little peace and quiet wouldn't hurt.

"Here," Cathal said as he dropped something into my lap.

I frowned, staring down at my silver sundial watch in surprise, only just now realizing it hadn't been on my wrist. Christ, when had I dropped it? I glanced up over my shoulder at Cathal. "How long have ye had this?"

"You left it on the battlefield. Must have come off. It reeks of magic." His nose twitched, the furrows between his eyes bunching together. "Where you go, it goes."

I grunted and reached for the watch, studying it, praying that the gnomon would inch even just a tad—a sign that I had some residual magic stored up. But it didn't; my fuel reserves were empty. My shoulders slumped, but something caught my eye before I could wallow too long. I frowned, turning the watch this way and that beneath the moonlight. At last, I realized what was bothering me about it; the face had changed shape. Rather than a flat disk, it seemed beveled, slightly thicker in the middle. "Oy," I nudged Cathal, "what d'ye do to me watch?"

"Besides return it to you, unasked and unthanked?" Cathal replied, scathingly.

I bit back my response. Yeah, probably not a good idea to berate the messenger, in this case. Even if he *had* bent the damn thing in the process of returning it to me. Except, it didn't *feel* bent. I probed the circumference of the watch, fingertips sliding along the grooves and seams until I felt something give—a tiny clasp I hadn't been able to make out in the gloom.

The sundial popped open like a pocket watch.

"Huh," I said, staring down at the watch's interior—an interior that definitely had never been there before. I held it up, marveling at the intricate designs: a minute hand shaped like a spear, the hour a sword, the upper and lower quadrants decorated with what looked like a cauldron and a dolmen. And yet—more interesting to me—was what lay behind: three, neatly divided sections that depicted crows, though each was posed distinctly from the other. The upper right, upon which the two hands were pointed, showed a crow in flight. The upper left a crow swooping down, claws outstretched, cawing as it sought its prey. The lower third a crow nesting.

Before I could study the watch further, however, we were enveloped in a thick, cloying fog that made it nearly impossible to see, let alone distinguish etchings at night, no matter how bright the full moon overhead. I snapped the watch closed and was in the process of sliding it back onto my wrist when it occurred to me that Cathal had no pockets.

"And where exactly d'ye keep this t'ing?" I asked, holding up the watch with the tips of my fingers, fearing the worst.

"In my mouth."

Well, I guess that wasn't the *worst* place he could have kept it for several months.

But it certainly wasn't the best, either.

I let the watch dangle for a moment before resolving to put it on. They say a dog's mouth is cleaner than a human's, right? I shook my head, muttering to myself about the shabby state of my life, before finally turning my attention to the mist. It was impossibly dense, so much so that when I finally let my arm drop, I could feel condensation sticking to my arm. "This better not be ye," I insisted, waving my hand idly at the roiling fog.

"Or what?"

"Or..." I began, then thought better of it, realizing I was just picking on Cathal to pass the time—anything to avoid ending up alone with my thoughts. "Nevermind. Sorry, I was tryin' to be funny. Make a little conversation."

"How's that working for you?"

I balled my fists, glaring up at the bastard. "Are ye always such a jerk?"

"Usually," Cathal replied, though he didn't seem to take any offense to the moniker.

"Why'd ye decide to come, then?" I demanded. "Too proud to let me wander off on me own? Or did Manannan threaten to have ye fixed if ye failed?"

"Fixed?"

"Neutered," I clarified. "Ye know, snip snip." I made a scissoring motion with my fingers. "Bye bye, balls."

"Are you referring to castration?"

I smirked at the disgust in his voice. "Aye, now you're catchin' on."

Cathal growled, the low rumble of his chest against my back reminding me of a mall chair massage. He shook himself, the boat rocking a little in the process. "I'd like to see someone try."

"Well then, what is it?" I demanded.

"The reason I'm here?" Cathal licked his chops with an awful slurping sound. "I owed the sea god a favor."

"Why? Did he save ye from a bath once?" I asked, grinning.

"He saved me from being murdered along with the rest of my kin, after our master's death."

I stopped grinning. "Oh, well that was nice of him."

"Nice?" Cathal snorted. "No. Manannan saw that I could be useful. Nice would have been killing off the humans who hunted us long before I was the only one left."

I frowned, wondering if Cathal knew what the word "nice" actually meant. But I wasn't about to correct him. Know your audience, people. "Ye blame 'em, then? The humans? Is that why ye hate our kind?"

Cathal grunted. "No, I've learned to hate your kind for other reasons. Besides, I don't blame them for what they did. I blame our master."

"Why's that?"

"Because he created us but did nothing to protect us. Gave us voices and minds of our own, then abandoned us to the whims of lesser creatures. It was…cruel."

Cruel. The word was laced with regret, so much so that I didn't even

155

need to see Cathal's face to know how much he despised what had been done to him and the rest of his kind. But I still wasn't sure I understood. Why hate the one who made you rather than the ones who took everything from you? "You'd rather have stayed mindless?" I asked, finally, steering the conversation to safer waters.

"I don't know," he admitted after a lengthy pause. "I doubt I'd have cared, had I remained a beast. But now I'm alone."

"I thought being alone wasn't so bad," I teased.

"There *are* worse things."

"Like what?"

"Like sharing a tiny boat with a foul-smelling human."

Now it was my turn to grunt. I surreptitiously raised my arms and sniffed but couldn't make out anything worth noting. Granted, I hadn't exactly been smothering myself in deodorant and perfume these last few months, but I'd washed regularly, from what I could recall. Maybe it was just his hypersensitive nose?

"It's your wound," Cathal explained.

I gritted my teeth, reminded of the nagging sensation at the base of my spine—a sensation that tended to dwindle so long as I didn't think too hard about it. "How bad is it, really?"

"I used fire to seal it, to clear out some of the rot, but it's bad. It'll fester soon. Your stamina will fade, and, eventually, you'll pass out from the pain."

"Great." I took a long, deep breath. "And ye t'ink me mother's ghost will be able to cure me?"

"I have no idea."

I whirled to face the hound, though in the end all I got for my trouble was a face full of wiry hair and a sudden flaring of pain along my spine. "What d'ye mean, ye have no idea?" I asked through clenched teeth.

"Exactly what I said. Honestly, are all humans from your realm as ignorant as you are?"

I felt my cheeks flush in anger at the insult, though it wasn't merely the snub that got me so heated—it was the lie. I felt feathers brushing against my cheeks, forcing me to shut my eyes. The fact that he'd lied to our face— that he'd given us a false sense of hope—set something off inside us, something vicious and savage. Before we knew it, we'd head-butted the mutt as hard as we could, the boat threatening to capsize with the force of the blow.

Cathal snarled and pressed a paw against our chest, pinning us down with his ridiculous weight.

"Enough!" he roared.

But we weren't done. We reached up to claw at that leg, to make it bleed. Pain. We wanted Cathal to suffer as we suffered. To fear as we feared. To carve—

I drew back, hands over my eyes, blinking away the streaks in my vision. The brilliant light bursting from Cathal's marks faded almost immediately, the effect remarkably like a stun grenade. I wiped away tears, my eyes on fire. "What the hell was that?" I groaned.

"A warning," Cathal replied. "Your wild side, the *awen* the bard spoke of, is growing reckless."

I tapped on Cathal's leg, an invitation to remove it from my chest. He did, though slowly, gingerly. I noticed he was favoring the one side, and I wondered if that headbutt had done serious damage; even without magic to call upon, it seemed I remained inhumanly strong. "It does that," I replied. "Are ye hurt?"

"I'm fine," Cathal said, though his tone said otherwise.

"Let me have a look," I insisted.

"No. Just know that next time you try a stunt like that I'll take a chunk out of you."

I gulped, imagining myself caught between those powerful jaws. "Well, don't be a dick, then," I insisted, defensively.

"I—what did you just call me?"

"A dick. You're a dick." I held up a hand. "Don't even try to deny it. First ye lie to me. Then ye tell me ye don't even know if I'm goin' to survive, no matter what we do, and ye expect me to—what? Say t'anks?"

"You would've preferred I continued lying to you?"

"No, I'd prefer it if ye didn't provoke me for your own amusement," I countered.

Cathal's ears flicked about for a minute before he finally looked away. "Fine. I'll try to be less..." he drifted off.

"Dickish," I provided.

"If," Cathal added, "you promise to get yourself under control. And fast."

I ground my teeth and turned away, my frustration getting the better of me. After all, how was I supposed to get myself under control? I wasn't even entirely sure who or what I was at this point—even if I couldn't admit it out loud. Quinn, yes, but for how long? How long until my wild side took over to revel in slaughter and mayhem? Or would it be Ceara, weaseling her way into my thoughts and emotions, thrusting her alien sentiments to the surface?

"I—"

Cathal's ears perked up, his body going rigid, hackles rising. "We're here."

3 1

*T*he Blighted Lands were nothing like I'd expected. I don't know why, but some part of my imagination—the same part which flashed on images of skulls shattering beneath the metal toes of a Terminator whenever anyone brought up Judgment Day or pictured a fiery lava pit whenever anyone mentioned Hell—had assumed we'd step out onto the shore of a nuclear wasteland. A place utterly devoid of life. You know, a *blighted* place.

But the truth—the reality—was far worse than I ever could have imagined. Instead of a barren wilderness, an endless desert, or whatever the hell I'd been envisioning, we stepped onto a beach, the yellow-green sand strewn with rotting seaweed, littered with the hollow carapaces of dead crabs. The stench alone threatened to overpower me—something between decay and decomposition, like formaldehyde mixed with bile. Beyond the shoreline, almost lost amidst the clouds of roiling, sickeningly thick vapor, were withered trees, bark sloughing off like a discarded reptilian skin, revealing nothing but rotten heartwood beneath.

I pressed a hand over my mouth and nose, fighting the urge to gag.

"How do you think I feel?" Cathal asked, nonplussed at my expression.

But it wasn't only the smell bothering me. There was something to this place, something diseased, that made me want to crawl back into our boat and accept my fate. Better to die on the open sea than to linger in a place like this, I decided. Except the boat was already gone by the time I thought to look for it.

Guess it didn't want to be here, either.

"Well, shit."

"It was your choice," the hound chastised.

I didn't bother informing the mutt that it hadn't been a choice at all; I doubted he'd understand even if I could articulate what Blair had meant to my Other self—not to mention the fact that literally removing someone's eyes was a little much, even for me. "Come on," I replied instead, hiking up the sloped beach, accompanied by the brittle snap of shells shattering beneath my feet.

"Of the two of us, who is supposed to be the guide?" Cathal asked.

I turned. "Am I goin' the wrong way?"

The giant hound pushed past me, bumping me with his broad shoulders. "This way."

"That's the way I was goin'!" I contested, trailing after him.

"Even humans get lucky sometimes," he replied, tail wagging.

I realized he was baiting me, trying to get my mind off the locale, and so I left it alone; if he could keep me alive long enough to get me out of this place, then I could handle a little teasing. "How far is it, anyway?"

"To the Hall of Lives?" Cathal studied the ground as he padded forward, clearly agitated to find nothing but carcasses beneath his paws. "We'll have to pass through the Forest of the Damned, the Desert of Despair, and through the tunnels beneath the mountain."

I balked at the various landscapes Cathal had named, my imagination spiraling almost immediately out of control. I mean, who the hell had the cartographer been for this place, Wednesday Addams? "So, the mountain," I said, "let me guess...Mount Doom?"

"No. They call it Mount Never Rest."

"Great, just great," I mumbled. "And how long will all that take, d'ye t'ink?"

"Weeks, if we're lucky."

"Weeks?! I thought ye said me mother's ghost only had a few days?!"

"And how would I know something like that?" The hound snorted after catching the irate expression on my face before continuing onward. "Look, I was tasked with getting you there. That's it. I told you what I thought would get you up and moving fastest. Deal with it."

I gaped at the hound's retreating backside. "You're just a big, hairy liar, that's what ye are!" I accused, pointing.

Cathal didn't even bother turning. "I told you what you needed to hear. Maybe I should have said hours. Then you'd have been properly motivated, and we wouldn't have had to cross the Dagda-damned *Blighted Lands*."

I frowned at his tone. "Ye keep talkin' like this place is...I don't know. Hell? Worse than hell?" I took a look around and shuddered. "I mean it's awful, but still, I don't get—"

Cathal barked a laugh. "What, you think this is as bad as it gets?"

I coughed into my hand, declining to answer.

"You have no idea what we're in for, human. The only reason we weren't attacked on sight is because I asked Manannan to drop us off on the far shore. This is the land of exiles. Home to every creature in existence that we've forgotten or chosen to forget. Creatures without names. Creatures recalled only in nightmares. And we'll be running from all of them, because you're too damn fragile to survive, otherwise."

I opened my mouth, then closed it. Opened it again. No, nevermind; what good would it do to argue? Cathal was right. This was definitely going to suck. And, if we survived, I doubted either of us would make it through unscathed. I sighed and trailed after the miserable bastard, trying to ignore the popping sounds beneath my feet as we ascended towards the tree line, breathing judiciously through my mouth.

"T'anks for taggin' along," I said, a few minutes later.

"Thank me if we live," Cathal grumbled.

I dove for cover behind the relative shelter of a time-worn rock formation, the blistering sun overhead literally scorching the earth—white-hot flames danced along the ground wherever the light touched, threatening to burn the hems of the pants I'd stolen off a corpse we'd discovered in a cave on the fringes of the desert. Not the most sanitary decision I'd ever made, but—after traipsing through the Forest of the Damned in a swiftly deteriorating dress for several days, not to mention the stubble that my legs had accumulated during that span—I wasn't about to be too picky. Besides, I'd ripped them off the bleached bones of a skeleton, no doubt a victim of this miserable desert and its soul-searing sun; at this temperature, I doubted even germs could survive for long.

And yet we'd managed it for, what? A week? Two?

Time felt like such a strange, obscure measurement in this place.

"Where is it?" Cathal asked, huddled beside me, his massive body barely shielded from view behind the weathered, sizzling stone.

"It went left," I whispered, scanning the ravine we'd opted to pass through as we headed for Mount Never Rest—a great big stain on the horizon that never seemed to get any bigger no matter how long we trudged.

Or—on days like today—ran.

"How'd you spot it?" Cathal asked, scenting the air, his once shiny black nose turned a dingy grey, the pebbled flesh cracked and ashy. My lips, I knew, were just as bad; the blistered sores kept me up at night, the taste of blood whenever I probed them making the thirst that much worse. Cathal had insisted we couldn't die of starvation or thirst here, but I was beginning to suspect that was a torture in and of itself—being so hungry, so thirsty that you could die and then being forced to carry on like that, struck by waves of mind-crippling nausea, not to mention being constantly reminded of the crippling ache in your throat.

Let's just say it gave Hell a whole new meaning.

"Didn't," I replied. "It caught me." I showed Cathal my arm and the red welt already spreading across my skin. Soon, especially if I kept moving, the raised flesh would split open, the pressure too much for the skin to bear. Not that I'd mind by then.

Better to be bleeding than dead, right?

Cathal cursed. "Can you run?"

I nodded, though I knew it would be a long-shot; I was tapped out, unable to muster much in the way of anything for the last day or so. At best, I could tell my legs to move and see if they felt like playing along. If so, we stood a chance. If not, the sun wraith—what I called the nearly invisible creatures that haunted this godsforsaken desert, their whip-like limbs flailing about like the arms of an inflatable tube man—would find us. At this point, though, I wasn't sure it mattered.

Because Cathal, my guide and last hope of surviving this place, was dying faster than I was.

"When I say go, we go."

"Are ye sure?" I asked, eyeing the jagged wound that ran along Cathal's side and flank. It was a nasty thing, pus-riddled and festering—the handiwork of a particularly horrifying, two-headed primate we'd encountered in the forest the night before we stumbled out onto this rocky desert. Together, we'd managed to escape, but not before Cathal took a blow meant for me, the creature's feral claws gouging deep into the hound's side.

"What choice do we have?" Cathal asked, bunching those massive shoulders of his, ducking his head for a moment in defiance of our situation. I didn't have the energy or the will to argue. Hadn't had either for days, now. Instead, I nodded, rising to a crouch.

"Alright, go!"

We ran. Well, Cathal ran; the hound raced ahead, favoring one side, but still able to move with remarkable speed, especially considering the fact that I could hear his paws sizzling as they brushed patches where the sun hit directly—the heat so intense it had actually tried to eat away at the leather of my boots over the past several days, leaving my footwear faintly lopsided.

I, meanwhile, jogged at a slow, measured pace. I kept my head down, focusing on putting one foot in front of the other rather than scouring the ravine for the sun wraith. One, because it wouldn't do me any good—the wraiths were almost impossible to see so long as the sun was up and frighteningly fast besides. And two, because I was more concerned with falling flat on my face and being unable to get back up.

As I loped, I tried to remember how long we'd been stuck here. How many days had we spent avoiding the sun, how many nights fleeing from the creatures that called this place home? It felt like an eternity, but couldn't have been more than a week, surely. Two at most. Except my top told a different story—my former dress had been reduced to almost nothing, the ends so frayed and shredded that it rode me like a man's oversized T-shirt. Partly that was because I'd torn some of the material to cover my exposed bits, especially my hands—tying the cloth over my scraped palms. But for some reason the top appeared more worn down, more aged than it should have.

Before I could worry about what that meant, however, I practically stumbled on Cathal at the far end of the ravine, lying on his side, his breathing irregular, chest sinking drastically from the force of his exhales. His tongue—pale, almost white—lolled out of his mouth, his eyes so wide I thought they might pop out of his skull.

I skidded to a stop and sagged to my knees beside him, pressing my hand against that massive chest. His heart beat frighteningly fast beneath my hand, his fur slick with sweat. A fever, maybe? His injuries must have finally gotten to him, I realized, the infection too much for his body to withstand. I cursed through broken, bleeding lips. If only I had a way to save him, to seal the wound the way he had mine. Part of me—the twisted part that still remembered how to laugh, even in this horrid place—truly wished I did; it would have been fair play to cauterize the literal son of a bitch.

"Cathal," I rasped, throat so parched I thought it might shrivel up and cave in, "ye have to get up." I shook him, but there was no response. "Cathy," I insisted. "Get up, Cathy."

But not even mocking the mutt was going to get him back on his feet. Not now. I lay my head against that shuddering body, listened to his ragged breathing, and tried to think of something nice to say. A eulogy, of some sort. "Cathal..." I said, at last, voice breaking. "I wish I'd never dragged ye into this. I'm so sorry. Ye deserved better."

Almost in response, so distant I thought I must have imagined it, I heard a horn. Then again, two notes rising to reverberate throughout the ravine, crashing over us in waves. I glanced up to find the cliffs on either side swarming with figures in black, their features nearly impossible to see beyond the glare of the sun at their backs. I squinted and raised an arm to block out the light but caught sight only of a faintly lizard-like creature, skin reflecting light like glass, scuttling past, its long, thin arms swinging around to catch me across the chest. Another sun wraith, or the same one? Either way, it didn't matter; the instant the limbs collided with my chest, I felt agony crack across skin and fell, unable to breathe, clutching at the raised flesh, crumpled in the fetal position, wishing I could die.

Which was exactly how Rhys found me.

I thought I'd seen the very worst the Blighted Lands had to offer. That—between the desiccated foliage and maggot-filled corpses of the Forest of the Damned and the savage, sun- scorched Desert of Despair—I had truly grasped the horrors of this realm. I wasn't so naive as to believe there wouldn't be other horrifying creatures out there, other environments eager to soak up the blood of the living, but never in my wildest nightmares would I have believed anything like *this* was possible.

"Move," Rhys said, jabbing me with a jagged length of metal affixed to a crude wooden handle by a strip of knotted cloth—the Blighted Land's prison shiv equivalent, I guessed. I did what I was told, shuffling forward, my hands bound behind my back. But I couldn't stop staring at the valley in front of me, at the Blighted Land's bloodcurdling underbelly—Slavers Vale, Rhys had called it, a huge gorge tucked away on the outskirts of the desert that led all the way to the sea.

From the cliffs above, I could make out the milling crowds, peppered by many of the men Rhys worked for—bandits in black, fallen warriors all, if I were to hazard a guess. I could also see rusty cages full to bursting with haggard, half-naked people. Creatures of all shapes and sizes were kept in closely guarded pens, like animals at some improbable zoo. I found myself cringing as we approached, the noise appalling even from this high up, though nothing could have compared to the wafting odor of unwashed, diseased bodies left to bake beneath the sun. I would have gagged, but I was too exhausted, my skin throbbing, head aching. Frankly, it was all I could do to stay upright.

And yet, that still meant I was in better shape than Cathal; the bandits were dragging him across the ground on a makeshift wagon, the uneven, wooden wheels groaning beneath his weight. One of the bandits had flushed the hound's wound at Rhys' command, and I could tell he still breathed, though I wasn't sure how much longer he would last like this. But then, as I studied the cruel conditions below, I realized it may have been preferable had he died out on that ravine.

At this rate, it wasn't like we had anything to look forward to.

"Take the dog to the Handler," Rhys barked. "Get him in a cage, then make sure he's up and on his feet. We want him to look dangerous."

Two of the bandits nodded and wandered off towards the men dragging Cathal. As one, the group broke away, moving briskly down a steep decline which led directly to the valley floor. The rest of us, meanwhile, seemed to be taking the scenic route; a wide, winding path had been carved into the cliffs, snaking inexorably downward.

Not for the first time, I considered trying to appeal to Rhys, to convince him to let us go, but—after the black eye and busted lip he'd given me last time—I wasn't that tempted. If there was one thing the Blighted Lands were short of, even more so than water and food, it was sympathy. This land was a hard, hellish place that seemed to drag everyone down, to encourage your worst impulses, your shittiest self. So much so, in fact, that it seemed the only civilization these people could carve out for themselves was predicated on slavery.

"How did you get here?" Rhys asked, for perhaps the dozenth time, as we started down the path.

"By boat," I croaked.

The bastard kicked me from behind, right behind the knee. I stumbled, cursing as I collided with the rocky wall, my shoulder screaming in pain. But that was nothing new; my lower back no longer ached but burned—the wound's poison seeping deeper and deeper to the point that now I only wondered how much longer I had before it took me completely.

"You didn't come through the port," Rhys continued, dragging me upright with a savage tug. "Which is where all the boats come in. So, I'll ask you again, how did you get here?"

"Magic carpet," I replied. "No, wait. It was a time travelin' Delorean circa 1985." I coughed, throat too sore to laugh.

Rhys punched me in the gut, hard enough to drive the air from my lungs and make me want to puke. I curled up around that fist and leaned into the man. A rush of something, some alien emotion, washed over me as I smelled the peculiar, off-putting scent of his sweaty body—familiar in its own way. "Oh, Rhys Two Tusks," I said, in a voice so much gentler than my own, "how far you've fallen."

Rhys jerked back, then clenched his fists, face purpling with anger. "Do not call me that."

"Why not? It's your name, isn't it?"

Rhys just stared at me, his anger leaking out to reveal something cold, something raptorial, in his eyes. "I'm not sure what cruel twist of fate brought you into my life, Ceara, but I will make you pay for what you did to me." His mouth twitched in a smirk that sent chills down my spine despite the heat. "Just wait."

I sighed and turned to follow the train of bandits, ignoring the man, which seemed to piss him off more; he grabbed me by the hair before I could take two steps. "We aren't done, Ceara!" he insisted.

"It's Quinn, actually," I replied through clenched teeth. Then, with a savage yank of my own, I tore myself free from the man's grasp, strands of my hair poking out from between his fingers. Though I was off-balance and so weak I felt like I might fall down any second, I felt a surge of satisfaction at seeing the man's disbelieving expression.

At least until he recovered and punched me in the face.

Well, you win some, you lose some, I guess.

3 4

orced to breathe through my mouth, my nose broken, my mouth and chin covered in dried blood, I shambled forward under the watchful eye of one of Rhys' men; apparently the bastard didn't trust himself not to kill me, which meant I'd needed a different handler.

Didn't want to ruin the merchandise, I guess.

Either way, I was glad for the change—whereas Rhys had monitored my every move, my new captor seemed content to leave me be so long as I didn't mouth off or wander. Neither of which, truthfully, I felt compelled to do; the blood smeared across my face was a solid deterrent against speaking, and a crowded valley full of malicious slavers wasn't the sort of place I wanted to explore alone with my hands tied behind my back.

Still, I made an effort to look around as we went, scanning the crowds, hoping to catch sight of where they'd taken Cathal. For some reason, I hated the idea of him being carted off and dying without me almost as much as I hated the idea of being stuck here alone. I couldn't tell if that was me being selfish or not. Frankly, I couldn't have cared less.

"This way," my captor instructed, tapping my thigh with the flat of his sword—a crooked, shoddy thing with just enough edge to keep me from teasing him. Together, we adjusted our trajectory, heading for the cluster of fighting pits I hadn't spotted from up above. They reminded me of gladiatorial arenas, though shabbier—great big holes dug into the earth where combatants would face off and potentially kill each other for the amusement of the audience above.

Not great.

"Am I to fight, then?" I asked, the blood caked on my face tugging awkwardly at my skin.

"Eventually. They'll clean you up first," my guard replied. He eyed me sideways. "To be honest, I don't think you'll last beyond the first match. But Rhys says otherwise."

I grunted, not bothering to respond, as I pondered why Rhys had kept my identity—my time with the Curaitl—a secret. I frowned, realizing I was likely to become his ringer. The giant, half-dead redhead. Part of me wondered if I should simply throw my first fight and die just to spite the bastard—at least that way I'd die with a smile on my face. But, deep down, I knew I wouldn't. I definitely had my faults but being a martyr sure as shit wasn't one of them.

"Who am I supposed to be fightin'?" I asked.

The slaver chuckled. "Does it matter? The Masters will decide. Bets will be taken. You'll either kill or be killed." He waved a hand about as if he were describing something as mundane as the weather, face practically bisected by his gap-toothed grin.

"What's the point?" I asked, dubiously.

"The point?"

"Aye. Are we fightin' for our freedom? For food? Water?" I racked my brain trying to come up with anything else I might want, but that was as far as I got before my brain shut down, unwilling to think about all the other amenities I'd once taken for granted.

The slaver belted out a laugh, shoving aside a group of regular citizens who'd gotten too close, brandishing his sword about to intimidate them. "You fight to survive. Or you don't," he replied, with a shrug. "Either way, we get paid."

Great.

"Weapons?" I asked, hopeful.

The bandit's eyes narrowed, flicking up and down my body, assessing me with more intelligence than I'd given him credit for. "The Masters decide that, too." He gestured to a pile of what I'd mistaken for trash not far from the fighting pits. "That's where they keep the junk."

Turned out "the junk" referred to just about every type of weapon I'd ever seen—albeit each and every one in the sorriest condition imaginable. Rusted swords, shattered spears, broken shields, you name it. None of it looked remotely serviceable, and yet I'd have given anything for even one of those in easy reach. Sadly, it seemed the pile of semi-lethal garbage was guarded by at least a dozen men, each wielding weapons of a slightly better quality—though not by much.

"Ye all should invest in a freakin' blacksmith," I muttered.

"What was that?"

I shook my head. "Nevermind."

"Rhys warned me not to let you talk too much," the bandit admitted, reaching out to drag me close by my bound wrists, pressing the line of his body against mine in a way that made my flesh crawl. "Probably best if you shut up until we get to the cages."

"Cages?" I asked. But it seemed my captor was done talking, leaving me to wonder what it would be like to be put in a cage like an animal.

The experience turned out to be even worse than I thought; pressed up against iron bars by the weight of emaciated bodies—slaves who looked somehow even more feeble than I did—I had just enough room to avoid touching the hive-inducing metal, though it meant standing with my shoulders slumped, arms folded down the length of my body. Unable to do much else, I distracted myself from my sorry state by people watching; now that I had time to stop and think, I couldn't help but wonder where all these men and women had come from. Were they all exiles, like Rhys? Or had some grown up here, a whole population surviving the Blighted Lands long enough to reach adulthood? The infrastructure—not to mention the fortitude—necessary to make that possible made me sick to my stomach. Imagine being a child in a place like this, where terrifying creatures roamed freely and fights to the death were the chief form of entertainment. I shuddered, unable to comprehend the sort of person who could thrive here.

"What's wrong, Ceara?" Rhys asked, sidling up to the bars of my cage and running his secondhand dagger across them. The hands of fellow captives darted away lest they get sliced, even as the sound of metal on metal pealed away. "Don't you like your new accommodations?"

I ignored the bastard. Now that I was caged, I had that luxury; if he came after me through the bars, I'd snap his arm in half, even if my heart gave out in the process.

"I want to show you something," he continued.

"Go away, ye miserable shit."

"Now, is that any way to talk to the man who saved you?" Rhys asked, face souring. "If it weren't for me, you and the hound would have died out there." He gestured in the general direction of the desert, and I realized we'd inadvertently ended up much closer to the mountain—not that it mattered, now.

"Saved me so ye could have me fight for me life in the pits," I replied, snorting. "Aye, t'anks for the hospitality, ye dick."

"Oh, but it wasn't just you I saved." Rhys retrieved a key from his belt and thrust it into the lock, eyeing the other slaves until they shied away from the door to the cage. "Don't you want to see your pup's first fight?"

I felt my skin prickle with dread. Cathal, fighting? Already? But he'd been dying only a couple hours ago. Like on death's damned doorstep—a fucking welcome mat with "Here Lies Cathal: He Really Was an Asshole" splashed across his chest. What kind of fight could the poor guy even put up? "Let me out," I growled, resisting the urge to snatch at the bars—no need for Rhys to see the effect of raw iron on my skin.

Rhys smirked, but held up a finger. "If you try anything, I'll kill you."

"If ye do that, ye won't get much of a return on your investment," I challenged, leaning close enough so that only he could hear me. "If ye expect to get your money's worth, I mean."

"That would be a shame," Rhys said, though the gleam in his eye told me something had changed. That, on some level, Rhys wanted me to try something. That he was itching to kill me.

And yet...Cathal.

"Fine, let's go."

35

The crowd around the fighting pit Rhys led me to consisted of jeering men and women in ragged clothes, most of whom looked only a hair better than the slaves they intended to watch die for their amusement. Blood frenzy rode the air as spittle flew from their mouths, fists pumping as if they were worshipping some primordial rock 'n roll god. But they weren't.

They were cheering the beast below.

Cathal, collared and chained to the side of the pit, roared in defiance, frothing at the mouth, his druidic markings ashen, bright eyes glazed over. The wound on his side seemed to have healed, patched by the elderly man who whispered soothingly in the hound's ear—the Handler, if I had to guess. The man reached out and ran a hand along Cathal's neck, petting him, as he applied a salve to that wounded side.

The sight made me sick to my stomach.

For a proud, standoffish creature like Cathal, I could only imagine that one gentle stroke was as much a violation as groping me would have been. And the fact that he hadn't reacted at all meant the Handler either had the hound firmly under his control using some sort of spell, or Cathal was drugged. Neither boded well.

"What d'ye do to him?" I yelled at Rhys, gripping the man's forearm.

He'd bound me but left my hands in front this time—as if daring me to try something.

But Rhys wasn't listening. Instead, he stared down at the other side of the pit, where a lone challenger had been literally thrown into the ring. The woman rose to her feet clutching a long spear, her hair pulled back tight in a side braid, sporting the very same leathers I'd seen her in last. She looked haggard and defeated, her shoulders slumped, but a dim fire raged behind her eyes. A passion I'd seen ignited more than once and knew better than to underestimate.

Blair.

"She came for you," Rhys said, refusing to look away.

I turned to him in horror while a voice inside my head screamed. I clamped down on it, refusing to let Ceara's hysteria overwhelm me. Rational. I had to be rational. So, Blair—the godsdamned fool—had followed me, somehow, to the Blighted Lands. I felt a sudden burst of pride from Ceara at the thought. My Other self was proud that she'd defied us, that she'd chosen to fight for us, no matter the odds.

In essence? Pure, romantic drivel.

"Ye have to get her out of there," I hissed.

"She got here days before you did," he went on, as if I hadn't spoken. "By the time I saw her, she didn't even look human. The things she'd done to survive..." he trailed off, then grunted. "I nursed her back to health. Gave her water, and food. Returned her clothes and even got her a spear. But all she ever talked about was you. About how you betrayed her. How you'd come to the Blighted Lands and how she'd find you, one day."

I grimaced. "Now's not the time," I insisted, pointing down at the pit. "Cathal *will* kill her, especially considerin' the state he's in."

Rhys nodded absentmindedly. "Yes, I know. I'm the one who suggested she fight the beast. She seems to blame the hound for you regaining your memories. Or maybe she thinks she can interrogate him, figure out what happened to you." He flicked his eyes to me. "She doesn't know you're here, after all."

I gaped at the man, struggling to understand why he was telling me all this. Was it all some elaborate plot? Vengeance, pure and simple? But if so, why not just kill me when he had the chance? And why nurse Blair back to health? None of it made any sense. "I don't understand," I admitted. "D'ye want her to die? Is that it?"

His lips tightened to a thin line. "I thought things might be different, here. That Blair would rely on me, let me take care of her. And she did, until she saw that damned hound. Until she was reminded of you, of her *purpose*." Rhys spat to one side, and his ensuing smile was crooked, wrong somehow —more like a dog baring its teeth than a reflection of joy. "But that's alright. I guess I'll simply have to settle for watching you suffer as your lover and your pet try to kill each other."

I swung my gaze back to the pit, where already several slaves were stepping nervously forward to remove Cathal's collar, shying away from the beast's snapping jaws. Blair, meanwhile, was twirling her spear in slow circles, warming up the muscles in her back and shoulders. The sands upon which both stood were stained from what I could only assume was spilled blood, the splatter patterns sporadic and yet oddly easy to track, like some twisted version of a Rorschach test.

No, I decided. Not like this.

It couldn't happen like this.

I...no, not merely I. A familiar brush of feathers against my skin, the sound of birds cawing loud in my ears. But this time I relished in them, embraced the sensations. *We* weren't about to let this happen. We *couldn't* let it happen. And yet...and yet I resisted. I fought against the unrelenting pressure of my wild side, unwilling to lose myself a second time. I ground my teeth so hard I felt my jaw threaten to lock. What if I lost control again? What if I couldn't come back this time? Dear God, who would I become in a place like this?

That thought alone chilled me to my core.

Together.

Ceara's voice filled my mind like smoke rising in an empty room, her emotions enveloping me like a warm blanket. Her panic, yes, but also her resolve. Her willingness to sacrifice herself—to sacrifice anything—if it meant saving Blair. I swore I could hear my wild side purr in response as my Other self coaxed out all those animalistic, primitive urges and gave them a focus, a direction—something I'd never been able to do.

Together.

That word again, only this time I realized it meant something else. Ceara wasn't proposing we work in tandem. No. She was offering a melding—a blending of our three disparate personalities. A partnership. Part of me balked at the idea, frightened of the notion that—by saying yes—I'd become someone else altogether. Someone who treated people better, maybe, or someone who made friends easily, sure...but then I wouldn't be *me*.

And the problem was, I realized, I *liked* me.

So do we.

The thought made me frown, then laugh. A laugh that started as a slight chuckle, but quickly gave way to something much more obnoxious—a knee-slapping, tear-jerking chortle that had me bent over double. I laughed so hard, in fact, that Rhys must have felt compelled to snatch me by the throat; he stared into my eyes from inches away, his fetid breath stinging my nostrils.

"What's so funny?" he snarled.

"Me," I replied, shaking my head, forcing the word out from beneath the pressure of his hand. I realized I sounded crazy, but that was okay; it wasn't like Rhys needed to know what was happening inside my head. Besides, I *was* crazy...or maybe slow was a better word.

Because, at some point, I'd forgotten the oh-so-simple truth I'd learned when I'd gone to Fae so long ago: my wild side and I were one and the same. Granted, I think I'd always known that, intellectually, but I hadn't given any consideration as to what it actually *meant*.

What it meant was that I *didn't* have multiple personalities ringing about in my head. Not really. I simply had multiple *Me's* in my head. A version of myself who intended to survive at all costs, for example—the thrill-seeking maniac who refused to back down from a challenge. Or the version who preferred harmony—the good-natured people-pleaser who made friends easily, who believed she actually *deserved* love.

"What does that even mean?" Rhys growled.

I closed my fingers around the man's forearm and squeezed—squeezed so hard I felt the bones pop and shatter beneath the sudden surge of strength. Rhys screamed in agony, but the sound of his voice was lost among the crowd's roar. "It means *I* am the Morrigan's daughter," I replied, silkily. "And the Morrigan," I added, wrenching the man forward to ram his face into my knee, "is a triple-headed goddess."

I laughed again as Rhys crumpled to the ground, and in that laughter, I heard my wild side's raucous joy intermingle with Ceara's indefatigable hope and my own relief. The sounds merged, harmonized, became one. Around me, spectators shrank away, flinching as if my laughter were descending upon them like whips and chains.

"What's she doing?" a woman asked.

The man beside her shook his head, his face pained. I let the laughter die, realizing these poor people probably hadn't heard joy in so long it stung, like bright sunlight on the pale skin of a hermit. A few of those gathered around swiftly spotted Rhys at my feet and began pointing, jabbering away amongst themselves, the space around me growing larger with each passing moment, as if I were carrying some sort of plague. Though, to be honest, that suited me just fine.

Because this bitch was going to need some room.

36

I hustled forward, shoving people aside as I went, casually ignoring their shouts and half-hearted threats. The slaves below were still in the process of releasing Cathal, but I knew I had to find a way down into the pit before that happened if I hoped to stand any chance of stopping the two from tearing into each other. Which is why, when I finally reached the edge only to find the perimeter guarded by one of the bandits in black, I didn't even hesitate.

I simply Spartan kicked the bastard over the brink.

His shrieks died the moment he hit the floor of the pit. Coincidentally, so did everyone else's; as one, the crowd turned to look at me, my chest still heaving from having thrust my way to the pit's edge. Even the slaves below paused to look up, their fingers coiled around Cathal's collar. I noticed Blair, too, her jaw practically brushing the blood-soaked floor as she stared up at me in utter disbelief.

"What's this?" a man cried, stepping forward, the crowd parting before him with far less effort than I'd have thought possible. "A new challenger?"

A few whoops and catcalls rode the air.

"Aye," I yelled, mind racing, realizing this could work to my advantage if I played my cards right. How better to get down into the pit than to be invited, after all? "I've come to fight."

The man—robed and looking far wealthier than those around him, his

178

cheeks bulging with fat, hair slicked back and oiled—clapped his hands joyously as though I hadn't just killed one of the pit's guards. "Another volunteer! That makes two in the same day. How marvelous."

"Is that wise, Aeron?" another man cried as he emerged from the crowd some dozen feet away, similarly robed, though his was a shade of blue, not scarlet. I wondered if these men were the Masters I'd heard mentioned—the slavers who employed the bandits and hosted these battles to the death. Given the way the crowd responded to them, it seemed likely.

Aeron waved a hand magnanimously. "You've seen the beast for yourself." He raised both arms, his flabby skin wobbling back and forth. "How about it, citizens? Would you all like to see the hound take on two at once?"

The crowd erupted.

Aeron made a gesture as if to say, "I told you so," and the other man shrugged. I felt a tension ease out of my shoulders; it seemed they were going to let me fight. Of course, that solved my immediate problem of getting below, but not the other, perhaps larger, concern...how not to get eaten once I made it down there.

Two bandits emerged, grabbing me roughly by the arms as if to drag me away, clearly pissed that I'd knocked off one of their own—pun intended. "Wait!" I cried, earning me the full attention of both Masters. "Don't I get a weapon?" I asked, jerking my chin towards the pile of discarded junk I'd seen on our way in.

Aeron studied me, undoubtedly noting my ragged appearance, not to mention my many visible wounds, and sniffed. "Yes," he said, then raised a stubby finger to point at the men holding me, "and get her changed into something more appropriate while you're at it. I'm sure we can wait a few extra minutes." He surveyed the crowd as if anticipating an argument, but no one dared speak up.

I nodded, feeling relieved. A weapon would be...wait, had he said something about getting *changed*? I glared at the guards holding me, both of whom seemed suddenly more than happy to help a girl in need. I shook them off with a curse and made for the pile in the distance, the crowd parting just enough so that people could run their hands along my body, the way fans try to do at ball games—a form of hero worship I'd never entirely understood, but had ironically engaged in a few times, myself, Boston being the sports town that it was; Tom Brady was practically an acknowledged demigod, and we'd gone so far as to give the Red Sox player the nickname "bearded Jesus" for Christ's sake.

Behind me, I could hear Aeron barking out new orders, which I took to mean Blair and Cathal were at least reasonably safe, for now. But they wouldn't stay that way unless I came up with a plan. Luckily, I had a place to start.

I broke through the crowd and approached the mound of weaponry, rummaging through the stack, under the watchful gaze of my two would-be stylists, cursing as I went. I yanked the shaft of a spear free only to have it rot away in my hands. Next, I raised a sword missing its tip. A trident with only one prong. A bow with no string. I hung my head, wondering if any of these would even hold up long enough to *look* threatening.

"Hurry up!" one of the bandits called.

I cursed once more, turning away, but that's when something caught my eye. I frowned, then began climbing the pile, eyes locked onto an odd protrusion which poked out from between two warped shields. Locked onto something that really, truly didn't belong.

And, as I got closer, I found myself smiling very, very wide.

"I'm comin'" I called back, voice breathy with exhilaration. "Oh, I'm comin'."

37

I strolled out onto the sands of the squalid arena in a pair of black leather pants, boots, and a black tank top, my hair pulled into a high ponytail, with a duffel bag riding the base of my spine, strap wound casually over one shoulder. I'd cleaned off most of the dried blood that had stained my face and chest using the grungy dishwater the bandits had given me before I threatened to gouge out their eyes if they watched me change—a threat I really should be more judicious with, I realized, afterwards. I'd also thrown gauze and bandages over the various scrapes and cuts I could reach, taking extra care with the festering wound at the base of my spine. Of course, the end result—somewhere between badass biker chick and rotting mummy—wasn't exactly fashionable, but it sure beat the shit out of the rags I'd been wearing.

And, bonus, Blair seemed to like it just fine.

She launched herself at me mere seconds after I stepped into the pit, her arms wrapped around me so tight it bruised what were likely already broken ribs. I wheezed a hello, awkwardly patting her back.

She broke away, uncertainly. "Quinn?"

"Aye, Blair. Quinn. Always Quinn," I replied, though my answering smile was genuine as I squeezed her arm. "I see ye took it upon yourself to find me."

Blair snorted indignantly. "You never knew me at all if you thought I would let something like you getting exiled stop me from finding you." But her eyes were unsure as she drew away, hugging herself.

I took a step forward, closing the distance between us, and pressed my forehead gently against hers. "No promises from here on out," I said, lips brushing her cheek, "but, assumin' we make it through this in one piece, ye and I will have us a talk. A real one. Alright?"

"What's this?" Aeron cried from above, interrupting our brief reunion. "Do the two combatants know each other?!" The crowd howled its disapproval, but the robed man waved them away as if fighting off a horde of bees. "No, citizens! This is even better than we could have hoped! A true team effort. Perhaps they might even stand a chance at defeating the beast," he added, dubiously.

The howls became cheers once more, and I felt something brush my senses—a faint breath of magic, but wrong somehow. Tainted. Aeron spoke again, and I could see it hanging about him like a faint miasma—a diseased spell he wove over the crowd as he spoke. Like poisonous gas, it drifted into the air, swallowed by the screaming masses "Citizens of the Vale, witness the spear-bearer and the..." Aeron trailed off, eyeing my empty hands and strange clothing for perhaps the first time. "The spear-bearer and the giant-ess!" he finished, with a flair. "Watch as they take on the Cù-Sìth for your pleasure!"

More thunderous applause.

"Quinn..." Blair said, my name seeming to stick to the roof of her mouth. "Where's your weapon?"

I patted the impossible duffel bag with one hand. "I have everythin' I need right here." She cocked her head, frowning in confusion, but I didn't elaborate; I wasn't sure she'd understand even if I did. Instead, I took her by the arm, whispering the plan I'd come up with the moment I'd laid eyes on the duffel—a plan which would either get all of us executed, or secure us a way out of this hellhole once and for all.

"I don't understand," Blair said, once I'd finished, "why are they going to let us go?"

"Well, first we'll have to kill some of 'em," I admitted, sheepishly.

Blair took in the restless, bloodthirsty crowd. "How many?"

"However many it takes."

Blair's eyes widened, but she nodded. "Alright, I'll follow your lead."

"Wouldn't be the first time," I teased, jabbing her in the ribs good-naturedly.

She grunted, eyes widening further, and finally grinned. "I'm looking forward to that talk."

I rolled my eyes, though I felt a blush spreading across my cheeks. "Keep your head in the game, girl, sheesh."

But it turned out Blair didn't need me to tell her one way or the other; the crowd had fallen deathly silent, and as one Blair and I turned to find Cathal's handlers had left the pit.

Which meant, while we'd been discussing our plan, the hound had been freed.

"Shit," I cursed, a moment before Cathal struck.

Guess there went plan A.

*P*lan B involved scrambling madly from one side of the pit to the other—largely because doing anything else was sure to get either or both of us killed. Fortunately, Cathal didn't seem inclined to pick us off one by one. If anything, he seemed to be operating on pure instinct, launching himself at us whenever he saw an opening, but also dancing away the second we darted in his direction. In essence, the mangy bastard was all impulse, his ears flicking about with every scream from above, no doubt struggling to process all the sights and sounds and smells.

"Can ye keep him busy for a few minutes?" I asked Blair, between breaths; even with the bit of food and water I'd consumed before heading to the pit, I was still running insanely low on energy. And playing keep-away with a possessed puppy the size of a freaking pony wasn't helping.

Blair scoffed. "I can give you maybe thirty seconds."

"Never could last long," I muttered under my breath.

"One minute," Blair snarled, slapping my ass before sprinting towards the hound, jabbing at him with her spear. She was good—maybe not as fluid as Aife had been, or as strong as Tristan—but she knew how to move, relying on her quick reaction time and those fast twitch muscle fibers which lent her body a corded, almost masculine silhouette. I shook my head, reminding myself not to get distracted, and whipped the duffel bag around.

But no, not simply *the* duffel bag, I amended.

My duffel bag.

Improbably, perhaps miraculously, I'd spotted the black nylon duffel tucked away amongst the remains of inferior weapons—a bag I'd packed and subsequently lost above the island of Neverland during my last visit to Fae. Honestly, I had no idea how it had ended up here, other than the possibility that all discarded things eventually did. It would make sense, given how rundown everything—and everyone—was. But the why hadn't interested me nearly as much as its contents; I'd already donned the emergency stash of clothes within and made use the First Aid kit, but that was mere icing on the proverbial cake, considering what the bag had been designed to carry.

I hurriedly unzipped the duffel and reached inside, feeling about until I had the stock and barrel of a familiar weapon beneath my hands. I withdrew the subcompact machine gun, cradling the MP5 to my chest like it was a sleeping babe, and rocked slightly from side to side.

"Hush now, I've got ye," I whispered. Then I flipped the gun around, tucked the extended stock into the crook of my shoulder, and leveled the barrel at the crowd. I sighted until I found Aeron's blue robes, then drew a bead on the man's face—he was grinning, bloodshot eyes locked on Blair and Cathal's battle, ignoring me completely. His mistake.

I pulled the trigger.

38

*E*veryone ducked—as people tend to do whenever live ammunition is fired repeatedly in the air. Aeron, meanwhile, had fallen to his knees, hands clasped over his ears, staring at me as if I'd called down thunder and bolts of lightning. Of course, in the eyes of these primitive people, I may as well have done precisely that. I raised my rifle to my shoulder and turned it on Cathal, who shied away from the boom stick like any dog would, dancing backwards, barking savagely at me.

"Good boy," I muttered. "Now," I shouted, ignoring Blair's stupefied expression for the time being, "ye all have a choice!" I did my best to imitate Aeron's showmanship as I turned in a slow circle, making sure everyone in attendance could see my resolve. "Either ye let the three of us walk out of here, never to bother ye again. Or...I use this," I touted my rifle, "to kill every single one of ye where ye stand."

A tense hush fell over the crowd, so silent I expected to hear crickets. But apparently even crickets knew better than to live in this godsforsaken shithole, because it wasn't until Aeron rose to his feet, his face a mask of self-assurance, wearing his arrogance like a cloak, that I finally had my answer. "Citizens of the Vale, do not listen to—" he began.

"Wrong answer," I said, with a sigh. This time, when I fired in his direction, I made sure not to let the barrel rise; the spray of bullets took the Master in the chest and throat. Blood blossomed, barely distinguishable from the man's scarlet robes, as he toppled. As we watched, he grasped at his injured body, only to fall flat on his face.

Silence. Then one long, ragged scream split the air.

Dozens turned to flee, tripping over themselves and trampling each other to get away from the line of fire. I let them, less than eager to mow down a bunch of civilians, even if they were despicable human beings. "In case I wasn't clear, I'll say it again!" I bellowed, swinging the rifle around until I spotted the man known as the Handler—an aged gentleman in rough leathers, his body absolutely smothered in scars and bite marks—among those who remained. "We would like to leave. So tell me, old man, what d'ye give me friend?" I asked, jerking my chin towards Cathal.

The Handler shook his head, eyes downcast, and opened his mouth to speak...but he couldn't, I realized, because the man had no tongue. Indeed, even his teeth were missing, and I knew in that instant that I was looking at another slave. A master of beasts, perhaps, but still a slave. I cursed, swiveling my rifle, looking for my only other target—the only other person I'd seen with any authority.

But I was too late.

"Get her!" The man in blue robes screamed, ducking behind a cluster of bandits. "Kill them all!"

I watched the bandits guarding the perimeter exchange concerned glances, clearly wary of both my rifle and the megaton canine still prowling the edges of the pit. For a moment, I actually thought we might be able to bluff our way out of this mess. Hell, I might not even have to kill anyone else, for once. That is until a wretchedly familiar face fought his way to the fore, glaring down at us, bloody teeth bared.

"You heard him, men!" Rhys roared. "Let's kill the bitch!"

As one, the bandits turned, their momentary indecision giving way to a shared resolve as they brandished their weapons. I felt something inside me break as I aimed my rifle at Rhys, prepared to end the miserable shit if it was the last thing I did.

Except suddenly there was Blair, thrusting my rifle aside, screaming, "No!"

"What the hell are ye doin'?" I shouted.

She grabbed my shoulder. "He saved me," Blair insisted, adamantly. "He found me and kept me safe."

I shrugged her off, but didn't have time to argue, to tell her the truth about the man she'd just saved. Instead, I grabbed her wrist. "We need to get Cathal!"

"The hound?" Blair spun around to find Cathal still foaming at the mouth, hackles up, looking even more dangerous now that he'd been forced into a corner. "How?!"

It was a good question.

I sighed, looking around for inspiration, but already a few of the bolder bandits were scrambling down the steep slope of the pit, using their blades as climbing tools, while still others had doubled back to enter through the tunnels that I'd used. I shook my head, wishing I'd thought of this sooner. That I'd found something, anything, to bring Cathal to his senses.

But that's when I noted a certain tongueless man had also entered the arena and was beckoning to me frantically, gesturing meaningfully at the snarling hound. I gritted my teeth and shoved the gun into Blair's hands. "Take this." I thrust her hand over the stock, slid her finger over the trigger gingerly, and pointed her in the right direction. "Just make this motion," I crooked my finger, "and point it at the ones ye want to die."

Blair looked like she was about to throw up. "Is that all?"

I wished I had about three days to walk her through basic gun etiquette and safety protocols, but we simply didn't have the time. "It will jump on ye, a lot, at first. Just try to keep it steady, and don't point it at anyone ye want to stay alive. Try to shoot in quick bursts." I made the motion with my finger again. "Pull, release. Pull, release. Alright?"

Blair's chin bobbed.

"Oh, and if ye see Rhys? Kill him," I insisted.

"But—"

"Blair," I said, gripping the back of her neck, the gun pressed horizontally between us, "trust me. Kill. Him." Then, without waiting for a response, I stole a kiss, pressing my lips firmly against hers for one long, juicy moment before ducking down to retrieve the other two lovelies from my duffel bag—a pair of sawed-off shotguns with enough staying power to put down a horse at close range. Or a hound the size of a horse, if it came to that.

Though I was really hoping it wouldn't.

39

The staccato sound of rifle fire made me want to turn and make sure Blair was alright, but I knew I couldn't afford to; I was too busy working my way across the pit, warily trailing the Handler as he approached Cathal. The man moved like a bobbing snake, hands splayed and held non-threateningly in front of him, making cooing noises. I mimicked the motions and gestures, my shotguns dangling off my thumbs by their trigger guards, but that was about it; for all I knew my version of baby talk would translate into something extremely counterproductive, like "get 'em boy," or "sic balls, Chopper!"

Still, despite our creeping pace, Cathal snapped and lunged wildly, barking so loudly it practically harmonized with the sound of gunfire, his snout bunched to reveal rows of savage teeth. Honestly, I wasn't sure what the Handler had in mind that could calm the bastard down, but I did know time was running out; if the bandits managed to circle around Blair or she ran out of bullets, we'd be done for. Granted, my shotguns were damn lethal in close quarters, but they definitely weren't going to be enough to mow down a small army of black-clad bastards.

Before I could dwell on our fate should it come to that, the Handler grabbed me by the arm, drawing me forward until we both stood only a few feet outside the hound's radius. I cringed, eyes drawn to those slobber-coated lips and Cathal's startlingly white teeth. Dear Lord, I thought, I hoped the Handler's plan didn't involve us getting gnawed on…

But, apparently, it did.

Because the elderly bastard turned to me, raised my arm, and made to bite it.

"Oy!" I hissed.

Cathal growled a warning, hackles rising.

The Handler shook me a little, imploring me to relax with his eyes. I stopped fighting him, easing the tension in my arm, realizing I was being ridiculous. So what if he tried to bite me? The man had no teeth; at best he'd drool all over my arm. Gross, but not exactly lethal. But the Handler didn't go that route. Instead, he mimed the bite, gesturing from my arm to Cathal. Then again. Fake bite. Me. Cathal.

He…wanted the freaking hound to bite me.

"No fuckin' way," I said, adamantly.

He let my arm drop, shrugging as if to say, "this is the only way I can think of." Somehow, I doubted this was the *only* way…but maybe the hoary bastard knew something I didn't. Maybe Cathal's instability was tied to his bloodlust, somehow? I had no idea. But—while getting chomped on definitely wasn't my idea of a good time—I owed Cathal. He'd saved me, risked himself for me, so many times, and I couldn't leave him here to die.

Not if there was some way to save him.

I jerked my chin in a curt nod and shuffled forward, switching my second shotgun awkwardly to my other hand in the process. I held out my arm like an offering, beads of sweat sliding down my brow as I inched closer. The sounds of rifle fire faded as I stared into Cathal's eyes, willing that spark—his spark—to return. "C'mon, Cathy, I know you've thought about it," I muttered.

And that's when Cathal pounced, snapping his maw shut over my forearm.

*C*athal drew back almost immediately, my blood dripping from the tips of his fangs, shaking his shaggy head back and forth as if I'd slapped him on the nose. I, meanwhile, clutched my wounded arm to my chest, staring down at the neat imprint he'd left behind—the indentations from his teeth quickly filling up with blood. I hissed through my teeth at the pain, but honestly, I was simply glad to still have an arm at all.

"What..." Cathal said, blinking rapidly, nose twitching.

I smiled.

But then a sound—one I'd been dreading since I'd handed Blair the assault rifle—brought me back around as the MP5 clicked empty. I saw a cluster of bandits working their way towards her, murder in their eyes, as she continued to pull the trigger, clearly panicked.

Not good.

"Get out of here!" I shouted at the Handler, only to find him scurrying away as fast as his old feet could carry him. I grunted, spared the bewildered hound a brief glance, and then whirled to race towards Blair, transferring the shotgun back to my other hand in the process, though I found it was all I could do to grip it under the circumstances.

"Down!" I screamed. Blair ducked as I closed the space between us, revealing the cutthroats who'd come to claim our lives. I wasn't sure how many of their number Blair had taken out, but the instant they saw me hoisting the shotgun with my good arm, they froze, eyes wide with fear—and it was this immediate skittishness, this inability to act, which cost them their lives.

I unloaded both barrels. Three of the men tumbled, taken out by the blast. Two others fell, screaming in agony, caught in the blast radius. The others scrambled, fleeing, tripping over themselves in their rush to escape. But not just themselves, I realized as I stared out at the carnage. Bodies littered the floor of the pit. Bandits, but also citizens. So many I wondered how Blair hadn't run out of bullets sooner. I turned my head to the side and spat, disgusted.

"Blair, it's time to go," I insisted, turning to the woman, hoping to return to Cathal and get the hell out of here before we were forced to kill anyone else.

But she wasn't there.

"Blair isn't going anywhere with you," Rhys said, dragging Blair back with one hand latched over her mouth, the other holding his crude knife, the blade nestled in the hollow of her throat.

I switched my remaining shotgun to my uninjured side and pointed it at Rhys' head, but the man ducked behind Blair, peeking out like a child hiding behind his mother's skirt. Not that it mattered; I couldn't risk firing a sawed-off without taking Blair out in the process.

Shotguns were messy like that.

"Let her go, ye rat bastard," I snarled.

Blair struggled, eyes wide, screaming words into the man's hand. But he didn't remove it. Instead, he shook her, viciously. "That's enough," he chided. "You two…" Rhys let the words hang in the air as he flicked his eyes from one dead body to the next. "You've ruined everything."

"Oh, sure, because *we* were the ones who started this," I replied, rolling my eyes.

"You started this!" Rhys screamed, spit spewing from his lips, his grip on Blair's mouth tightening so much I could see tears in her eyes. "You!"

"Listen, Rhys, I'm—" I began, prepared to apologize if it saved Blair's life.

"Enough," Rhys hissed, removing his hand from Blair's mouth to savagely yank on her braid, exposing the long, slender line of her neck. "I'm tired of talking. To both of you." And—so slowly it didn't even seem real— he ran the dagger across Blair's throat.

"No," I whispered, dropping my arm, the shotgun falling from my numb, useless fingers. Rhys laughed at my expression and released my former lover's limp body with a flourish, stepping back with a wide, manic smile painted on his face.

It was, I found myself thinking, the most heartbreaking smile I'd ever seen.

Not that it lasted long; as Blair fell to the ground, tumbling forward in what seemed like slow motion, Cathal appeared, leaping to take Rhys' head in his powerful jaws. The hound landed and whipped his head back and forth, dragging Rhys around like a ragdoll, working at the bastard like a fucking chew toy. In seconds, Rhys' headless corpse lay only a few feet from Blair's.

Except his body wasn't glowing.

And Blair's was.

I took a few steps forward, reaching out with my good arm, staring at the body. Blair's body. I fell to my knees beside her, hoping to cradle her in my arms, to see it had all been some elaborate, cosmic joke. Except those eyes—those captivating eyes—were open, glassy. Staring at nothing. I felt a sob rise up as I reached out to touch her, to run my fingers through her hair. But the instant my fingertips closed the distance between us, that glow exploded, forcing me to shield my eyes.

When I looked back, Blair was gone, though her blood—so much blood —still littered the ground. Dazed, I took a handful of that coarse, wet sand and squeezed, letting it crumble through my fingertips. Something prodded me from behind, and I looked up to find the hound looming over one shoulder, nudging me with his blood-drenched muzzle, mouth open in a silent scream.

No, not silent, I realized.

"Get up!" he was shouting. "Now!"

But I couldn't. I couldn't move. "Just go," I whispered, staring at the blood spattered on the ground, unable to process what had just happened. But Cathal didn't; instead, the bastard clamped his teeth down on my shirt and began pulling, drawing me away. I struggled, kicking and screaming at the indignity of being dragged. At last, he let me go, shoving his face menacingly into mine.

"Get on then," Cathal growled, dropping his belly to the sand.

Too numb to think straight, I did as he suggested, rising to clamber onto his back. In moments, I was forced to grab hold of his powerful neck as the hound rose and headed directly for the steep slope of the pit. I blinked, realizing he was going to try and run straight up the wall. At last, my self-preservation instincts kicked in.

"What the fuck are ye doin'?!" I shouted.

"Getting us out of here," Cathal replied. He jumped before I could question his methods, paws pounding as he charged the slope, four legs pumping like those of a sprinting greyhound. It was all I could do to hang on, my heart in my throat, as we cleared the pit. Cathal charged forward, ignoring the screaming masses as they fought to escape the nightmare that had emerged from their would-be entertainment, their guards no longer around to save them.

Or, I realized, to keep them in line.

"Cathal!" I screamed as the hound hunted for any path that would take us out of the Vale, haphazardly knocking down anyone who got in his way. "Cathal, ye have to go back! The slaves, we could—"

"There's nothing for us here!" Cathal bellowed, his irritation clear. "This is the Blighted Lands. These people might as well be dead."

His words hit me like a slap in the face. Indeed, the instant we cleared the decrepit settlement, I realized he was right. There *was* nothing for us here. Nothing but exiles and slaves and bandits and death. Hell, the only worthwhile creature in this whole, godsforsaken place—a beautiful woman with eyes you could lose yourself in—was gone. Lost in a flash of light, her lifeblood staining the sand. Overwhelmed by the thought that I would never see Blair again, I ducked my head into the hound's shoulder and sobbed as he ran, and ran, and ran.

But I knew we'd never get far enough to forget.

Because some memories you simply can't run away from.

40

The tunnel beneath Mount Never Rest was gloomy and bone-chilling, though for all I knew that was merely the shock of everything I'd been through leveling up, hitting me physically from yet another angle; I'd already bawled my eyes out, drained to the point I could barely raise my head. Watching Blair die before my very eyes—only to watch her disappear without even being able to say goodbye—had been far harder on me than I thought it would. Honestly, part of me wished Cathal had simply left me behind. That way—instead of finally ending this insane journey and meeting my mother's ghost within the Hall of Lives, assuming she was still alive—I'd have ended up in a festering cage, left alone long enough to wallow and mourn on my own time.

It all felt like it was happening too fast.

But he hadn't, and—no matter how wiped I felt right now—I still wanted answers. I wanted to know how my mother could let the Blessed People fumble around in the dark without at least a little guidance from their gods, for one thing. I also wanted to know why the Blighted Lands—that awful, hideous place—existed, why they were *allowed* to exist. I owed Blair, owed everyone I'd met, that much.

"How much farther?" I asked, hugging the hound's back, nestling up against the markings that whorled through his fur; they shone with a dim white light, emitting the faintest heat, which made me really rethink

Cathal's value as a companion. After all, part nightlight, part heated blanket? If it weren't for that mouth of his, he'd be perfect.

"It speaks," Cathal rumbled.

"Don't make me hurt ye," I replied testily, though we both knew the threat was unfounded; I was insanely weakened after nearly a day's ride from the Vale to the mountain. My various wounds, especially the festering sore, were so bad that—the one time I'd tried to walk on my own several hours before—I'd nearly collapsed. Cathal had taken one piteous look at me before offering his back once more, which had told me all I needed to know about my sorry state.

"It's not much farther," Cathal said. "Save your strength. I'll get you there, as promised."

I found myself nodding, absentmindedly. "You're a good boy, Cathy," I mumbled, feeling oddly sleepy as that frigid cold gave way to warmth. My body became weightless in increments, the pain from my wounds diminishing with each step until I finally let out a ragged sigh of relief.

And that's when Cathal tossed me off his back.

"Motherfucker!" I yelled, startled. "What was that for?" I began rubbing my poor backside, glaring up at the demented dog.

"You were falling asleep. Don't do that. Get up and lean on me. It's not far, now."

Too tired to argue, I rose, fumbling a bit, my knees wobbly, legs practically asleep after such a long ride on the back of an animal. At last, I found Cathal's shoulder and leaned into him, taking one precarious step after another as he padded beside me. "Say, Cathy, what happened to ye in the pits?" I asked, recalling the instant he'd pierced my skin and what had looked like a damn allergic reaction. "When ye bit me?" I added.

Cathal froze, muscles twitching, the movement so sudden I nearly toppled. "I did what?"

I reminded him what had happened—how the Handler had insisted I let him snack on my arm, how I'd sacrificed my limb so nobly for his sake because I was freaking awesome like that. Of course, the moment I said that I realized my "injured" arm felt completely fine, especially compared to how it had felt in the pits. But then, maybe my body was too broken down to care, too shocked to notice, at this point? What was one more injury amongst dozens, after all?

Cathal hesitated, before shuffling forward once more, the rippling muscles of his back moving like rocks coated in silk beneath my hand. "I must have been under a spell," he said, at last. "Your blood must have broken it."

I nodded like that made all the sense in the world, my mind too foggy to wonder why my blood had done the trick, as opposed to someone else's; at this point, it was the most I could do to keep moving. Each lurching step quickly became its own tiny accomplishment, especially once the cold returned in force, the temperature dropping the farther into the tunnel we got.

"I was cold when this all started," I recalled, giggling a little to myself as I thought back to that early morning walk with Scathach, what felt like years ago. "Ye know, I don't even know how long I've been gone for..." I felt my skin prickle as I realized how very true that actually was. How much time *had* passed since Scotland? Months? Or had it been longer? What about everyone on the outside? Names began popping up in my head—a long list of people I'd liked to have at least warned before I disappeared without a word. Christoff, Othello, Robin, Scathach, Max, Eve.

Oh God, Eve.

"She's goin' to kill me," I murmured, realizing I'd left my morose house-plant behind without so much as a goodbye. Still, there was some comfort in knowing she wouldn't be entirely alone; I'd given both Scathach and Othello keys to my apartment—not that either would have had any qualms about breaking down my door if the need arose. I was fairly certain they'd check in on her, at least water her know-it-all ass, if nothing else.

"Time moves differently between realms," Cathal replied, seemingly unconcerned by my mutterings. "So, I couldn't tell you."

I nodded dumbly, still dreading what I'd find on my return. Would any of them even want to talk to me after disappearing on them for so long? God, I hoped so. For some reason, maybe because I'd accepted this alien part of me that actually *liked* people, that mattered to me more than it ever had before.

Cathal stilled, cocking his head to look at me. "You'll have to take the next few steps on your own."

I frowned. "Ye aren't comin'?"

"I can't. The Hall of Lives is a realm only the Tuatha de Danann can visit. And even they are sometimes turned away, if they are deemed unworthy or threatening."

"But...but what about ye?" I asked, dreading the idea of Cathal trying to make his way back to the sea from here. Granted, without me he stood a much better chance of surviving, but that didn't mean he was safe; the humans we'd left behind would likely be hunting for us, and there was no guarantee he wouldn't run into some other nightmarish creature, even *if* he eluded the slavers.

Cathal snorted. "Once you're gone, my debt to *Manannan* will be repaid," he said, putting odd emphasis on the sea god's name. "This tunnel branches off and leads to a river on the other side of the mountain. There'll be a boat there for me, I'm sure." The hound bumped into me, gently. "No need to worry," he added, voice oddly soft.

I nodded, hoping the mangy bastard was right; I'd feel awfully conflicted leaving him behind, otherwise. Not that I'd ever know—this was goodbye, after all. I turned and—before Cathal could step away—wrapped his neck in a fierce hug, pressing my face into his fur. He smelled like peat smoke tinged with something spicier, like aged whiskey.

"I'm sorry we humans suck," I murmured.

"You really do," Cathal replied, though his tone was oddly warm, even friendly. "Now, go." He wrenched himself free, took a few steps back, and thrust me forward with his paw before I could say anything else. I stumbled, tripped, and suddenly I was falling, falling without end.

41

I fell, but the sensation quickly became more like drifting, as if I were a leaf coasting inexorably downward, only slightly heavier than the air beneath me. I panicked at first, then relaxed as the blackness around me lightened in small, measurable increments to a murky shade of twilight. I took a few deep, calming breaths and studied the brightening tunnel, realizing that—far below—lay a semi-familiar cosmic landscape, an invisible hallway laden with impossible windows. In moments, I began to see planets and stars hovering all around me as if I were drifting across the universe. I coasted, leisurely closing the distance, descending like a deflated balloon, making out details I'd never noticed before in my dreams, or even when I'd accidentally stepped between realms. Like how the windows that hung in midair each had a frame of some sort, all distinct, if not inconceivable; the one nearest me seemed to bleed—the crimson liquid spilling down the frame over and over again like one of those never-ending waterfalls— while its neighbor flashed silver beneath an uneven coat of black tar.

I landed gently on my feet, my exhaustion fading almost immediately, the pain of my wound a distant thing. It wasn't gone, just…held at bay. By something, or someone.

"Took you long enough," my mother's ghost rasped.

I spun, finding the woman leaning against the transparent wall, her face significantly gaunter than when I'd last seen her, her flesh sickly pale. Her eyes, once flaming, had dulled to mere embers. She looked worn down, as if she hadn't slept well in weeks. I cringed as I met her smoldering gaze, realizing she hadn't been exaggerating; she was dying.

Still, the bitch had some nerve.

"It wasn't exactly easy gettin' here," I growled, my irritation flaring. I glared at the lingering memory of the goddess my mother had been, wondering what I should accuse her of first. I had so many things to say, so many points to make, so many questions to ask. And, of course, beneath all that lay the gut-wrenching knowledge that Blair was gone, that she and I would never get to have that talk—the guilt of which made me want to reach out and shake the demented woman who'd started it all until she begged me to stop.

But I didn't get a chance to do any of that.

Instead, my mother's ghost threw herself away from the wall with visible effort and stumbled towards me, snatching my wrist in the process. "Come with me, we're running low on time."

"Wait a damned second, I—"

But she ignored me, tugging harder, her grip surprisingly strong despite how frail she appeared. "Be a brat later," she hissed. "I'll answer all your questions, in time. But first I need to show you things. Things I couldn't before. It's important."

I snapped my mouth shut. Important, huh? Fine. Let her show me whatever she had to show me, *then* I'd grill her about Blair, about the Otherworlders and the Blighted Land, about just what in the hell she and her fellow gods had been thinking when they created this mess of a world.

My mother's ghost drew me close, switching her hand to my shoulder, and spun me to face a window framed in obsidian—so polished I could almost see my reflection in it. The woman reached for a lever and yanked, slamming it down, the window itself blew open as if buffeted by an errant wind. "Look," she insisted, her grip on my shoulder tightening.

I did, though I was defiant about it, glaring back at her before facing the gaping window. I frowned, recognizing the all-too-familiar layout of a dive bar. I didn't recognize the interior, but the vibe was eerily reminiscent of the worst holes I'd wandered into before finally carving out a place for myself at Christoff's. The sort of place most people avoided without even thinking about it, a testament to Darwinism in action, if you asked me.

Grungy music that might have been country, garage band metal, or some combination of the two, could barely be heard over the general ruckus, and a fight near the bar was seconds from breaking out. The bartender was hurriedly waving over the bouncer by the door, face panicked. But there was no point—this was going to be an ugly one. Because at the center of the bar stood a lone woman whose sole purpose—if I had to guess—was to ruin everyone's good time.

Or make it better, depending on your persuasion.

Badb, my mother's sister and therefore my aunt, one third of the triumvirate who the world knew as the Morrigan—Queen of Air and Darkness—thrust two fingers into the chest of the biggest, beefiest son of a bitch in the bar. "What are you going to do about it, fatty?" she said, her accent faintly Southern. Probably an affectation of some kind—something to make the locals more comfortable. But the locals *weren't* comfortable. In fact, the whole bar suddenly looked downright agitated, like a pack of dogs scenting something worse coming their way.

Of course, that something worse was the goddess they'd inadvertently let into their bar. I frowned, studying the leather-clad maven, noting the not-so-subtle go fuck yourself style she'd opted for; half her head was shaved, the other half a spill of raven black locks, her lips painted purple, pale skin flashing bright beneath a whole cattle farm's worth of leather, with enough silver studs and piercings on display to tempt a jewelry thief.

Oh, and she was grinning.

The beefy man shared a concerned look with his friends, probably shocked to hear anyone—let alone a woman nearly a foot shorter and a couple hundred pounds lighter—talk to him like that. I didn't blame him; the only people who were that in your face were typically either convicts, or soon-to-be convicts. No one else had that kind of edge, the sheer brazenness to spit on cops and cuss out court judges.

My mother's ghost leaned in over my shoulder, resting her chin on it, though one look told me it was from exhaustion, not affection—which is all that kept me from shrugging her off. "Badb," she said, then snorted. "Always picking fights. Of the three of us, she is the closest to what you might call a war goddess. Her bloodthirst is legendary, her battle prowess unmatched. She is the tempest."

I frowned, thinking of my wild side, of that part of me which arose whenever a fight broke out—especially if I was the cause of said fight. I felt the woman behind me nod, as if I'd spoken aloud. Then again, maybe I had. "Yes," she noted, "that is her power. Residual, but yes."

"But why would I have *her* power?" I turned in confusion. "Aren't ye..."

My mother's ghost straightened. "Your mother birthed you alone. But even though you know us as separate entities, we three *are* one. We kept ourselves apart only because to do otherwise would mean stepping away from the world entirely, as many of the most powerful gods have been forced to do. And because we have, clearly," she said, glancing over my shoulder at what lay beyond the window, "different tastes."

"But what about the others," I began, thinking of those gods I *knew* were still around, "did they—"

"Some of the Old Ones," she interjected, "felt the need to stick around, that's all. Come." She dragged me away from the window, which closed slowly, allowing the briefest glimpse of a brawl the likes of which I'd rarely seen; Badb was riding piggyback on the beefy man's shoulders, punching him in the head over and over as she cackled, lashing out with her feet whenever one of the other patrons wandered close enough, her steel toe boots occasionally knocking out teeth.

The window shut, cutting her laughter off abruptly.

"Does she do that a lot?" I asked.

"It keeps her busy," my mother's ghost replied, as if that were answer enough. She stopped a moment later before another window, this one made not of obsidian, but veined marble. She lowered the lever more judiciously this time, the window spreading wide slowly to reveal a hallway in a hospital. Like the bar, I recognized the surroundings immediately; hospitals were too bland, too sanitized to be anything else. Signs hung from the ceiling overhead, tiny overturned triangles indicating the various wings, and elevators at the end of the hall hummed with use. As I watched, a woman's back came into view, her blonde hair piled high on her head, navy blue scrubs obscuring what I assumed would be a remarkably lithe and attractive body, judging by the muscles displayed in her arms as she pushed a man in a wheelchair, his head lolling about as if he'd forgotten what his neck was there for. She walked to the elevator, turned him sideways to wait, and reached out to flick the button.

"Macha," I said, recognizing the woman's face the instant I caught her profile. Aunt number two and, therefore, the second part of my mother's triumvirate. But my mother's ghost was silent as Macha leaned in, brushing

201

her cheek against the man's salt-n-pepper stubble, to whisper something in his ear. The man's head shot up so suddenly it was like she'd woken him from a deep sleep. He craned his neck to stare at the would-be nurse, mouth gaping. She smiled, patted his shoulder, and the two returned to studying the elevator as though nothing had happened—there was an intelligence, a determination—in the man's eyes that hadn't been there before.

"This time it'll stick," my mother's ghost said, bobbing her head.

"What will?"

"That man's been using his whole adult life. Overdosed twice before. This was the third time and should have killed him. And yet, after today, he'll recover. He'll even stay clean. It'll be hard, but with her blessing, not impossible." She raised the lever, letting the window snap shut.

"So that makes Macha...what? The ghost of Christmas presents?"

The woman stared blankly at me.

"Nevermind," I said, coughing into my hand. "What I meant was, what's her aspect? If Badb is war and strife, that is."

"Life. Nature. Motherhood." My mother's ghost waved a hand. "The three are intertwined more often than not. Besides, Macha doesn't distinguish between the three. She likes to wander, helping mortals as a nurse or midwife or gardener or what have you. She channels wellness and recovery the way Badb channels battle lust. She is the air that fills mortal lungs, giving them hope."

Sounded like Ceara, I thought, acknowledging the similarities between my aunt's nature and that piece of myself. The piece who had embraced the Curaitl and made her home among them. The piece who genuinely cared for people—even those I'd resolved to hate.

I found my mother's ghost nodding in agreement and frowned. "And what about ye?" I asked, realizing she'd shown me her two sisters to prove a point, or at least clue me in to...I wasn't sure what. Something. "Which part of the Morrigan are ye?"

"That depends on who you ask," my mother's ghost replied, looking away, her eyes reduced to hot cinders. "In the past, mortals came to us asking for different things they needed. Strength in battle," she gestured to Badb's obsidian window, "or the health of their child." This time to Macha's. "But there was one power the boldest, or perhaps the most foolish, sought from us. They pleaded, begged us to read their futures. To predict what might happen."

I frowned, realizing the woman was talking about fortune telling. No, not fortune telling—reading the future, she'd said. Prophecy. "I don't understand," I admitted.

"If Macha represents life, and Badb represents war, then your mother represented foresight. The ability to see into the possible futures and their various outcomes."

I shook my head. "But I didn't inherit any of that," I said, brow furrowed.

"Ah, but you have. You'll remember them as dreams, perhaps. Flashes. Whatever allowed you to come here in the first place."

I thought back and realized that was true; I had ended up in the Hall of Lives thanks to a bout of awful dreams that wouldn't go away—a series of restless nights I'd survived only by getting blackout drunk. I'd almost forgotten, given how much had happened since. "But," I held up a hand, "and no offense meant or anythin', but isn't that a bit...lame?"

"Lame?"

"Aye. I mean Badb is, ye know, the tempest or whatever. And Macha's aspect is life and air and all that. And I know you're sayin' me ma could read the future, but could she actually *do* anythin'?"

Her lips pursed. "I think you underestimate the power of prophecy." My mother's ghost held her arms wide. "Pick a window."

I sighed, suspecting the whole "no offense" approach had completely backfired on me, and eyed the windows. Two stood out, the first rimmed in a glittering, shimmering quartz, its edges dripping liquid gold. The second seemed bland by comparison, but ornate, the cherry wood decorated with some sort of crest. "Those two," I said, pointing.

My mother's ghost followed the trajectory of my finger and raised her brows in surprise, then grunted. "Yes, I suppose you would have chosen those. Come."

I followed her to the first window, wondering what this was all about while also wishing I'd kept my trap shut; it wasn't like I was trying to be dismissive of my mother's abilities, they just seemed to pale next to those of a war goddess who could decimate her enemies at will and a nature goddess capable of literally breathing new life into the sick or fallen.

My mother's ghost hesitated at the window, palm hovering over the opaque glass until—at last—she grasped the lever and pulled. I blinked, surprised to find the Fae realm on the other side. The difference was easy to spot: where else would you find mushrooms as big as trees, their stalks the color of peaches, their caps glowing beneath a moonlit sky? And those unfamiliar stars, forming alien constellations—a night sky streaming with tendrils of multi-colored light that never decorated our own. It was stunning. Breathtaking.

Until one of those stars exploded.

The sound of the gunshot made me flinch and duck out of habit before I realized it had come from the Fae side of the window. I glanced back to find that the star, meanwhile, had shattered into a million pieces of broken light, hanging about in the sky like leftover confetti, a firework trapped in a never-ending explosion. I quickly studied the landscape for the source of the shot only to find a man sprawled out on a luminescent mushroom cap, drawing back a massive silver-plated handgun to blow smoke off the barrel, eyeing his handiwork. I squinted, then felt my eyes widen in recognition.

Nate Temple.

And yet...there was something different about him. As I watched, he held out his hand, crooking his fingers just so—as if he might reach out and touch the shattered star. It reminded me of the way I used to pinch the moon as a child, perspective making the impossible possible. Except what happened next was decidedly *not* a trick of perspective. As I stood there gaping, Nate Temple began *reassembling* the star, idly probing and tweaking until each bursting bit of light returned to its usual place in the sky, like he was putting a puzzle back together.

"The Manling born in Fae," my mother's ghost intoned. "Seems he's embraced his wild side, his past self." She glanced at me and smirked. "In a way, he's further along than you are."

I scowled at her. "What's that supposed to mean?"

"It means we need to hurry." She shut the window, but not before I glimpsed a small huddle of others joining Nate—a gargantuan wolf-man and a black, winged alicorn I thought I recognized, trailed by a spear-wielding catman, a little girl, and a...very, very handsome young man.

"Who—" I began.

"Stay away from him," my mother's ghost called back, not bothering to turn around. "Best to avoid the Pendragons, as a rule."

"Wait, that was—"

"Hush, there's no time for that." She gestured to the second window, which she'd already opened, but held up a hand before I could peer through. "You wanted to know how our power compares to those of our sisters?

Before you look through this, let me ask you something. Imagine you come to me, begging to know if you'll find love."

I opened my mouth to reject that ridiculous hypothesis, but the weight of her glare stopped me cold. I shrugged. "Fine, whatever ye say."

"Now," she continued, "let's say I tell you that you'll have three great loves in your life. That one will die, that one *you* will kill, and that the other will leave you."

"Morbid," I noted. "But sure."

"Tell me, what would happen?"

I sighed, not the least bit interested in this hypothetical scenario, but decided to give it some actual thought since it seemed so important. I considered her prophecy, my frown deepening the longer I did so. "Nothin' good," I answered, at last.

She nodded. "And why not?"

"Because I'd be worried the whole time. Afraid to fall for anyone. Would they die on me? Leave me? Why would I have to kill 'em?"

"Precisely. Now, let's say you probed me for more information. I go on to tell you that your first love would die in battle. That your second would leave because he never felt he could compare to the first. And that the third would ask you to help him pass late into the course of your lives."

"Why not just say that, then, in the first place?" I asked, baffled by this turn in conversation.

"Ah, but the consequences." She raised a finger in warning. "What if she tried to stop the first love from ever going off to battle? Eventually, he resents her and leaves. The second is bitter about never being enough and beat you until one day you strike back, ending your days behind bars. The third love dies alone, never having met the woman he would have spent most of his life with. The prophecy remains fulfilled, but you end up miserable and broken."

"Are ye always this optimistic?" I asked, dryly.

"My point is that fate *can* be a weapon. It can also be a shield. Knowing one's future can mean salvation, or damnation, depending on the path we take." And, with that very cryptic comment, she waved me forward to look through the window.

I frowned, but did as she asked, stepping forward to see the central aisle of a magnificent private library, the lights dimmed, but bright enough to reveal four shadowy figures standing around a pedestal that contained what appeared to be a book.

"So it's true," one of the two men present muttered, barely audible from this distance. "The Catalyst...all of it."

I jerked away from the sound of that voice, recognizing it from a memory I'd seen here before. "Is that—"

"Your father, Merlin, yes. But pay attention."

I turned back to the window and saw that the two couples had stepped away from the pedestal, and that the book was gone. The man who'd spoken, my father, faced away from the others, shoulders bunched, face lost entirely to the shadows.

"Is there a reason ye called us here?" one woman asked, her voice ringing out as if she'd never been shushed by a librarian in her life. My mother, in the flesh, standing not five feet from Merlin. I hugged myself to see my parents together—something I'd never hoped to do in my lifetime.

The other woman present turned to her companion. "Calvin, maybe you should show them."

The man beside her nodded and held out something—an hourglass, maybe? Either way, my parents' reactions were immediate; they each glared hatefully at the other, pointing accusingly.

"I knew this was a trick," Merlin hissed.

"The next time me sisters and I find ye, wizard, we'll kill ye," my mother retorted.

"This isn't a trick," the other man, Calvin, insisted, stepping between the two. "It's an offer. A...chance. Perhaps the only chance any of us has."

The unnamed woman ran a hand over her belly self-consciously. "We know what we're asking will be difficult. That you may not understand it all, but the Catalyst needs a protector. Someone powerful enough to do what must be done should the time come."

My parents turned to the woman, though it was clear by their posture both were fixated on her slight paunch of a belly. "Is it true?" Merlin asked, voice laced with trepidation, but also the faintest degree of...hope.

"What is it ye wish of us?" my mother asked.

"Makayla," Calvin said, turning to the woman, "why don't you explain it?"

Makayla smiled. "Well, that's the tricky part..."

My mother's ghost shut the window so abruptly I actually stumbled back in surprise. "That's enough," she said.

I glared at her. "What the hell d'ye mean 'that's enough'?!" I demanded. "What were they goin' to ask of me parents? And who were those two, anyway?"

"Calvin and Makayla Temple." She shook her head mournfully. "Your mother never trusted them, not entirely, but she saw the necessity in what they were doing. In what they asked of her and the wizard."

I blinked a half dozen times, trying to process those names. Calvin and Makayla Temple. "But why..." I trailed off, bewildered.

"They asked your mother and father to provide them with a protector," my mother's ghost supplied. "For their son. Nathin Laurent Temple."

"A...what? Wait, *me*?!" I jabbed a finger into my own chest, too incredulous to do more than stammer.

"That was your intended purpose, yes." My mother's ghost gave me a sad smile. "And now you know how powerful the gift of foresight is. What will you do with the knowledge you've just been given, I wonder?" She looked away, staring at the crest emblazoned on the window frame. "Will this knowledge destroy you? Define you? I suppose only time will tell."

I shook my head, and finally slumped to the floor, clutching my knees to my chest. Nate Temple's *protector*? I couldn't imagine how that was even possible, let alone what it meant. I mean sure, I knew the guy, tangentially—as a friend-of-a-friend—but I'd only met him twice. Once when he'd hijacked my Uber so he could make it to his date on time, and the second when he'd broken into my apartment on a whim and subsequently trashed it. Frankly, the guy had always behaved like a class A jerk around me...and yet he had a ton of very loyal friends whose opinions I valued. Still, that hadn't stopped me from agreeing to confront the bastard on behalf of the Winter Queen—one of the three Fae powerhouses who ruled that realm.

A confrontation I'd yet to have.

"But that would mean..." I drifted off, my emotions in turmoil.

"I have one last thing to show you," my mother's ghost said, drawing me laboriously to my feet.

"I don't t'ink I can handle any more surprises," I admitted.

"Just trust me."

I almost scoffed but held it back; it wasn't this creature's fault I'd chosen to look at that window, to witness that particular exchange. In fact, I was fairly certain some part of me had wanted to know the truth, to know what had brought my parents together. But to find out it had been nothing but obligation, that I had been engineered...

Another thought occurred to me, this one so dark I almost didn't voice it for fear of what the answer would be. "Did they love me? Me parents?" I asked, staring down at the celestial bodies beneath our feet as we shuffled down the hallway, my steps leaden.

"Until the day she gave birth to you," she replied, thoughtfully, "*that* was the one thing your mother distrusted most about the Temple duo."

I looked up in confusion. "Wait, what?"

My mother's ghost was studying the stars above absentmindedly. "How could they know, do you think, that the time-bending wizard and the prophetic goddess would fall in love—as much as they were capable—and truly cherish the child they would never meet?" She shook her head. "At times, I wonder still if the Temple's were gods themselves, or at least blessed with a vision of the future that was far clearer than even your mother's had been."

She tugged me along, and I fell back into my own thoughts, but I could feel a slight smile creeping across my face as I realized what she'd told me just now: my parents *had* loved each other, and I hadn't been solely a means to an end, solely the Catalyst's protector.

Whatever the hell that meant.

42

The final window my mother's ghost led me to seemed to be made of black ice, its corners licked by frost. She merely stood beside it this time, however, watching me, waiting. But for what I wasn't sure. "Are ye goin' to open it?" I asked, gesturing to the window.

"No. This one belongs to you."

I frowned at her choice of words, but eventually reached for the lever, drawing it down as I'd seen her do a handful of times already. The window swung open with a bang as if drawn inward, and a sudden blast of frigid air hit me, causing the flesh on my arms to pebble up. I rubbed at my exposed skin, surprised to find my breath fogging up. Beyond the frame lay darkness —an unlit, windowless room, perhaps. Maybe a meat locker, I thought, given the cold? That, or somewhere below the surface of the earth, like a cave in the mountains or a military bunker.

But it turned out to be neither; a flash of radiant azure light emerged from one corner of the room, and I realized I was staring at a bank vault.

A very familiar bank vault.

A man stepped into the middle of the room cradling that chilly blue light, his skin the pale white of freshly fallen snow, lips the color of black ice. His electric, blue eyes scoured the safety deposit boxes on either side as he turned a slow, lazy circle. But I already knew which one he was looking for.

"Ryan!" I cursed, staring at the pointy-eared bastard who I'd called a friend before he'd begun abducting Chancery members and torturing his own kind in pursuit of vengeance. On the one hand, I supposed it could be considered good news that Ryan had traded in mutilation for bank robbery. On the other hand, however, this was *my* bank.

And I had a sinking feeling Ryan knew that.

"The new Jack Frost," my mother's ghost said, studying Ryan. "He's better looking than the last one," she noted, dryly.

I stared at the woman, studying her, trying to decipher her expression. At last, I decided to ask a question that had been lingering in the back of my mind for a long time now, a question I'd left unasked for fear of what it might mean. "Is Ryan me brother?"

My mother's ghost raised both eyebrows. "What?"

I gestured to the open window even as Ryan began probing the boxes with his fingertips, ice spreading in thin tendrils along the many seams. "Ryan O'Rye..." I trailed off, then sighed. "I know me ma had another child, before me. And...I don't know. Ryan and I always had this odd connection. Like..."

"Like you were destined to find each other?"

I rolled my eyes. "Not like *that*, Jesus, just—"

"No, you're right."

I felt my jaw drop, but my mother's ghost was already shaking her head in denial. "Not about him being your long, lost brother. That's ludicrous. But you two *were* destined to find each other."

When she didn't elaborate, I reached out, gripping her shoulder the way she had mine not so long ago. "And what is that supposed to mean?" I asked the question sweetly but let her feel the strength in my fingers as I dug them deeper into the meat above her clavicle.

She batted my hand away as though a bug had landed on her shoulder. "It means you will be tested. Not by me," she added hurriedly. "But by fate. It also means you must make choices. This new Jack Frost, and what you do with him, will be one of many."

I gritted my teeth. "Well, isn't that cryptic as hell."

She pointed, ignoring my tone altogether. "Look, this is what you needed to see."

I did as she insisted, though under duress, only to find Ryan pilfering through my safety deposit box as if I'd left a note asking him to make as big a mess as possible; he tossed item after item to the ground, clearly searching for something in particular. I winced as each piece hit the ground, the monetary value of each artifact—and that's precisely what they were—enough to make a tycoon's eyes boggle. But Ryan wasn't looking for something as mundane as magic wands or ancient tablets or scrolls that shouldn't exist. Hell, he casually dismissed the lead box containing Balor's Eye—the very artifact I'd bargained for when I'd agreed to confront Nate Temple in the first place—tossing it aside like it was yesterday's newspaper.

Seconds later, however, he seemed to have found his prize.

He withdrew the multi-faceted stone with a reverent sigh, cradling it in the palm of his hand, caressing its luminous surface with one finger. I actually thought I could hear him crooning at it like an infant.

I almost felt embarrassed for him.

"The devourer," my mother's ghost said, tilting her chin towards that tiny, unbelievably powerful stone. "One of the last that remains in this world."

"Ye mean Balor's replacement eye?" I asked, recalling vividly the flashes of brilliant light bursting from the Fomorians' eye as he wiped out a whole fleet of ships, that radiance ensuring nothing but a brutal, immediate execution.

"It was given to Balor, taken from its rightful resting place by a man with too much time and too little sense," my mother's ghost replied, eyes distant. She shook herself and looked at me appraisingly. "It will be your task to retrieve it and return it to where it belongs, when the time comes."

"I—wait, what?" I stammered.

She indicated I should shut the window, though I wasn't quite done watching the capricious little thief; I glared at the frostbitten fucker, pissed beyond words that he'd robbed me, but even more so that he'd tossed away my other valuables like garbage.

It always pissed me off when people refused to appreciate nice things.

I reached out and flicked the lever, letting the window close, wishing I could step through and strangle the bastard. Too late, I realized I'd missed my opportunity. "Wait, can we," I pointed at the window, "can we go through these?"

"Absolutely not. And don't you ever try it," she chastised.

I sighed. Of course not; that would have been too easy. "Alright, well, what was it ye were sayin' before? Ye want me to steal back me stone?"

"The devourer. Yes. But that's only a small piece of it. Let's sit, I'm growing tired." She waved and two chairs materialized out of thin air, seeming to float as they settled on an invisible floor, casting no shadows. She settled on one with a huff, clearly drained. I took a seat as well, trying not to dwell too hard on the bizarre physics of this place; I'd done that before and knew it would only make me nauseous. Instead, I turned to her, expectantly.

"What do you know of the Four Jewels of the Tuatha de Danann?" my mother's ghost asked, catching my look.

I reached up and unbound my hair as I considered that, recalling tales of the legendary items associated with my mother's people—tales I'd unearthed while researching the various myths associated with my extended family. "They're apocalypse memorabilia," I said, at last, slipping the hair tie around my wrist and running a hand through the tangled mess.

"They—what?"

I shrugged. "That's what I call anythin' so powerful it could destroy the world if used improperly. Or used at all, in some cases. There's a bunch of 'em out there accordin' to the myths, but few have been recovered. Thank God."

My mother's ghost gave me a considering look before nodding. "Apocalypse memorabilia. I see...because they're all that will be left behind when the world ends?"

I gave her a thumbs up with my free hand.

"Do you know their names? The Four Treasures, I mean."

I thought about that. "Aye, though some have different names dependin' on the story. There's Nuada's sword. The Stone of Destiny. The Dagda's Cauldron. And—"

"Lugh's Spear," she finished for me, nodding. "Very good."

I mimed brushing my shoulder off. "It's not me profession for nothin'," I replied.

"No, no it isn't." She gave me a look I couldn't decipher, though her tone suggested there was something more to her words than what was on the surface. "Anyway," she continued, "that devourer, the one Balor used, the one Jack Frost stole, is part of Lugh's Spear. An integral part. Without it, the weapon is practically useless. Harmless, even, by comparison. With it, the wielder would be impossible to defeat, able to cut down any foe..." she trailed off meaningfully.

"Are ye sayin' Ryan took me stone to power up that spear?" I frowned, considering the possibility that Ryan was still gunning for Nate Temple—still trying to avenge his father's murder, though I had reason to believe there was more to that story. "Does Ryan have it, then?" I asked, the implications making me shift nervously in my seat.

"No. Long ago, when we put Lugh to rest, we entrusted the spear to a man, a wizard we thought we could trust." She shook her head. "But, since the devourer was clearly taken, and I don't know what became of its guardian, I can only assume the spear is unprotected, although still far out of reach for most."

I snorted. "Are ye bein' vague on purpose? Or is it just hard for ye to use proper nouns?"

"Atlantis," she replied, eyes narrowed.

My eyebrows shot up all on their own. "Seriously? And the guardian?"

"Merlin. Your father."

I cursed, sensing the strings of fate tugging at me from every which way and wishing the woman across from me didn't look so frail, so I could deck her. "I see, so ye expect me to go runnin' off after Ryan to freakin' Atlantis, and—what—check in on dear ol' da while I'm there?"

But she was already shaking her head vehemently. "It won't be that simple. As for your father, I believe his absence will be explained in time. According to your mother's memories, he was as bad as the Temple's when it came to plotting. In fact, it would be fair to say he had as much a hand in their schemes as anyone—especially after he gave them that godsforsaken Round Table. A present for his godson, indeed," she muttered, rolling her eyes.

I blinked rapidly, trying to process what I was hearing. Merlin, my father, had given Nate Temple's parents the fucking *Round Table*? And he was Nate Temple's *godfather*? I felt jealousy stir, my skin prickling with it. "That's it," I hissed. "I'm done here." I stood to leave, too emotionally drained to handle even one more revelation—but my mother's ghost snatched my wrist.

"Sit down," she commanded, "we aren't done."

"The hell we aren't," I snarled, reeling back from her tone, prying my wrist from her weakened fingers. "Ye t'ink I'm goin' to just run off and do what ye want? After all this?" I waved at the windows absently, cheeks flushed with anger. "I'm not some playthin' for ye to order about! I deserve the truth. All of it, not just crumbs ye toss out whenever ye feel like sharin.'"

"You're right."

I folded my arms over my stomach, scowling, biting off my next tirade. "What was that?"

"I said you're right. You've been patient. Ask your questions. But hurry."

I took a long, deep, calming breath. I tried to sort through all the questions I had, most of which had cropped up in the last hour but decided all that could wait; I felt compelled to stick to my original questions out of sheer obstinance. "Blair," I began, the mere mention of her name enough to make my stomach lurch. "What happened to her?"

"The woman your Other self fell in love with?" My mother's ghost cocked her head as if listening to something in the distance. "She's been returned to her people."

I felt something inside me shift uncomfortably. "Have they buried her, then?"

"You misunderstand. She's been returned—alive. Blair was never truly in exile. She was sent back and revived as all Otherworlders eventually are— even now she searches for you, though she knows deep down you've departed from their realm." Her eyes flicked over my shoulder, and I turned to find a window framed in foliage, the leaves long and frond-like.

I took a step towards the window but felt a hand brush mine. I glanced down and saw the woman's chiding expression, her smoldering eyes imploring me to stay put. "Now isn't the time. Ask your questions."

I bit my lip but nodded. "The Otherworlders...the Blighted Lands...why?"

She raised an eyebrow. "Why, what?"

"Why d'ye leave 'em like that?" I shuddered, recalling the horrors of the Blighted Lands, not to mention the prolonged, seemingly meaningless existence of the Otherworlders. "How could their gods let t'ings end up so...wrong?"

My mother's ghost made a considering sound in her throat. "I see. And what would you have us do? To fix things."

I shook my head; I had given that a great deal of thought over the last few weeks. "Confront the leaders," I said. "Tell 'em to let their people live their lives in peace."

"And the Blighted Lands?"

"Heal 'em. Let the people there redeem themselves, somehow."

She nodded. "Suggestions the Tuatha de Danann considered in the past. And yet, what is life without uncertainty? And how do you expect selflessness to survive without repercussions?" She turned away, studying the cosmos. "You see, if their gods tell them what to do, we take away their ability to decide for themselves. To feel as though they have a say in their own lives. And, if we abolish their prison, we force the good to host the bad." The heartfelt sigh she let out seemed genuine. "And so their gods left them to their own devices, giving them very few rules."

"But why are they there at all?" I challenged, recalling Amergin's request that I question the validity of the Otherworld's intended purpose.

"They will be needed," she replied, as if that explained everything. "And so will you."

I held out a hand. "Enough of that nonsense, alright?"

"But it's true, Quinn MacKenna. Quinn Light-Eater, Morrigan's daughter." She turned those flickering eyes to me and smiled, though it was a sad, paltry attempt. "Ask your last question. We may only have time for one more."

I clenched my fists, deciding not to rise to the bait, not to ask her what my role was supposed to be in all this, to discover what plans fate had in store for little old me. Frankly, I wasn't sure I wanted to know. Maybe I was getting smarter with age, after all.

"My sibling," I said, at last. "Who is it?"

"It?"

"He, she, whatever," I replied, waving my hands about.

"She," my mother's ghost said, "*was*. Not is. Your sister died before you were born. It was a tragedy your mother never entirely recovered from, though she did manage to find a human shoulder to cry on, if memory serves. Desdemona Jones."

The sound of my aunt Dez's full name spoken aloud made my insides clench. I looked away, quietly mourning a sibling I'd never even known existed until recently, that grief melding with the complicated emotions talk of Dez always brought up. After a prolonged silence, I finally asked the only other question I could think of. "What's next?"

My mother's ghost sighed, rising slowly to her feet to brush absentmindedly at her dress—a remarkably human gesture. "Well, I think it's time I died."

43

I turned away, less than eager to watch my last tenuous link to my mother fade away like a mirage, never to be seen or heard from again. But it seemed she wasn't going to make it easy on me; the woman wrapped her arms around me from behind, pressing her face against my shoulder. "If you leave this place as you are, you'll die," she whispered, breath cool against my skin, sending shivers up my spine.

It took me a minute to realize what she was talking about. The wound. I realized I'd forgotten all about it, what with all the revelations and stimuli. This place seemed to be sustaining me, for now, but I sensed she was telling me the truth; I'd been so very close to falling asleep for good back in the tunnel with Cathal. "Wait, is Cathal safe?" I asked, concerned for the fate of my guide.

"The Hound of Ulster has returned to the place of his birth. He mourns his brothers and sisters, fixating on death. He, too, needs a purpose."

I tried to turn in her arms to look at the woman, wondering what had gotten into her all the sudden. Why was she talking like that? Was she just trying to prove a point, to provoke me for some reason? But that hug got tighter, making it nearly impossible to move. "What's happenin'?" I rasped. "Let me go."

"Long ago," she said, ignoring me, "your father blessed you with a power too great to be let loose on the world. And so your mother bound you with

216

her own lifeforce, containing your ability to move through time until you could use it responsibly." She paused, taking a deep, shuddering breath I could feel against my spine. "But she also removed a piece of herself from you, the piece you were meant to inherit as the child of a goddess, a power all your own. And she made of that power a specter, a ghost formed from her memories, to guide you. To warn you."

I felt hot tears spill down my back and stiffened with surprise. "What are ye sayin'?" I whispered.

"Your new guardian watched over you, doing her best to fulfill her duties and give you advice. To be what you needed. Once, there may have been time to explain the purpose of this power and how to use it, but that time has passed. For the specter is fading, and your power—the power of a goddess—must return to its rightful place."

"I don't—"

"You asked once," she interrupted, "about your mother's power. The ability to see, yes...but that's not all. As Badb embodied the tempest, and Macha the air, so too was your mother blessed. Blessed with power over the darkness, for the dark has always been associated with the unknown. *This* was to be your legacy. And now, it is my duty to return what was taken... with my love."

"Wait, I—" But that was as far as I got before the power hit me. Although, to be fair, *hit* might have been the wrong word. *Ravaged*, I decided. The power was *ravaging* me, tearing at me like a wild animal trying to climb its way inside, burrowing into my bones like vultures hunting for marrow, pulling my ligaments apart like taffy, splitting open my muscles as though they were overripe melons bursting beneath the summer sun. My skin burned, then ached, then burned again, nerves wailing as wave after wave of mind-melting agony crashed into me.

Or maybe I was the one wailing.

And then, as suddenly as the pain had come, pleasure followed. I felt it tingle in my fingertips, on my tongue. It caressed my brain with the touch of a lover and slid across my lips like honey. I almost went limp with it, trapped in that pure, glorious afterglow. It was like sex, but more somehow, more than caffeine or nicotine or opiates. It was like waking from a euphoric dream, huddled beneath warm covers with all the time in the world to simply lay there and languish in the knowledge that the world wasn't this fucked up, awful place. Not today. Not for me.

217

Not ever.

I fell to my knees, skin glowing with power. So much power. Enough power to blow up the moon, or spin the Earth the opposite direction, or... but no. That wasn't how this power worked; I could sense that it was a subtle thing, not meant for anything flashy. The opposite, perhaps.

A power forged in darkness.

I held out my hand and watched in fascination as shadows danced down my arm to leap from my fingertips like flames, hovering, their inky tongues darting this way and that. I rose and turned, realizing I was no longer being held against my will, and opened my mouth to ask my mother's ghost what she'd done to me. But there was no one. She was gone, and I was alone.

Again.

I lowered my arms, crestfallen, but something—an instinct stronger than those I'd felt when choosing the windows before—urged me to walk. And so I did, led by the burgeoning power almost as surely as I had been by my mother's ghost, my eyes locked on a frame that seemed to glow before my eyes. Indeed, I passed window after window until, at last, I found the one I was meant to open—a gilded, blue steel frame patterned with frozen roses.

I pressed my hand to the window's glass surface and watched shadows play across it at odd angles, as if they couldn't decide where to go or what to do. I drew back, flexing my fingers one at a time, and finally reached out to pull the lever down, though it took me several tries; the lever seemed to move all on its own.

"You were successful?"

The voice belonged to the Fae Queen within the window, her imperious tone easy to place. The Winter Queen sat on a throne of ice in a stately room I'd never seen before—new digs, I guessed. Before her stood two Faelings. The first was a child I didn't recognize. The second was an attractive, blonde Faeling who I thought looked familiar, but couldn't place.

"Yes, my Queen," the child replied. The voice made my breath catch; it was the same as the one I'd heard after I'd been stabbed. The voice of my attacker.

"Good. I'm glad one of you managed not to fail me."

The blonde ducked her head. "I apologize, my Queen. As I said before, I have no idea how she escaped us. I saw her pass beneath the branch, myself. I made sure of it."

"Enough excuses," the Winter Queen hissed, clawing idly at one arm of her icy chair, flicking chips of frozen liquid in the blonde's general direction. "It is done."

But it wasn't done. *I* wasn't done. I let my hand drop from the lever, afraid I might snap it in two as angry as I was, and realized my skin was glowing brighter with each passing second. I seethed, staring at the trio. The Queen. The child with the knife. Bubblegum Barbie, the Faeling I'd met in Scotland—Mabel, I believed her name had been. *They* were the ones who'd tried to bring me over into Fae against my will. *They* were the ones who had attacked me. And why? Because I hadn't gone after Nate Temple as I'd said I would? Or had my tiff with Ryan—with the new Jack Frost—earned me a one-way ticket to the afterlife?

Regardless of their reasons, I felt suddenly very compelled to go knock on someone's fucking door. No, not knock. To bang that fucker down and nail someone to it. Surprisingly, the instant I thought that, I could feel the power inside me roil, skin dimming entirely as a shadow spread out in front of me like a path, only to stop a mere few feet ahead. No, not a path, I realized.

A doorway.

Somehow, I knew all I had to do was take a single step and I'd fall right in, traveling directly to the Winter Queen's throne room the way only I—Quinn MacKenna, Morrigan's daughter—could. I took one look at the child and the blonde bowing and scraping as they left the throne room and felt my anger rise another notch. I strode into the darkness, prepared to give her Majesty and all her pissant minions a taste of the hell they'd put me through.

Because karma may be a real bitch.

But I was more punctual.

44

J materialized within the very room I'd seen in the mirror, emerging from the shadows cast by the throne as if I were rising from the depths of the ocean, darkness sloughing off my skin in rivulets to puddle around my feet like ink. Frankly, I wasn't sure how I'd done it—especially how I'd managed to appear in this exact location despite having no idea where the hell I actually was—only that I had.

But I could explore my new abilities later, I decided. Right now my priority was having a little tête-à-tête with a certain frosty bitch before someone else came out of the woodwork with a dagger aimed at my back. I flexed the fingers of my right hand and smiled as shadows pooled around the grooves of my knuckles, swarming over my skin like ants.

This was going to be a *good* conversation.

I stepped out from behind the throne, fully aware of just how intimidating I'd seem appearing out of nowhere after being presumed dead. In fact, I was counting on it, prepared to scare the living...*befreezus* out of the Winter Queen and her lackeys.

Except, rather than step out in all my nebulous glory, I tripped and fell flat on my face.

"Motherfu—" I began, cutting the curse off as I groaned, trying to climb back to my feet. But I couldn't. Or, rather, my body wasn't cooperating. In fact, it felt as though every ounce of energy I'd had roaring inside me only a moment ago had suddenly fled, taking with it even my own reserves, leaving me drained and exhausted and...weak.

So very, very weak.

"Guards!" the Winter Queen shrieked, startled by my sudden appearance and subsequent collapse. I glanced over, taking particular note of her tastelessly tall heels and dainty ankles before I felt a beefy hand push me flat to the ground. I grunted, finding it suddenly hard to breathe, my ribs pressed so tight against the stone floor I thought they might shatter.

"Get her up," the queen commanded, snapping her fingers.

The hand gripped the back of my neck like I was a naughty kitten, drawing me to my feet. It was freaking embarrassing, but personally I was glad for the order; at least this way I wouldn't die from lack of oxygen. And yet I was having trouble even standing on my own two feet.

Dear God, what was wrong with me?

Had I overdone it with my mother's magic, somehow?

"You!" the Winter Queen gasped as her bodyguard—a blue-skinned, red-furred troll with filed teeth—propped me up against his shoulder.

"Me," I replied, lamely, waving one hand.

"But how?!" the child assassin cried, running up to us, apparently drawn by the ruckus I'd caused. Except he wasn't a child, at all. He was a beardless dwarf, his features slightly too robust to belong to a kid. "I stabbed her, my Queen, I swear it!"

"Clearly you should have stabbed her again," the Winter Queen drawled, studying me. "No matter." She strutted forward, those high heels clicking against the stone, loud enough to set my teeth on edge, and placed one freezing hand on the pulse of my throat. She ran it down, fingers trailing, and I shivered, turning this way and that in an attempt to get away from her glacial touch. But, with the troll holding me fast by my neck, I simply wasn't strong enough to free myself.

Only...since when had I been too weak to break out of a hold, even from one of the Fae? I scowled, realizing that something—something not related to my mother's power and the possible magical overload—was very, very wrong.

The Winter Queen's eyes met mine and a slow, languid smile split her face practically in two. She licked those cobalt-coated lips and tapped my breastbone thoughtfully with a slender finger, nail breaking skin with each descent to leave bloody half-moon welts on my chest. I winced, shying from her touch, but remained unable to get away. "Oh, child..." she said, seductively, "what promise did *you* break?"

*T*he Winter Queen's dungeon was freaking cold.
Big surprise.

I leaned back against the iron bars of my cell, unconcerned whether or not the metal brushed my skin since it seemed to have no effect on me currently, still beating myself up for being so monumentally stupid. *What promise did you break?* I felt like those words may as well have been etched onto the back of my eyelids for as many times as I'd reflected on them—on what they meant for me. But then, I wasn't the only one getting screwed over right now.

There was Eve, too.

My poor, potted houseplant, who I'd promised—on my godsforsaken *power*—to bring to Fae the next time I visited. And yet, what had I done? I'd stepped right into the freaking lair of the Fae Queen trying to have me assassinated without an ounce of fucking sense and lost everything, including the advantage of surprise and, naturally, my dignity.

To say I was feeling low would be an understatement. Truthfully, I felt like a fool, yes, but worse, I felt like I'd betrayed Eve. Betrayed someone I'd come to care about because I'd been too shortsighted, too eager to kick ass and take names. And now, not only had I broken my vow, but I'd gotten myself captured by a race of creatures who thought of time as a malleable law of physics, who equated decades with hours—which meant, at this rate, Eve may never get her wish, at all.

I groaned, letting my head fall back to clang against the bars of my cell, grimacing at the sudden spike of pain. Then again. "Stupid, stupid, stupid..." I muttered.

"I told you, halfling," a voice said, slithering out from the dim hallway outside my cell, "you'll never beat us. You simply don't have what it takes."

I spun around on instinct, kicking my way across the floor just in time to avoid the knife thrust I'd sensed coming. The blade gleamed with some infernal light, casting shadows in all directions, but it was enough to make out my attacker. Mabel, the elven girl who'd insulted me before the race in Scotland. Ryan's fangirl. In hindsight, her presence made all the sense in the world; Ryan must have recruited her when he'd gone to work for the Winter Queen. Turned her into a spy, using her to dig up dirt on the Chancery. I scowled, wondering how many other traitors we had hiding out among our members. Wait, our members? I laughed at the momentary slip-up, acknowledging to myself that not only was I not a member of the Chancery, but that—at the moment—I wasn't much of anything.

I was a mere mortal. Fragile. Weak.

"Having a good time?" Mabel asked.

I shrugged, glad the cell was large enough that I could at least stay well out of her reach. I pretended to take a long look around as she withdrew her blade. "I mean, it's not the Ritz," I replied, thoughtfully, "but I've stayed in worse places." Frankly, I wasn't sure that was entirely true, but I *had* spent a couple months sleeping on the floor of a friend's closet in New York City…at least this wasn't my choice. Less embarrassing that way, maybe.

"Oh, I doubt that," Mabel replied. She dropped to a squat, staring at me from about eye-level, her smile malevolent. "They've been debating what to do with you for a while now. The Queen and King Oberon, that is."

I perked up at that, something like hope fluttering in my chest. Granted, Oberon and I hadn't exactly been pals following our little run-in with Balor and his army…but we hadn't been enemies, either. As things stood, the Goblin King, as he was sometimes known, might be my only chance of making it out of this place alive. "And?" I asked, trying to sound casual.

The elven girl shrugged, coolly. "They go back and forth. Torture you, leave you to rot for a few hundred years…" She trailed off, waving her dagger about as if there was little difference between the two. "That's why I figured I'd stop by, first."

I studied that odd, glowing dagger. "Ye wanted to kill me, instead?"

"Oh no. Personally, I'd have preferred what the others had in store for you," she admitted, eyes flicking down the hall. "But Ryan made me promise not to let you talk."

"Why?" I asked, incredulously. Thing was, while Ryan and I had found ourselves on opposite sides of the field, I certainly hadn't expected him to try and have me killed. Especially not for something as mundane as talking to his boss. Hell, that made even less sense; wouldn't he *want* them to pry every ounce of information out of me?

"Ryan wouldn't say," she admitted, looking a tad petulant.

"He doesn't trust ye?"

Mabel tensed, her smile vanishing so swiftly I thought I must have imagined it. "He *loves* me."

Oh, here we go.

"Well, you're probably right," I said, shrugging. "I mean, I always thought trust was integral to any healthy relationship. But that must just be a human t'ing. Don't mind me."

Mabel's cheeks flushed. "It's not important why. Ryan trusts me to do what he asks, that's all. If I'd wanted to know, he'd have told me." She pressed one hand flat to the ground, hunkering forward until her face almost touched the bars. "But I do want to know one thing before I cut you open," she purred. "How did you escape? That day at the race, why didn't you end up here like you were supposed to?"

I grunted. "And why would I tell ye?"

The Faeling blinked owlishly as if she hadn't considered that.

"Is there like a standardized test out there ye lot take to figure out who among ye is the dumbest?" I asked, cocking an eyebrow.

"What?"

I shook my head. "Nevermind. Listen, I don't know what you've got planned here, but unless ye can get past iron bars, I can promise ye I'm not gettin' close enough to let ye stab me with that t'ing."

Mabel laughed, the sound akin to birdsong—an awfully pretty sound to come out of such an ugly, malicious person, I decided. Then she casually reached back with her free hand and drew a set of keys from somewhere, dangling them for me to see. "Don't worry, Quinn MacKenna, if you can't come to me, I'll come to you."

Well, Mabel may have been dumber than pixie dust...

But she certainly had a flair for villainous delivery.

45

I was already on my feet by the time Mabel found the right key—a process which took at least five ridiculously long, excruciating minutes. At that point, the elven hussy was so pissed she was spitting; it probably hadn't helped that I'd mocked her the entire time for not being able to put the right key in the appropriate hole. I may or may not have alluded to Ryan putting his key in a lot of holes to see which fit best...not my proudest moment, or even one of my best jokes, but what can I say?

I'd gotten bored.

"Oy, tell me, can a Faelin' catch anythin' from humans? Ye know, if he's especially promiscuous?" I asked good-naturedly, as if I were inquiring about the weather or picking an appetizer off a menu.

Mabel snarled, twisting the key so savagely I seriously thought it might break.

"Imagine that conversation with a doctor, am I right? Can ye even imagine what bang slang they'd come up with for that one?" I cocked my head thoughtfully, finger pressed to my lips. "Oh wait, why am I askin' ye like ye don't already know?"

"I will *kill* you," she hissed, throwing open the door.

"Ye said that already," I drawled. "Lesson number one when threatenin' someone? Try not to lead off with death. Doesn't leave ye much wiggle room." I said all this as she stepped inside, but before she advanced too far into the cell and effectively cornered me. Then I did the only thing I could do under the circumstances; I rushed her.

Mabel, so angry she probably couldn't even see straight, lashed out with her dagger, baring her perfectly straight teeth—but I was already moving. I pivoted to the side, relying not on the speed and strength I'd gotten so used to of late, but on my hard-earned reflexes—years and years of hand-to-hand training which rendered even Mabel's superior Fae genetics momentarily useless—as I dipped my shoulder, I snatched her outstretched arm and slammed it into the nearest iron bar. Once, twice. She shrieked, flesh sizzling, and dropped the knife.

Which was all I'd been waiting for.

I snatched up the knife, whirled, and plunged it deep into Mabel's thigh. I'd have preferred a more lethal strike, personally, but my options were limited; even without the blade, the elven girl could snap my neck with hardly any effort, assuming she didn't feel like plucking off my limbs one at a time like some demented toddler with her least favorite Barbie. But none of that turned out to matter because—the instant the blade struck her flesh —Mabel promptly disappeared.

And, of course, *that's* when the alarms went off.

I stood in front of two of Fae's most powerful rulers, wrists and ankles shackled, two armed guards on either side watching my every move. To be completely honest I was kind of flattered, feeling a little like Il Duce from *The Boondock Saints*. With one notable difference, of course; I wasn't about to be released to exact my own personal brand of vengeance anytime soon. If ever.

"I'll ask you again," the Winter Queen said imperiously, "how did you escape?"

I sighed. "I told ye, I didn't escape. The Pink Ranger tried to kill me."

"Mabel," she clarified, nodding along as if she'd heard it all before—because she had. "And yet none of my people can find her. Although doing so should be easy, if what you're saying is true."

"She disappeared into thin air," I explained.

"How convenient of her," the queen drawled.

I rolled my eyes. "Look, I stabbed her with the dagger she came at me with, and she went poof. I don't know what else ye expect me to say." I shrugged, chains clinking, and was rewarded to see my guards flinch. So touchy.

"Neither do I," the queen retorted, waving her hand dismissively. "Especially not from someone who breaks her vows as easily as you do."

That made me wince. "Listen, I—"

"Why *haven't* you gone after Nate Temple?" Oberon interjected. The Goblin King wore his favorite disguise—a goblin meatsack that hid his true form, a gargantuan, horned creature with all the presence of a god—and sat in a gaudy chair the queen must have procured for him. His eyes glinted with amusement to see me in irons, though there was a tension in the way he held himself that made me wonder just what I'd wandered into, here.

"I..." I trailed off, considering the question. Why *hadn't* I gone after Temple? I'd been freakishly busy after leaving Fae, for one thing, but I'd had enough downtime since then to seek him out. Hell, to track down Callie or Othello or anyone else I knew who would be eager to see me break bread with the bastard. But I hadn't. In fact, after returning from Moscow, I'd made an effort not to associate with any of them. To avoid Nate altogether, even tangentially. But why? Was it this "protector" business? Or something else?

"Well?" the Winter Queen barked.

I scratched idly at the skin of my forearm before answering. "Nate Temple and I..." I shook my head. "There's somethin' between us. Somethin' I need to sort out before I see him again."

Oberon cocked his head, studying me carefully. His royal companion, meanwhile, was leaning forward, face outraged. "That is not what we agreed upon!" she hissed.

I snorted. "Oh? And did ye put a time limit on our meetin', then?" I rubbed at the chafed skin beneath my manacles in agitation. "Because I don't seem to recall that. I also don't recall ye warnin' me that, unless I did what ye asked, you'd try to have me killed."

Oberon sat up a little straighter at that. "You didn't—" he began.

"She needed an incentive," the Winter Queen hissed, wheeling to face her companion. "How else are we to stop this madness? Soon all of Fae will be a battleground. Their war threatens us all!"

I frowned and raised a hand, though I didn't get very far what with the manacles. "And whose war would that be?"

"Mordred," Oberon answered. "Mordred Pendragon has declared war on Nate Temple. Indeed, I've been told he's awakened the Knights of the Round Table and that they are in his service."

I felt my jaw drop at that bit of news. Mordred Pendragon...as in King Arthur's son? The one Morgana and the Green Knight had gone off to find? What kind of batshit craziness had I walked into, here? And wait, what about that man...the one my mother had called Pendragon, could he have been...?

"Is that why ye sent Ryan to Boston?" I asked, shaking my head in an effort to clear it. "To stop the war, I mean."

"Ryan?" the Winter Queen echoed.

"Jack Frost," I clarified. "The new Jack Frost."

Oberon stiffened, then. "You claimed a new Jack Frost?" His tone was somehow icier than any I'd heard from the Winter Queen, and I could see her shifting uncomfortably in her seat beneath Oberon's stare.

"It is my right."

"It is your *privilege*," Oberon clarified. "Is the Summer Queen aware of this?"

The object of Oberon's scorn refused to meet his gaze, her eyes tight with anger. "She has her own affairs to tend to, as you well know. Not to mention a Jack of her own. She wouldn't begrudge me mine."

Oberon made a disgusted noise. "And what's this about letting your Jack roam the mortal realm? I seem to recall that being a rather *bad* idea last time."

The Winter Queen swung a hateful glare his way, then held her chin up in the air. "She must be mistaken. My Jack has not traveled to the mortal realm, not on my orders."

I laughed, fidgeting with the shackles. "Your *Jack* has been galavantin' all over the mortal realm. He kidnapped, tortured, and mutilated Fae exiles to create a monster specifically designed to kill Nate Temple. Hell, he just stole a devourer from me private bank!" I exclaimed, raising my hands as far as they would go.

The guards shuffled forward, latching onto my arms as if I were in immediate danger of breaking free from my shackles. I snarled at them, but didn't resist; as weak I was, there was no point. Except...except there *was* something going on. I glanced down at my arm to see faint marks appearing, glowing from within as if lit by smoldering coals, that faint itch becoming worse with each passing moment. But, when I looked back up, I realized the two royals hadn't taken any notice. Instead, they were staring at each other in utter shock, as if I'd dropped an F bomb in the middle of communion and they were trying to decide who was going to punish me.

"Did you say 'devourer'?" Oberon asked, turning back to me, voice so soft I barely heard him.

"That's not possible," the Winter Queen replied, shrilly. "She lies. She would say anything to save herself!"

But I wasn't lying. And, what's more, I wasn't entirely sure I needed to say anything, at this point. Because the marks on my flesh had solidified, forming a familiar arc—the dental imprint of a certain hound, flaring up so bright the guards had taken notice, pointing in wordless surprise. Not that I was trying to hide it, or anything.

After all, that would be rather pointless.

What with Cathal howling just outside the throne room door.

*Y*ou could say a lot of things about Cathal—most of which revolved around him being a sarcastic, pessimistic asshole and smelling like a stiff drink—but there was one thing I had to admit I loved about the mangy mutt.

He sure knew how to make a fucking entrance.

The throne room doors were literally blown apart as the blue-skinned troll who'd Faehandled me earlier came sailing through them, rolling end over end, clutching his ragged mess of a leg. Cathal, seeming somehow even bigger than I'd seen him last, shoulders so broad he almost couldn't fit through the gaping doorway, padded in with all the grace and ferocity of a lion. Hackles raised, his druidic markings burning the same shade of fiery orange as the marks on my forearm, the hound would have made any sane creature piss themselves with fright.

"What is the meaning of this?" Oberon shouted, hopping off his chair, chest puffed in indignation.

"Guards!" the Winter Queen shrieked, jabbing her finger towards the hound. "Kill this intruder!"

Cathal growled, amber eyes flashing with pent-up excitement as he studied the two guards who stood quivering beside me. He juked their direction, then yipped as they fell back, too scared to do anything but assume the position—the fetal position, people.

"Boo," Cathal said, licking his chops.

The Winter Queen made to rise up out of her seat, likely to do something monumentally stupid, like attack, but the Goblin King was already there, arm held out to stay her.

"Wait," he said, his voice full of awe. "Hound!" he called.

Cathal's ears perked up as he shifted his attention from the guards to the Goblin King, markings flaring for just an instant. "My *name* is Cathal."

"But he prefers to go by Cathy," I chimed in.

"I do not."

I mimed a series of nods with my finger held to my lips, winking, but the Goblin King ignored me completely. "It's true then? A Hound of Ulster survived the culling?" he asked.

I frowned, recalling the Goblin King's true nature for just a moment. Because Oberon wasn't merely one of the rulers of Fae, he was also the leader of the Wild Hunt. Which meant it was more than likely he knew precisely what Cathal was.

"That's not possible," the Winter Queen hissed.

"Ye keep sayin' that," I retorted, raising an eyebrow, "and ye keep soundin' like a fool."

"What of it?" Cathal asked, ignoring us both, locking eyes with the Goblin King, who shook himself.

"It's good to see one of Cú Chulainn's pups, that's all," Oberon explained, then frowned. "But why are you here?"

"My Queen called," Cathal replied, though he sounded awfully bitter about it.

All eyes swiveled to the Winter Queen, who appeared almost as baffled as she'd been angry only a moment before. "I...wasn't aware I'd called you," she said, thoughtfully.

"Not you, you moron. Her." He jerked his head towards...me. His Queen. I coughed as all eyes swung to me. "Um, Cathy dearest, as much as I appreciate bein' dubbed 'Your Royal Hotness,' I t'ink ye must have me confused with someone else."

Cathal huffed, rolling his eyes. "Trust me, I wouldn't say it if it weren't true." He swung that shaggy head to look at me, his markings dimming slightly. "Turns out I serve *you* now." He eyed my arm meaningfully.

I stared down at the mark in surprise. "I don't understand," I admitted.

"May I?" Oberon asked.

I scowled, realizing just how ridiculous this had all become, but unwilling to bring attention to it lest we all go back to fighting. So, I raised my shackled hands in exasperation. "Be me guest."

Oberon bowed as if I'd said something nicer than I'd intended, then strolled past Cathal, though I could tell he was resisting the temptation to reach out and brush his hand along Cathal's flank, clutching his arms to his chest the same way dog lovers do at a park lest they start petting every pooch in sight. Still, he seemed to have recovered his composure by the time he reached out to study my arm; after a moment, he gasped. "You've bound him!" He dropped my wrist as if I'd burnt him, staring at me in utter shock. "But how?"

"She is my Queen," Cathal drawled. He looked at me over the Goblin King's head. "I take it back. Humans are brilliant. It's the Fae I worry about."

I coughed a laugh, careful not to show too much amusement with Oberon standing close enough to tear my throat out on a whim. "Cathy," I chastised. "Not nice."

Cathal rolled his eyes. "Don't you two get it?" he asked, glancing back and forth between the two rulers. "She's my *Queen*. Which makes her yours, too."

Now *that* was funny. I snorted a laugh, unable to hold back this time, throwing my head back in the process. Except...no one else seemed to be laughing with me. I cleared my throat, studying the two rulers, both of whom had backed considerably away from me.

"I didn't see it before," the Winter Queen whispered, hand hovering over her mouth in horror as she hid behind her throne. Oberon made a noise, and she glared at him. "I didn't! Her power was stripped away, how was I supposed to see it?!"

"See what?" I interjected, mouth suddenly dry.

"You've accepted your mother's mantle," Cathal explained, pawing idly at the floor. "You are the third sister. Morrigan reforged. The Phantom Queen reborn."

*E*ven with the chains off, I decided I still felt like a prisoner. Though, if I was being honest with myself, the majority of my angst stemmed from the royal label Cathal had so generously bestowed upon me —a title the Goblin King and Winter Queen weren't stipulating. All four of us sat in the throne room, now, though my seat was the floor, my back propped up against Cathal; he'd begrudgingly allowed it as my first royal decree.

"So, what the hell does me bein' the Phantom Queen even mean?" I asked, addressing the Jabberwocky in the room. Cathal gnawed on the long-bone of a creature somehow larger than he was, procured for him by Oberon, who seemed inclined to fawn over the hound the way some pet owners do their prized poodles. As I waited for the response to my question, the mutt chomped, wrenching free a sliver of bone.

"Would ye quiet down?" I asked, elbowing him in the side.

Cathal grunted. "That a command?"

I rolled my eyes. "No."

He bit down harder this time, the ensuing snap of marrow that much louder.

"It's more an unofficial title," Oberon explained, ignoring our banter. "Your mother and your aunts were once rulers among the Tuatha de Danann, but more in name than actual fact. Their combined power was such that they were obeyed, even as they appointed others to look after the Fae they left behind." He and the Winter Queen exchanged glances. "The Tuatha de Danann were concerned with their own pursuits, more often than not. We don't expect that to change."

I frowned, reading between the lines. "Are ye suggestin' I might try and overthrow ye, or somethin'? Meanin' I should, what? Pretend this never happened?"

"I'm suggesting you think long and hard before you share that title outside this room," Oberon clarified, shaking his head. "You may not understand the way we do things here, and that's precisely why you should listen to me, now. Trust me when I say that you don't want to be responsible for the Fae. Not really."

The Winter Queen sniffed, scowling at Oberon. "Besides, what good have the Tuatha de Danann ever done us?"

"Amen," I replied absentmindedly as I mulled over what the Goblin King was saying. I realized he was right: the fewer people who knew what I'd become, the better. I already had enough of that "my Lady" bullshit back in Boston; I could only imagine how obnoxious it would be to be treated like a freaking Queen. I nodded to myself, resolved, only to find the Winter Queen glaring at me when I looked back up.

"What was that?" she asked.

It took me a second to realize what she was asking, but eventually I waved a hand. "Oh, I was agreein' with ye. See, I've been stuck in the Otherworld for months t'anks to their machinations, not to mention *yours*," I added, eyeing the Winter Queen from the corner of my vision. "And I'm not sure if the Tuatha de Danann deserve to rule anythin', at this rate." I thought about the state of the Otherworld, the Blighted Lands, and my mother's flimsy defense of their choices in both instances. I scoffed, shaking my head at the preposterous notion that the Tuatha de Danann should have any say at all in what happened from now on. "Would ye believe me ma's ghost actually insisted I chase after Ryan to find Lugh's Spear?"

"She said *what?!*" Oberon bellowed, rising to his feet, his wild side appearing like a clap of thunder, sprouting horns that brushed the ceiling, eyes aflame, hulking body towering over us all like an ominous rain cloud about to break and ruin our entire day.

Cathal raised his head and stared, bone spilling from his open mouth.

"Uh, Lugh's Spear," I repeated, quailing a bit beneath the monstrous figure, my current fragility even more in focus now that I was figuratively standing before Oberon's true self. "She wanted me to find it. To get back the devourer..." I coughed, sensing the sudden uptick in tension.

"*Your* Jack," Oberon said, rounding on the Winter Queen.

"I didn't know," she insisted. "He must be working with someone else." Her eyes narrowed, expression turning hateful. "Never before has Jack Frost crossed me."

"Oh? And how many of your Jack's took the position just to kill a single man?" I asked, an errant thought crossing my mind.

"What are you saying?" she asked.

"Nate Temple." I looked up, locking gazes with the Winter Queen.

She blinked first.

"I don't follow," Oberon replied, flopping back into his seat, a diminutive goblin once more, glancing back and forth between the two of us with suddenly bloodshot eyes, seemingly exhausted from even the brief revelation of himself.

I filed that away for later.

"Was he angry with ye? For not takin' on Temple yourself?" I asked scanning the queen's face. A curt nod was all I received. "So," I mused, "it's possible he sought out someone who *was* goin' after Temple. A certain Pendragon."

Oberon hissed through his teeth as he realized what I was implying. "You think he's going after one of the Four Jewels for *Mordred?*"

I shrugged, though there was some sense to it. My mother's ghost *had* inadvertently named me Nate Temple's protector, not to mention dubbed Ryan a fated enemy. There certainly seemed some cosmic hand in all this, engineering our confrontation. But where was it all leading?

"Where is the spear?" Oberon asked, when none of us immediately spoke up.

"Atlantis," I replied, deciding in that moment—not to trust these two, necessarily—but at the very least to open up to them. Frankly, I was beginning to sense there was no alternative, especially if I wanted to truly discover more about my legacy, my role among the Fae. Maybe learn more about the duties of the Phantom Queen reborn...whatever the hell they might be.

Oberon barked a laugh. "That's impossible. No one can even get there, anymore. Not unless they..." he drifted off, shaking his head.

"Unless they what?" I asked.

"There *is* a way," the Goblin King said in a hushed voice, huddled in his seat. "A path through the Greek realm. A backdoor. My...other self knew of it."

I frowned at the use of the past tense, wondering what "other self" he was referring to, but decided not to ask; something in the Goblin King's haunted expression told me the answer would be one of those sad stories you never really want to hear, but people tell you anyway just to make themselves feel better. Indeed, looking down at his hands, I could see them straining, the wood of his chair splintered beneath his fingers. Something passed between us, then—an errant blast of power that set my teeth on edge. "Well, how do I get there?" I asked, instead, choosing to ignore the brush of power.

The Goblin King glanced up, meeting my even stare, and grunted. "You'll need a guide."

"Where can I find one?"

"I can take care of that," Oberon said, sighing. "I still have some...pull, with that side. But you'll also need a ship."

I raised an eyebrow at that.

"She can take a few of mine," the Winter Queen suggested. "I'll even give her troops. I want that traitor executed for what he's done."

"No," Oberon said, leaning back in his chair, rapping his fingers against the wood thoughtfully. "No, I believe she's got a ship of her own. Don't you, Quinn MacKenna?" That gleam flickered to life behind Oberon's eyes, and I realized I knew exactly what—who—he was talking about.

A certain ragtag group of pirates...and maybe a few Lost People.

"Aye, I may indeed have a ship. And a crew, if they'll sail with me," I replied, thoughtfully.

Oberon held out his hands as if all were settled, grinning like a merchant who'd just sold his finest piece of junk for a small fortune.

"But first," I said, resting my head on the hound at my back, "I really need to stop by me apartment and take care of me plant." I eyed the Goblin King, expectantly.

He cleared his throat. "I think we can arrange something."

"Aye. Had a feelin' we might."

DON'T FORGET! VIP's get early access to all sorts of Temple-Verse goodies, including signed copies, private giveaways, and advance notice of future projects. AND A FREE NOVELLA! Click the image or join here:
www.shaynesilvers.com/l/38599

Q *uinn   returns   in   SEA   BREEZE.   Get   your   copy   online!*
http://www.shaynesilvers.com/l/812060

Turn the page to read a sample of **<u>OBSIDIAN SON</u>** *- Nate Temple Book 1 - or*
BUY ONLINE (It's FREE with a Kindle Unlimited subscription). *Nate Temple is a billionaire wizard from St. Louis. He rides a bloodthirsty unicorn and drinks with the Four Horsemen. He even cow-tipped the Minotaur. Once...*

TRY: OBSIDIAN SON (NATE TEMPLE #1)

*T*here was no room for emotion in a hate crime. I had to be cold. Heartless. This was just another victim. Nothing more. No face, no name.

Frosted blades of grass crunched under my feet, sounding to my ears like the symbolic glass that one would shatter under a napkin at a Jewish wedding. The noise would have threatened to give away my stealthy advance as I stalked through the moonlit field, but I was no novice and had planned accordingly. Being a wizard, I was able to muffle all sensory evidence with a fine cloud of magic—no sounds, and no smells. Nifty. But if I made the spell much stronger, the anomaly would be too obvious to my prey.

I knew the consequences for my dark deed tonight. If caught, jail time or possibly even a gruesome, painful death. But if I succeeded, the look of fear and surprise in my victim's eyes before his world collapsed around him, it was well worth the risk. I simply couldn't help myself; I had to take him down.

I knew the cops had been keeping tabs on my car, but I was confident that they hadn't followed me. I hadn't seen a tail on my way here but seeing as how they frowned on this kind of thing, I had taken a circuitous route just in case. I was safe. I hoped.

Then my phone chirped at me as I received a text.

I practically jumped out of my skin, hissing instinctively. "Motherf—" I cut off abruptly, remembering the whole stealth aspect of my mission. I was off to a stellar start. I had forgotten to silence the damned phone. *Stupid, stupid, stupid!*

My heart felt like it was on the verge of exploding inside my chest with such thunderous violence that I briefly envisioned a mystifying Rorschach blood-blot that would have made coroners and psychologists drool.

My body remained tense as I swept my gaze over the field, fearing that I had been made. Precious seconds ticked by without any change in my surroundings, and my breathing finally began to slow as my pulse returned to normal. Hopefully, my magic had muted the phone and my resulting outburst. I glanced down at the phone to scan the text and then typed back a quick and angry response before I switched the cursed device to vibrate.

Now, where were we?

I continued on, the lining of my coat constricting my breathing. Or maybe it was because I was leaning forward in anticipation. *Breathe,* I chided myself. *He doesn't know you're here.* All this risk for a book. It had better be worth it.

I'm taller than most, and not abnormally handsome, but I knew how to play the genetic cards I had been dealt. I had shaggy, dirty blonde hair—leaning more towards brown with each passing year—and my frame was thick with well-earned muscle, yet I was still lean. I had once been told that my eyes were like twin emeralds pitted against the golden-brown tufts of my hair—a face like a jewelry box. Of course, that was two bottles of wine into a date, so I could have been a little foggy on her quote. Still, I liked to imagine that was how everyone saw me.

But tonight, all that was masked by magic.

I grinned broadly as the outline of the hairy hulk finally came into view. He was blessedly alone—no nearby sentries to give me away. That was always a risk when performing this ancient rite-of-passage. I tried to keep the grin on my face from dissolving into a maniacal cackle.

My skin danced with energy, both natural and unnatural, as I manipulated the threads of magic floating all around me. My victim stood just ahead, oblivious to the world of hurt that I was about to unleash. Even with his millennia of experience, he didn't stand a chance. I had done this so many times that the routine of it was my only enemy. I lost count of how many times I had been told not to do it again; those who knew declared it *cruel, evil, and sadistic.* But what fun wasn't? Regardless, that wasn't enough to stop me from doing it again. And again. And again.

It was an addiction.

The pungent smell of manure filled the air, latching onto my nostril hairs. I took another step, trying to calm my racing pulse. A glint of gold reflected in the silver moonlight, but my victim remained motionless, hopefully unaware or all was lost. I wouldn't make it out alive if he knew I was here. Timing was everything.

I carefully took the last two steps, a lifetime between each, watching the legendary monster's ears, anxious and terrified that I would catch even so much as a twitch in my direction. Seeing nothing, a fierce grin split my unshaven cheeks. My spell had worked! I raised my palms an inch away from their target, firmly planted my feet, and squared my shoulders. I took one silent, calming breath, and then heaved forward with every ounce of physical strength I could muster. As well as a teensy-weensy boost of magic. Enough to goose him good.

"*MOOO!!!*" The sound tore through the cool October night like an unstoppable freight train. *Thud-splat!* The beast collapsed sideways onto the frosted grass; straight into a steaming patty of cow shit, cow dung, or, if you really wanted to church it up, a Meadow Muffin. But to me, shit is, and always will be, shit.

Cow tipping. It doesn't get any better than that in Missouri.

Especially when you're tipping the *Minotaur.* Capital M. I'd tipped plenty of ordinary cows before, but never the legendary variety.

Razor-blade hooves tore at the frozen earth as the beast struggled to stand, his grunts of rage vibrating the air. I raised my arms triumphantly. "Boo-yah! Temple 1, Minotaur 0!" I crowed. Then I very bravely prepared to protect myself. Some people just couldn't take a joke. *Cruel, evil,* and *sadistic* cow tipping may be, but by hell, it was a *rush.* The legendary beast turned his gaze on me after gaining his feet, eyes ablaze as his body...*shifted* from his bull disguise into his notorious, well-known bipedal form. He unfolded to his full height on two tree trunk-thick legs, his hooves having magically transformed into heavily booted feet. The thick, gold ring dangling from his snotty snout quivered as the Minotaur panted, and his dense, corded muscles contracted over his now human-like chest. As I stared up into those brown eyes, I actually felt sorry...for, well, myself.

"I have killed greater men than you for lesser offense," he growled.

His voice sounded like an angry James Earl Jones—like Mufasa talking to Scar.

"You have shit on your shoulder, Asterion." I ignited a roiling ball of fire in my palm in order to see his eyes more clearly. By no means was it a defensive gesture on my part. It was just dark. Under the weight of his glare, I somehow managed to keep my face composed, even though my fraudulent, self-denial had curled up into the fetal position and started whimpering. I hoped using a form of his ancient name would give me brownie points. Or maybe just not-worthy-of-killing points.

The beast grunted, eyes tightening, and I sensed the barest hesitation. "Nate Temple...your name would look splendid on my already long list of slain idiots." Asterion took a threatening step forward, and I thrust out my palm in warning, my roiling flame blue now.

"You lost fair and square, Asterion. Yield or perish." The beast's shoulders sagged slightly. Then he finally nodded to himself in resignation, appraising me with the scrutiny of a worthy adversary. "Your time comes, Temple, but I will grant you this. You've got a pair of stones on you to rival Hercules."

I reflexively glanced in the direction of the myth's own crown jewels before jerking my gaze away. Some things you simply couldn't un-see. "Well, I won't be needing a wheelbarrow any time soon, but overcompensating today keeps future lower-back pain away."

The Minotaur blinked once, and then he bellowed out a deep, contagious, snorting laughter. Realizing I wasn't about to become a murder statistic, I couldn't help but join in. It felt good. It had been a while since I had allowed myself to experience genuine laughter.

In the harsh moonlight, his bulk was even more intimidating as he towered head and shoulders above me. This was the beast that had fed upon human sacrifices for countless years while imprisoned in Daedalus' Labyrinth in Greece. And all that protein had not gone to waste, forming a heavily woven musculature over the beast's body that made even Mr. Olympia look puny.

From the neck up, he was now entirely bull, but the rest of his body more closely resembled a thickly furred man. But, as shown moments ago, he could adapt his form to his environment, never appearing fully human, but able to make his entire form appear as a bull when necessary. For instance, how he had looked just before I tipped him. Maybe he had been scouting the field for heifers before I had so efficiently killed the mood.

His bull face was also covered in thick, coarse hair—he even sported a long, wavy beard of sorts, and his eyes were the deepest brown I had ever seen. Cow-shit brown. His snout jutted out, emphasizing the golden ring dangling from his glistening nostrils, and both glinted in the luminous glow of the moon. The metal was at least an inch thick and etched with runes of a language long forgotten. Wide, aged ivory horns sprouted from each temple, long enough to skewer a wizard with little effort. He was nude except for a massive beaded necklace and a pair of worn leather boots that were big enough to stomp a size twenty-five imprint in my face if he felt so inclined.

I hoped our blossoming friendship wouldn't end that way. I really did.

Because friends didn't let friends wear boots naked...

Get your copy of OBSIDIAN SON online today!
http://www.shaynesilvers.com/l/38474

Shayne has written a few other books without Cameron helping him. Some of them are marginally decent—easily a 4 out of 10.

Turn the page to read a sample of **UNCHAINED** *- Feathers and Fire Series Book 1, or* **BUY ONLINE (FREE with Kindle Unlimited subscription)**. *Callie Penrose is a wizard in Kansas City, MO who hunts monsters for the Vatican. She meets Nate Temple, and things devolve from there...*

(Note: Callie appears in the TempleVerse after Nate's book 6, TINY GODS...Full chronology of all books in the TempleVerse shown on the 'Books by the authors' page)

TRY: UNCHAINED (FEATHERS AND FIRE #1)

he rain pelted my hair, plastering loose strands of it to my forehead as I panted, eyes darting from tree to tree, terrified of each shifting branch, splash of water, and whistle of wind slipping through the nightscape around us. But… I was somewhat *excited*, too.

Somewhat.

"Easy, girl. All will be well," the big man creeping just ahead of me, murmured.

"You said we were going to get ice cream!" I hissed at him, failing to compose myself, but careful to keep my voice low and my eyes alert. "I'm not ready for this!" I had been trained to fight, with my hands, with weapons, and with my magic. But I had never taken an active role in a hunt before. I'd always been the getaway driver for my mentor.

The man grunted, grey eyes scanning the trees as he slipped through the tall grass. "And did we not get ice cream before coming here? Because I think I see some in your hair."

"You know what I mean, Roland. You tricked me." I checked the tips of my loose hair, saw nothing, and scowled at his back.

"The Lord does not give us a greater burden than we can shoulder."

I muttered dark things under my breath, wiping the water from my eyes. Again. My new shirt was going to be ruined. Silk never fared well in the rain. My choice of shoes wasn't much better. Boots, yes, but distressed, *fashionable* boots. Not work boots designed for the rain and mud. Definitely not monster hunting boots for our evening excursion through one of Kansas City's wooded parks. I realized I was forcibly distracting myself, keeping my mind busy with mundane thoughts to avoid my very real anxiety. Because whenever I grew nervous, an imagined nightmare always—

A church looming before me. Rain pouring down. Night sky and a glowing moon overhead. I was all alone. Crying on the cold, stone steps, an infant in a cardboard box—

I forced the nightmare away, breathing heavily. "You know I hate it when you talk like that," I whispered to him, trying to regain my composure. I wasn't angry with him, but was growing increasingly uncomfortable with our situation after my brief flashback of fear.

"Doesn't mean it shouldn't be said," he said kindly. "I think we're close. Be alert. Remember your training. Banish your fears. I am here. And the Lord is here. He always is."

So, he had noticed my sudden anxiety. "Maybe I should just go back to the car. I know I've trained, but I really don't think—"

A shape of fur, fangs, and claws launched from the shadows towards me, cutting off my words as it snarled, thirsty for my blood.

And my nightmare slipped back into my thoughts like a veiled assassin, a wraith hoping to hold me still for the monster to eat. I froze, unable to move. Twin sticks of power abruptly erupted into being in my clenched fists, but my fear swamped me with that stupid nightmare, the sticks held at my side, useless to save me.

Right before the beast's claws reached me, it grunted as something batted it from the air, sending it flying sideways. It struck a tree with another grunt and an angry whine of pain.

I fell to my knees right into a puddle, arms shaking, breathing fast.

My sticks crackled in the rain like live cattle prods, except their entire length was the electrical section — at least to anyone other than me. I could hold them without pain.

Magic was a part of me, coursing through my veins whether I wanted it or not, and Roland had spent many years teaching me how to master it. But I had never been able to fully master the nightmare inside me, and in moments of fear, it always won, overriding my training.

The fact that I had resorted to weapons — like the ones he had trained me with — rather than a burst of flame, was startling. It was good in the fact that my body's reflexes knew enough to call up a defense even without my direct command, but bad in the fact that it was the worst form of defense for the situation presented. I could have very easily done as Roland did, and hurt it from a distance. But I hadn't. Because of my stupid block.

Roland placed a calloused palm on my shoulder, and I flinched. "Easy, see? I am here." But he did frown at my choice of weapons, the reprimand silent but loud in my mind. I let out a shaky breath, forcing my fear back down. It was all in my head, but still, it wasn't easy. Fear could be like that.

I focused on Roland's implied lesson. Close combat weapons — even magically-powered ones — were for last resorts. I averted my eyes in very real shame. I knew these things. He didn't even need to tell me them. But when that damned nightmare caught hold of me, all my training went out the window. It haunted me like a shadow, waiting for moments just like this, as if trying to kill me. A form of psychological suicide? But it was why I constantly refused to join Roland on his hunts. He knew about it. And although he was trying to help me overcome that fear, he never pressed too hard.

Rain continued to sizzle as it struck my batons. I didn't let them go, using them as a totem to build my confidence back up. I slowly lifted my eyes to nod at him as I climbed back to my feet.

That's when I saw the second set of eyes in the shadows, right before they flew out of the darkness towards Roland's back. I threw one of my batons and missed, but that pretty much let Roland know that an unfriendly was behind him. Either that or I had just failed to murder my mentor at point-blank range. He whirled to confront the monster, expecting another aerial assault as he unleashed a ball of fire that splashed over the tree at chest height, washing the trunk in blue flames. But this monster was tricky. It hadn't planned on tackling Roland, but had merely jumped out of the darkness to get closer, no doubt learning from its fallen comrade, who still lay unmoving against the tree behind me.

His coat shone like midnight clouds with hints of lightning flashing in the depths of thick, wiry fur. The coat of dew dotting his fur reflected the moonlight, giving him a faint sheen as if covered in fresh oil. He was tall, easily hip height at the shoulder, and barrel chested, his rump much leaner than the rest of his body. He — I assumed male from the long, thick mane around his neck — had a very long snout, much longer and wider than any werewolf I had ever seen. Amazingly, and beyond my control, I realized he was beautiful.

But most of the natural world's lethal hunters were beautiful.

He landed in a wet puddle a pace in front of Roland, juked to the right, and then to the left, racing past the big man, biting into his hamstrings on his way by.

A wash of anger rolled over me at seeing my mentor injured, dousing my fear, and I swung my baton down as hard as I could. It struck the beast in the rump as it tried to dart back to cover — a typical wolf tactic. My blow singed his hair and shattered bone. The creature collapsed into a puddle of mud with a yelp, instinctively snapping his jaws over his shoulder to bite whatever had hit him.

I let him. But mostly out of dumb luck as I heard Roland hiss in pain, falling to the ground.

The monster's jaws clamped around my baton, and there was an immediate explosion of teeth and blood that sent him flying several feet away into the tall brush, yipping, screaming, and staggering. Before he slipped out of sight, I noticed that his lower jaw was simply *gone*, from the contact of his saliva on my electrified magical batons. Then he managed to limp into the woods with more pitiful yowls, but I had no mind to chase him. Roland — that titan of a man, my mentor — was hurt. I could smell copper in the air, and knew we had to get out of here. Fast. Because we had anticipated only one of the monsters. But there had been two of them, and they hadn't been the run-of-the-mill werewolves we had been warned about. If there were two, perhaps there were more. And they were evidently the prehistoric cousin of any werewolf I had ever seen or read about.

Roland hissed again as he stared down at his leg, growling with both pain and anger. My eyes darted back to the first monster, wary of another attack. It *almost* looked like a werewolf, but bigger. Much bigger. He didn't move, but I saw he was breathing. He had a notch in his right ear and a jagged scar on his long snout. Part of me wanted to go over to him and torture him. Slowly. Use his pain to finally drown my nightmare, my fear. The fear that had caused Roland's injury. My lack of inner-strength had not only put me in danger, but had hurt my mentor, my friend.

I shivered, forcing the thought away. That was *cold*. Not me. Sure, I was no stranger to fighting, but that had always been in a ring. Practicing. Sparring. Never life or death.

But I suddenly realized something very dark about myself in the chill, rainy night. Although I was terrified, I felt a deep ocean of anger manifest inside me, wanting only to dispense justice as I saw fit. To use that rage to battle my own demons. As if feeding one would starve the other, reminding me of the Cherokee Indian Legend Roland had once told me.

An old Cherokee man was teaching his grandson about life. "A fight is going on inside me," *he told the boy.* "It is a terrible fight between two wolves. One is evil — he is anger, envy, sorrow, regret, greed, arrogance, self-pity, guilt, resentment, inferiority, lies, false pride, superiority, and ego." *After a few moments to make sure he had the boy's undivided attention, he continued.*

"The other wolf is good — he is joy, peace, love, hope, serenity, humility, kindness, benevolence, empathy, generosity, truth, compassion, and faith. The same fight is going on inside of you, boy, and inside of every other person, too."

The grandson thought about this for a few minutes before replying. "Which wolf will win?"

The old Cherokee man simply said, "The one you feed, boy. The one you feed..."

And I felt like feeding one of my wolves today, by killing this one...

Get the full book ONLINE! http://www.shaynesilvers.com/l/38952

MAKE A DIFFERENCE

Reviews are the most powerful tools in our arsenal when it comes to getting attention for our books. Much as we'd like to, we don't have the financial muscle of a New York publisher.

But we do have something much more powerful and effective than that, and it's something that those publishers would kill to get their hands on.

A committed and loyal bunch of readers.

Honest reviews of our books help bring them to the attention of other readers.

If you've enjoyed this book, we would be very grateful if you could spend just five minutes leaving a review on our book's Amazon page.

Thank you very much in advance.

ACKNOWLEDGMENTS

From Cameron:

I'd like to thank Shayne, for paving the way in style. Kori, for an introduction that would change my life. My three wonderful sisters, for showing me what a strong, independent woman looks and sounds like. And, above all, my parents, for—literally—everything.

From Shayne (the self-proclaimed prettiest one):

Team Temple and the Den of Freaks on Facebook have become family to me. I couldn't do it without die-hard readers like them.

I would also like to thank you, the reader. I hope you enjoyed reading *SALTY DOG* as much as we enjoyed writing it. Be sure to check out the two crossover series in the TempleVerse: **The Nate Temple Series** and the **Feathers and Fire Series**.

And last, but definitely not least, I thank my wife, Lexy. Without your support, none of this would have been possible.

ABOUT CAMERON O'CONNELL

Cameron O'Connell is a Jack-of-All-Trades and Master of Some.

He writes The Phantom Queen Diaries, a series in The TempleVerse, about Quinn MacKenna, a mouthy black magic arms dealer trading favors in Boston. All she wants? A round-trip ticket to the Fae realm…and maybe a drink on the house.

A former member of the United States military, a professional model, and English teacher, Cameron finds time to write in the mornings after his first cup of coffee…and in the evenings after his thirty-seventh. Follow him, and the TempleVerse founder, Shayne Silvers, online for all sorts of insider tips, giveaways, and new release updates!

Get Down with Cameron Online

- facebook.com/Cameron-OConnell-788806397985289
- amazon.com/author/cameronoconnell
- bookbub.com/authors/cameron-o-connell
- twitter.com/thecamoconnell
- instagram.com/camoconnellauthor
- goodreads.com/cameronoconnell

ABOUT SHAYNE SILVERS

Shayne is a man of mystery and power, whose power is exceeded only by his mystery...

He currently writes the Amazon Bestselling **Nate Temple** Series, which features a foul-mouthed wizard from St. Louis. He rides a bloodthirsty unicorn, drinks with Achilles, and is pals with the Four Horsemen.

He also writes the Amazon Bestselling **Feathers and Fire** Series—a second series in the TempleVerse. The story follows a rookie spell-slinger named Callie Penrose who works for the Vatican in Kansas City. Her problem? Hell seems to know more about her past than she does.

He coauthors **The Phantom Queen Diaries**—a third series set in The TempleVerse—with Cameron O'Connell. The story follows Quinn MacKenna, a mouthy black magic arms dealer in Boston. All she wants? A round-trip ticket to the Fae realm...and maybe a drink on the house.

He also writes the **Shade of Devil Series**, which tells the story of Sorin Ambrogio—the world's FIRST vampire. He was put into a magical slumber by a Native American Medicine Man when the Americas were first discovered by Europeans. Sorin wakes up after five-hundred years to learn that his protege, Dracula, stole his reputation and that no one has ever even heard of Sorin Ambrogio. The streets of New York City will run with blood as Sorin reclaims his legend.

Shayne holds two high-ranking black belts, and can be found writing in a coffee shop, cackling madly into his computer screen while pounding shots of espresso. He's hard at work on the newest books in the TempleVerse—You can find updates on new releases or chronological reading order on the next page, his website, or any of his social media accounts. **Follow him online for all sorts of groovy goodies, giveaways, and new release updates:**

Get Down with Shayne Online
www.shaynesilvers.com
info@shaynesilvers.com

facebook.com/shaynesilversfanpage
amazon.com/author/shaynesilvers
bookbub.com/profile/shayne-silvers
instagram.com/shaynesilversofficial
twitter.com/shaynesilvers
goodreads.com/ShayneSilvers

BOOKS BY THE AUTHORS

CHRONOLOGY: All stories in the TempleVerse are shown in chronological order on the following page

PHANTOM QUEEN DIARIES

(Set in the TempleVerse)

by Cameron O'Connell & Shayne Silvers

COLLINS (Prequel novella #0 in the 'LAST CALL' anthology)

WHISKEY GINGER

COSMOPOLITAN

OLD FASHIONED

MOTHERLUCKER (Novella #3.5 in the 'LAST CALL' anthology)

DARK AND STORMY

MOSCOW MULE

WITCHES BREW

SALTY DOG

SEA BREEZE

HURRICANE

NATE TEMPLE SERIES

(Main series in the TempleVerse)

by Shayne Silvers

FAIRY TALE - FREE prequel novella #0 for my subscribers

OBSIDIAN SON

BLOOD DEBTS

GRIMM

SILVER TONGUE

BEAST MASTER

BEERLYMPIAN (Novella #5.5 in the 'LAST CALL' anthology)

TINY GODS

DADDY DUTY (Novella #6.5)

WILD SIDE

WAR HAMMER

NINE SOULS

HORSEMAN

LEGEND

KNIGHTMARE

ASCENSION

FEATHERS AND FIRE SERIES

(Also set in the TempleVerse)

by Shayne Silvers

UNCHAINED

RAGE

WHISPERS

ANGEL'S ROAR

MOTHERLUCKER (Novella #4.5 in the 'LAST CALL' anthology)

SINNER

BLACK SHEEP

GODLESS

CHRONOLOGICAL ORDER: TEMPLEVERSE

FAIRY TALE (TEMPLE PREQUEL)

OBSIDIAN SON (TEMPLE 1)

BLOOD DEBTS (TEMPLE 2)

GRIMM (TEMPLE 3)

SILVER TONGUE (TEMPLE 4)

BEAST MASTER (TEMPLE 5)

BEERLYMPIAN (TEMPLE 5.5)

TINY GODS (TEMPLE 6)

DADDY DUTY (TEMPLE NOVELLA 6.5)

UNCHAINED (FEATHERS... 1)

RAGE (FEATHERS... 2)

WILD SIDE (TEMPLE 7)

WAR HAMMER (TEMPLE 8)

WHISPERS (FEATHERS... 3)

COLLINS (PHANTOM 0)

WHISKEY GINGER (PHANTOM... 1)

NINE SOULS (TEMPLE 9)

COSMOPOLITAN (PHANTOM... 2)

ANGEL'S ROAR (FEATHERS... 4)

MOTHERLUCKER (FEATHERS 4.5, PHANTOM 3.5)

OLD FASHIONED (PHANTOM...3)

HORSEMAN (TEMPLE 10)

DARK AND STORMY (PHANTOM... 4)

MOSCOW MULE (PHANTOM...5)

SINNER (FEATHERS...5)

WITCHES BREW (PHANTOM...6)

LEGEND (TEMPLE...11)

SALTY DOG (PHANTOM...7)

BLACK SHEEP (FEATHERS...6)

GODLESS (FEATHERS...7)

KNIGHTMARE (TEMPLE 12)

ASCENSION (TEMPLE 13)

SEA BREEZE (PHANTOM...8)

HURRICANE (PHANTOM...9)

SHADE OF DEVIL SERIES

(Not part of the TempleVerse)

by Shayne Silvers

DEVIL'S DREAM

DEVIL'S CRY
DEVIL'S BLOOD

Made in the USA
Coppell, TX
11 July 2021

58820049R10156